THE CONJURERS

The Conjurers

DAVID GURNEY

NEW ENGLISH LIBRARY
TIMES MIRROR

First published in hardback in Great Britain by
New English Library Ltd., April 1972

*

FIRST NEL PAPERBACK EDITION SEPTEMBER 1973

*

NEL Books are published by The New English Library Limited from Barnard's Inn, Holborn, London E.C.1. Made and printed in Great Britain by C. Nicholls & Company Ltd

450015785

'I beseech you, though I show you the Way, call not upon the powers of darkness . . .'

OCTAVIUS GIBBER
(*The Grimorium Pristinum*)

*

'It is easy to call up demons, for they are always calling you . . .'

ALEISTER CROWLEY
(*Magick in Theory and Practice*)

Prologue

FORTY feet below, the sea fretted against the iron legs of the pier, sending ripples of reflected sunlight up through the narrow spaces between the boards. In the small dark cell in which the woman sat, this reflected brightness quivered against the ceiling as though a swarm of bright cherubim hung there with vibrating wings. As the sun moved, so the bright host shifted their position slightly against the black-painted roof of the cell, and it was possible, though only with a moderate degree of accuracy, to estimate the passing of the hours by marking this movement in the tiny pulsating ripples of golden light.

The cell was a wooden box, about three metres long by two metres wide, and barely high enough to permit anyone over normal height to stand upright. It was rented from the Council every season by Mrs. Fox-Modley, and each year it was repainted, inside and out, by her husband, Ted.

Josephine Fox-Modley had been married twice. By her first husband, long and violently dead, she had a son, Jimmy, now twenty-three; and by her second, Ted, she had two daughters, Janet and Sarah. Both daughters, at the time of the main events described in this book, were married; but Jimmy, who in his way was so very beautiful, was slow-witted, and still lived at home with his mother and step-father. Ted Modley worked in the Entertainments Department of the Town Council. In his spare time, he and Jimmy painted, cleaned, shopped, cooked and generally ran the house in Parrott Lane, behind the church. Josephine had no time for such routine chores. In winter in her own home, and in summer on the Pier in the small fresh-painted box, she gave her readings, conjured her spirits, and listened to her voices from the air. As Madame Joseph, she had played this perilous game for nearly thirty dangerous years, and even now she had no idea where it was about to lead her.

Jimmy, on that summer day, was at home, lying on the big double bed in his mother's room. His blue eyes were open, staring at the window. His long straw-coloured hair lay in a tangle on his step-father's pillow. Long and smooth, almost hairless, his beautiful body lay naked and tense under the moving hands and lips of a devil; a demon; a *succubus*, as such devils are called when they come in female shape. And this was a demon who came to him regularly, in the likeness of his half-sister, Sarah.

The tall, Victorian house was empty, quiet, sun-warmed. Through the open window, he could see the spire of the church of St. Luke, and beyond it the roof of the Royal Hotel. He had only to roll off the bed, cross the carpet in his bare feet, and lean out of the window, to see a segment of the vast blue saucer of the sea, trapped between these two familiar buildings. But even if the thought were to have crossed his mind, he would have been physically incapable of making the movement. He was chained to the bed by the touch of the demon's hands, by the urgency of its lips; by the pressure of its breasts and nipples and thighs, of its small brown chestnut stomach and the soft curling bush of light-brown hair between its legs.

"Jimmy," it said, over and over, and even its voice was the voice of Sarah. "Jimmy! Oh, Jimmy!"

He said nothing. He let it take the lead, as it always did. It seemed always to want it that way. Its hands and its lips moved over him, scampering like small lascivious mice over his beauiful body. His own movements were often clumsy, and he was afraid of hurting this lovely naked image, devil though he knew it to be.

In the box on the Pier, Madame Joseph told a frightened woman things that she would never dare repeat to a living soul. In a bar at the back of the Skating Rink, two men, one the husband of Sarah, the other married to her sister Janet, sat at a small table in an empty corner. Their heads almost touching, they were plotting disaster. Later, outside a precinct shop, a young woman will scream and scream, staring in horrified disbelief. Later still, blood will run, creaming redly along the blade of a silver knife. Words will be spoken. Words that for the most part would be meaningless to a casual listener. Words that are used as a key; a key to unlock the doors of power.

The succubus, in the shape of the nineteen-year-old Sarah, lying now on top of him, guided him in to its woman's shape. His blue eyes were unfocussed; blindly open still, but seeing nothing. The small white teeth of the succubus were sharp against the skin of his breast. The body of the succubus moved rhythmically, drawing the fire of his passion into a single white-hot flame. And against the naked skin above his heart, it whispered with the voice of Sarah, words that he only barely comprehended, but which filled him with a blind terror that he tried to throw aside, but could not. He was trapped by the weight of the demon on his body, and by the grip of his own passion. Over and over the words were repeated, and with them: "This you will do. For if you do not, you will die. And through all eternity you will never lie with me again."

Such was the power the succubus had over him, that it was the thought of losing it, even more than the threat of death, that made his fear unbearable, and terrible though the thing was that he had to do, he knew that he would do it. The demon knew it too, had known it from the beginning. The voice stopped. The small teeth bit deep, drawing a spurt of bright red blood. The pain of it, and the white flame in his loins, fused in a split second into the agony of the final thrust. Then down the long shuddering fall the demon rode him; down, down into the sweating pit of passion spent and flesh retracting; of fear of discovery, and the knowledge that he was trapped for ever. As the weight of the demon left him, he turned with a small hopeless cry, and buried his face in the pillow. Long shuddering sobs racked him, and a name was forced out from between his tight-clenched teeth. A name that was repeated, again and again. The warm air from the town moved gently in through the open windows. On his trembling body, the sweat of his passion dried like a second, invisible skin; while at the edge of the land, beyond the shimmering spire of St. Luke's, slowly, almost imperceptibly, the tide turned.

At last he quietened, lifted his head again. But the room was empty.

Background of Evil

CHAPTER ONE

(1)

MADAME JOSEPH, as she was generally known in the town, was small, intense, with eyes like dark polished stones. She had changed hardly at all with the passing of the years. Always, as far as the town remembered, she had had the same air of constant watchfulness, of listening. Seeing her for the first time, strangers were often deceived into thinking her deaf.

Jimmy's father had died in a pleasure-boat disaster, drowned off the Headland in the company of five holiday-makers and the boat-boy; on a calm heat-hazed day of mid-July. Why they drowned, no one ever knew; or almost no one. But after his death Madame Joseph had kept on the house in Parrott Lane, on which the mortgage had been paid off by the insurance company, and had looked carefully about her for someone to relieve her of the bother of keeping it going. Or so it had seemed. Ted Modley, for this purpose, the town agreed, had been a sitting duck. A friend of Skipper Roberts, he had been often enough to Parrott Lane, and when Skipper was decently buried, having been washed up in the Bay a full eight days after the drowning, he had moved in, first as lodger, then as husband.

It was a kindly gesture, some of the townspeople said, from an old friend of the drowned man. For Widow Joseph, who was unworldly, would surely need a man about the house; and despite the insurance, and the little that she made from her sittings, she would be glad of the extra money, what with Skipper Roberts' boy to bring up for the next fifteen years or more, to mention only one of the problems she had to face.

So said a few of the better-natured people of the town. But there were others who placed a different interpretation on the move. These were the uncharitable ones; those who had asked each other why Skipper Roberts' boat should have foundered in such a calm sea, and why no-one had been saved by using the life-jackets that every pleasure-boat is required by law to carry. These were the ones who said quite openly that Ted Modley was known to be in debt to the betting-shops of half the county, and to the liquor-shops of an even greater area. They also knew, or said that they knew, that Skipper Roberts had been spending more than he should on young Kathy Adeay, sister of the drowned boat-boy. Young Kathy was only fifteen, but she looked more, and local gossip had said that she would lie around with anyone in the town who could pay what she asked; which wasn't as cheap, it was also said, as might have been expected, considering her age. Her brother was the go-between, taking a small share of her earnings, and Skipper Roberts, so they said, had spent far too much of his time and money shut away with her in the small cabin of *Seamew*, with the boy on guard on deck. It was even rumoured that Madame Joseph knew about this, and when the story of the disaster first hit the little town, and even more when the bodies started drifting up on the shore, there were a few of the older townspeople who remembered the almost forgotten art of the raising of storms. *Certain words or ceremonies do seem at least to cause an alteration in the air or to raise tempests*, wrote Henry More, in 1653; putting into such few and simple words what many writers both before and after him have expressed at much greater length, yet no more clearly. Not only, said these old ones with absolute conviction, could a storm be raised, but it could be localised and directed. And though most of their neighbours said: *Nonsense!* as loudly as they dared, Madame Joseph's reputation underwent a subtle change. Those who believed in her, believed even more fervently, while openly defending her. Those who had so far denied knowledge of her, could no longer do so. While those others, the majority, who had regarded her with an amused tolerance, now edged their amusement with something that was not far removed from respect. It was not quite respect, though it was not so very different from it. It was perhaps only fear, which in some forms is almost the same thing. Secretly, they feared the possibility that in this small, intense creature, something of the old power might still exist.

No-one quite knew what had happened to Ted Modley. His debts were paid, not with spectacular suddenness, but slowly, regularly. No new debts were incurred, either to the betting-shops or to the liquor-merchants. He would be seen in a bar every now and again, it is true, but he rarely had much to spend, and never asked for credit. He drank what he could pay for, which wasn't much, and he appeared to get little or no enjoyment from it. In the Entertainments Department, where he had been unspectacularly employed since he left school, he worked no better and no worse than before, but now he shopped in his spare time for groceries, and hurried back to Parrott Lane as soon as his duty-rota permitted. There was some ribaldry at first among his mates, but he didn't rise to it, and after a while they left him alone. Every year, he became greyer, thinner, more ghost-like. And seeing him about the streets good Catholics would cross themselves openly as he passed.

(2)

Six months after the death of Skipper, Josephine Roberts had become Josephine Modley, and, soon afterwards, Josephine Fox-Modley, at least for professional purposes, for through her mother she was connected on the astral plane – or so she claimed – with the original Kate Fox, and Kate, as Mrs. Fox-Jencken, was one of the first of the modern mediums. Ted remained plain Modley, and so, when they arrived, were the two girls.

The girls were born within the first three years of this curious union; Janet first, when Jimmy was still only three; then Sarah Anne. Somehow – at first with a series of daily helps, but later, as the girls grew older and money grew short, alone – Ted Modley coped, in such spare time as he had, with the running of the house; while Madame Joseph's voices whispered their facts and prophecies increasingly into her inner ears. Sometimes, also, she saw visions, shades of the dead and the unborn. But, mostly, she was clair-audiant. She heard the voices of the spirit world, or so she claimed. And what they told her was often blindingly accurate, or at least appeared so to be.

As for the children, living in the same house, brother and sisters but not quite brother and sisters, virtually unsupervised for most of the time, they grew up as young animals do; satisfying their curiosity on each other; fighting a little; sleeping sometimes all together for warmth and companionship. Ted Modley had soon given up any pretence of parental control, and Madame Joseph appeared uninterested in her offspring. School was an unplanned, haphazard affair that was left to officials. The town swarmed with children, and was short of teachers. And so Jimmy, tall and soft, gentle as a young ox, sat almost unnoticed at the back of his too-big classes for far too long, before a harassed education department finally decided that he was mentally backward.

For a brief moment there had been realisation in the house at Parrott Lane; an acceptance, an inescapable awareness of truth. Then Madame Joseph, as always in a crisis, had written to her sister, married ten years earlier to a Canadian psychiatrist. West of Ottawa, the sister wrote back, on the Madawaska River, between Maynooth and Golden Lake, in Ontario Province, there is an excellent school run especially for boys like Jimmy. A ranch-type establishment, with a reputation for bringing-on, and training. Her husband had a certain influence, which he was prepared to exercise. And it was often an advantage in such cases for a clean break to be made with the influences of home . . .

And so, a month before his thirteenth birthday, Jimmy Roberts was put on a plane, met by his aunt, pushed into a train, met by strangers, shoved into a truck, and for the next six years was lost to his home in Parrott Lane. He was nearly nineteen when he returned, bringing with him a minimum of education, a small skill with basic tools, and a body that six years of Canadian weather, and the Canadian way of life, had moulded into a beautiful machine, imperfectly controlled.

Sarah and Janey had almost forgotten their awkward half-brother. Fifteen now, and sixteen, on his return, they were as unalike as sisters can be. Janey was dark and neat, quietly intense. More like her mother. Sarah's light-brown hair was bleached by the sun and the sea-wind. Her body had a certain grace, it is true, but she flung herself about the house like an untrained puppy, racing up the uncarpeted stairs, banging doors, leaving a trail of disorder in bedroom, bathroom, anywhere except in the séance room where Madame Joseph still kept a measure of control. Ted Modley had never interfered. Thinner, greyer, a little quieter each year, he moved about the house like a thin grey spirit that had been conjured into being by his wife's power, and was utterly dependent on it. He shook hands with Jimmy, and retreated to the kitchen. The girls stood side by side, staring at the stranger from Canada. Jimmy hung his handsome head, shifted his weight about as though unsure if the floor would bear it, and grinned as nervously as a chimpanzee.

Josephine said vaguely: "You remember Janey, of course. And Sam."

Sam? Why Sam? Sam was a boy's name, surely. It was only later that he realised that it was because she was Sarah Anne Modley. Calling her Sam was something new. But even in this, he was also to learn, there was no consistency. She answered equally to Sam, or to Sal; rarely to Sarah, and never to Anne.

Without waiting for a reply, Madame Joseph said: "Take him upstairs, girls. He's in his old room. I think it's ready for him."

She touched the stranger, who was unexpectedly her son – or was it her son who was inexplicably the stranger? – lightly with her finger-tips, then she disappeared into the séance-room.

Sal said: "Oh, come on, then," and hurled herself at the stairs. Jimmy picked up his cases and followed. Janey carried a couple of small parcels and his raincoat. At the top of the second flight, that was little more than a ladder to the roof-space, Sal was waiting, drumming a foot against the door of his room.

"Do you remember sleeping here? Before you went away?"

He edged his bulk through the narrow doorway, dropped his cases on the bare floor, looked about him indifferently.

"Yes, I remember."

"It isn't much of a room."

"It doesn't matter."

He thought back, briefly, to the dormitory block at West Star. Names came slowly into his mind. Jed in 3. Tom in 5. Chicka in 8. His own bed had been No. 7, with Chicka on his right as he lay on his back, and a French-Canadian boy they called Jonpy on his left in No. 6. He had hated Jonpy, who was mean as a jackal. Chicka was all right, soft-spoken and slow as Jimmy himself; and Tom and Jed were as close as thieves, or as lovers. He'd been neither happy nor unhappy there: he had accepted it, that was all. But already it seemed far away, in time as well as in space.

Did he really remember this room; this house; these silent, speculative girls? The vague woman downstairs?

The flickering shadow of a man who was his father, but not his father? He knew that he would accept them, as he had accepted the discipline of West Star; the plainness of the food; the long hours of dull, repetitive work relieved only by a burst of occasional violence from one of the staff, and the meannesses of Jonpy. He would accept them, because he had no alternative.

Janey put the parcels and the raincoat on his bed. She said: "The bathroom's on the floor below. Where it always was." He nodded, and went over to the window. The room was at the back of the house, overlooking a row of neglected gardens. Beyond was a car park, with the evening sun catching the rows of polished metal. A handful of gulls wheeled and fought over the yards at the back of the shops beyond the cars. When he turned away, Janey had gone; but Sal was sitting on his bed, swinging her long brown legs and looking up at him.

"Why did you go away? What was the matter with you?"

"Nothing was the matter."

He had never really questioned why he had spent all those years at West Star. He had been told that he was going, he had arrived, and he had stayed there, uncomplaining. Now he had returned to Parrott Lane. She might as well have said: "Why have you come back?" He had no idea of the answer to either question.

"Then why didn't you stay here, and go to school?"

He stared down at her without replying. Such a question and answer routine was of no interest to him. He was interested in very little beyond the ordinary business of living.

"Teddy says you're backward."

Teddy? Who was Teddy? The pale ghost who had married his mother? He hadn't remembered him ever being called Teddy. *Teddy says you're backward*. But even that didn't rouse him. He simply stood there, still shifting his weight about slightly, watching the young brown-skinned girl who was so unexpectedly on his bed.

At West Star, there were no young females. The ranch was way out of the nearest town, and all the staff lived on the estate. There was a nurse, and a couple of women cooks, but these were neither young nor attractive. Most of the work was done by the boys themselves, as part of their training. Two of the male staff were married, but their wives lived in town and they went home to them at weekends. The rest lived in bachelor quarters. Sex did not exist at West Star. Not officially, anyway.

Sal moved suddenly, stood in front of him. She stretched out a hand, touched his face. Then she said: "I like you, Jimmy. I'm glad you're back home." And: "Do you like girls?"

"I don't know."

There had been a couple of girls on the plane, about Sal's age, or maybe more. He'd kept looking at them all the way over. But he'd had the sense not to try anything. Not in there; not in that small vibrating cabin with all the hard-faced businessmen and grim-faced women travellers, and the mechanically smiling stewardesses endlessly passing and re-passing. But now, here, in his own room . . . He still couldn't believe that he really had his own room, all to himself. No Jed and Tom and Chicka and Jonpy and God knows who besides, ranged along the walls of the dormitory. No waking in the night and hearing the restless movements of the others, the snores and the gasps and the small whimpering cries either of those who slept and dreamed, or of those others who tried to bring substance into their dreams by coupling uneasily and inexpertly together.

"Did you know many girls in Canada?"

He shook his head. Why did she have to keep talking? Asking questions? Suddenly he reached out for her, put his arms around her shoulders, and bent his head to kiss her. It was a clumsy effort, but their lips found each other's, fumbled, then clung. She was almost as inexperienced as he, but for a while they remained locked together. Then she broke away, and he didn't try to stop her. And then Janey was calling up the stairs, saying that supper was ready, and in a flash she had gone, and he was left to follow her down, slowly, wondering if she would tell them. Uneasy as a dog who thinks he might be punished for some misdemeanour, he edged into the big kitchen on the ground floor. But no-one said anything, and gradually his fear died. It was all right, he told himself. It was only a kiss. He hadn't attacked her. If Sal kept quiet, it would be all right.

But it wasn't all right. Even that small incident, trivial as he assured himself it was, lent its shape inevitably towards the ultimate pattern of disaster and blind terror that was to involve them all.

(3)

Madame Joseph had a many-sided reputation in the town itself. There were a number who labelled her a cheap circus fraud, little better than the headless woman and the fish-tailed mermaid. There were others who professed to know nothing about her, but who came, none the less, to the side door of the séance room late at night, and in secret. There were the holiday-makers on the Pier. And there were her regulars, who came openly, sometimes as often as once a week, and who relied on her to guide them, comfort them, and in a macabre way to entertain them with her exchanges with the spirit world.

On the night of Jimmy's return from Canada, Ted Modley looked up several times from his supper, to see her staring at the boy as though she was unsure whether he was her son or not. She still wore the air of strained attention that she usually adopted when she was listening for her voices – especially if it was windy on the coast, for then reception was poorer – but her concentration for once seemed divided, as though she was fascinated by the problem of her own son, but was forced to listen to her voices at the same time.

Ted was not so much an active disbeliever in his wife's powers, as a man with so many responsibilities jostling for his strictly limited time that he had long ago closed his mind to anything that was not directly concerned with the daily scramble to satisfy the demands of his job, and of the millstone that was the house in Parrott Lane. What would happen now? he wondered vaguely. It was too early to make anything like a true assessment of Jimmy's capabilities. Would he be a help, or just another bloody liability, like those two useless girls? There was one thing, he'd he damned if he'd wait on *him*, as he had had to wait on the others. Making their bloody beds – when they got made, that was, which wasn't often. Cooking. Cleaning. Like a bloody housemaid. He'd tried to train Sal and Janey, but they were too wild by the time he'd got around to it. Now it was more trouble to keep chasing them than it was to do the job himself. It was easier still, of course, to leave the job undone. No-one else seemed to care, as long as there was food on the table, so why the hell should he? But there were times when he thought that Skipper Roberts, comfortably dead, might almost be better off.

Jimmy said very little He ate what was offered to him; not exactly wolfing it, but eating it steadily and fast. He looked up once or twice; a swift, shy, furtive glance that was dead almost before it was born. The first time, he caught Ted Modley looking at him as though he was the boy from Woolamooloo. But Ted looked away at once, as though he had been caught peeping through a gap in a curtain. The second time it was Josephine, her head on one side, staring at him with an air of puzzled concentration. She didn't look away, in embarrassment, as Ted had done, but her black polished eyes seemed curiously unfocussed, as though she was looking way beyond him. To the far Headland, perhaps, and the long-drowned bodies of Skipper Roberts; his five passengers; and the boat-boy, young Johnny Adeay from the cottages on the Rise. All of whom had perished on a day when the sun shone brilliantly above a slight haze, and the sea was as calm as milk in a cup. . . .

The third time he ventured his quick upward stabbing glance, it was to meet the light-brown stare of Sarah. She didn't look away, either; but neither was she looking beyond him, at the drowned ghosts of the past. She stared straight back at him, their glances locked, and he felt a sudden knotting in his stomach, and a lurching in his chest, that threatened between them to displace the newly-eaten food that he had stowed away. In all that time in Canada, from the thirteenth to the nineteenth years of his life, he had never been so close to a girl. She was just opposite him, across the table – exactly where Chicka had sat at West Star. He remembered their clumsy kiss, up there in his bedroom in the roof, and the food in his stomach shifted again. *Christ!* he thought in sudden panic. *Surely to God he wasn't going to throw up, not here in the kitchen, on his first night home. . . .* He began to sweat. He could feel it in his hands, clamped tight about his eating irons. He could feel it beginning to trickle, like melting ice, under his clothes. Like the ice that lined the banks of the Madawaska, when it started to give in the spring; when the little furtive trickles began, swelling to a flood as the season advanced. Did he actually try to lower his head, to break the contact? He didn't really know. He didn't think about it. He just stayed locked on to her, like an aircraft on a homing device. Once you're locked, you're fixed, until someone throws the bloody switch, or presses the button, or whatever it is they do. He was aware of no-one else in the room. There was a distant roaring that came and went, not unlike that of the sea when he'd first stumbled across it again on the way from the station, walking alone along the almost-forgotten promenade. No-one had been able or had taken the trouble to meet him, and he'd had to ask his way to Parrott Lane, so long was it ago. And he'd stopped often to rest the weight of his bags and to stare at the restless sea that was alarmingly at the flood, sucking and roaring against the land. The sound he now heard, though, was more familiar. It was the ordinary din of the world, rolling on its ordinary daily path. A jumble of tiny dins all flung together. He'd long ago given up the task of trying to separate them all, and most of the time he didn't even bother to try to pick out the one he was supposed to be listening for. The droning North American voice of one of the instructors at West Star, maybe, rasping on about mortices and tenons, or some simple bit of basic arithmetic. He would listen to it for a while, then it would blur and fade into the general cacophony, recede to a distant murmuring. His attention would be on something else. A patch of bright yellow sunlight, creeping across the dusty floor. A butterfly, outside the window. Or the way the hair grew round the open shirt-collar of the boy next to him at the bench. Until a belt on the side of his head would send him sprawling down into the sawdust, and he'd lie winded and confused. And then he'd crawl to his feet to stare, his mouth slackly open, at the shouting face of the instructor, and round him the sly grins of the rest of the class. And sometimes he'd be so confused that even then he wouldn't know what he had done wrong, or what was expected of him. And then, more likely than not, he'd get another savage blow, and down he would go again, down into the resinous dust, and sometimes he'd get a kick in the stomach as well, just for good measure. But after that they'd leave him alone, and after a while the pain and the confusion would die, and he'd pick up his tools and set to work as if it had never happened at all....

At last the switch was thrown by Sarah herself. He felt the current cut off, and suddenly the rest of the table came into focus. Janey was talking to her mother. Ted Modley was chasing bacon-fat around his plate with a piece of bread. Sarah reached for the butter. Still sweating, he bent his head over what was left of his food. But his heart was thumping painfully, and his mind was swinging in great clumsy leaps through trackless jungles that until that moment had been no more real than the fantasy stories some of the boys had told in the dormitory, stories based on ill-digested scraps flung at them by prurient staff or picked up from the magazines that circulated somehow, despite the rules.

Someone took his plate away, handed him another. Canned peaches and ice-cream. He sent his spoon skidding through a slab of what looked like melting latex, to slice into the soft flesh of the two half-peaches that lay under the fluff like breasts under a white-foam bra. Where that thought had come from, he had no idea. One of Jonpy's girlie mags? It could be. It was one of Jonpy's meanest tricks, to let him half-see the canned peaches in the mags he got from somewhere, to rouse him up and then not to let him see the rest of it. It was nearly always Jonpy who had them. He stole food from the kitchen, when he had the chance, and what he stole he swopped for the girlie mags, and for occasional cigarettes; but who he swopped with, Jimmy had never discovered. Someone on the outside staff, it could have been; one of the labourers from the settlement near the Falls. But he was cunning enough never to give it away, whoever it was.

The cutting edge of the metal sliced through the peach-soft flesh. Slowly he lifted a dripping gobbet to his mouth, where it lay smooth and slippery-cold against his tongue. He rolled it around, then bit into it, delicately. It was like a love-bite. But what had he ever known of love-bites, in the rough male dormitory at West Star? What had he ever known but sometimes the hard male flesh of Chicka furtive in his bed in the sleeping night? No flesh-soft peaches there. Chicka was hard and hairy, all bones and unexpected angles.

With the taste and the feel of the peach still in his mouth, he looked up again, quickly, furtively. Sarah was spreading jam on a slice of white bread, thickly buttered. She didn't look at him again. Janey was also eating peaches and ice-cream, shovelling it in as though she was starving. Madame Joseph had her head on one side, still listening. Ted Modley had lit a cigarette. His eyes were screwed up tightly against the smoke. They all seemed wholly absorbed in their own affairs, no longer even aware of the stranger from West Star. The moment, if there had ever been a moment, had passed.

(4)

The smallness of the room terrified him. For six years he had slept in a vast hangar-like space with twenty-three other boys, twelve down each side, feet facing towards the middle, lockers at the foot of each bed. Now he was in a box; a box with a lid that sloped alarmingly towards a window that nearly a century ago had been cut out of the steeply pitched roof to make an extra room from the dusty space between the bathroom and the rafters.

It had been used, no doubt, this small and airless box, by a succession of servants, in the last few years of the nineteenth century and the first two decades of the next; a procession of clumsy country girls from the inland villages. It had been a store-room when the Roberts had bought the house; and when Madame Jo had married again, and the girls were born, the three children for a long time had slept all in the same room, on the floor below, looking out over the back. It was not until Jimmy was ten, that he had been pushed up into the cleared attic.

Beyond the wooden wall, on the side away from the window, he could hear an occasional thunderous roar as the big metal storage tank took in its replenishment of water from the black reservoir hidden deep in the limestone hills to the north-west. Lying awake in the small odd-shaped space, the lights of the town reflected from the sky through the open window, he could hear the sounds made by the four strangers who were suddenly his family, as they prepared for bed. Water running in the bathroom below. The flush of the lavatory cistern; one, two, three, four times; followed by the dying thunder in the tank near his head. A murmur of voices. The closing of a door.

It had been after eleven when Ted Modley had finally switched off the television, and he had been told to go first to the bathroom. In and out, in forty seconds flat; then up to his room, his clothes flung anywhere on the floor. Naked, he had crawled into bed; naked, and only half-washed, as had been the general custom at West Star. But he couldn't sleep. Over there, it would still be the middle of the afternoon, so Ted Modley had told him, or maybe by now it was early evening. Whatever it was, he hadn't adjusted yet. Not that he understood exactly how this could be, but the simple fact remained – he was not yet ready for sleep, despite the journey.

Now that the tank was quiet, he could hear the distant murmuring of the sea; the sound of late traffic through the town; and a church clock banging out the quarters. And suddenly he was frightened; terrified at the strangeness of it all. The surroundings and the companions of six long years had vanished, like a company of ghosts at cock-crow, leaving only an empty churchyard, and the sound of a distant bell. Whimpering a little, like a half-grown puppy on its first night in a strange home, he crawled out from under the bedclothes and, naked as he was, went over to the window. It was a still, oppressive night, with summer lightning flickering over the inland hills, beyond the roofs of the little town. For a while he stood there, watching the crawling lights of occasional cars in the old town, and the sudden blaze of a late vehicle swinging down the hill road, a quarter of a mile away, momentarily pointing directly at him over the roofs below.

He wasn't actively unhappy. Happiness and unhappiness barely entered into his strictly limited emotions. But loneliness and fear, yes. And now he was both lonely and afraid; frightened by the strangeness; lonely for Chicka, and Jed, and all the others. Even for Jonpy, the mean little French bastard.

Staring out of the window, hypnotised by the moving lights, his mind preoccupied with his fear and his utter loneliness, he didn't hear the small sound that the door made, the click of the latch, the faint scrape of wood against wood. He wasn't aware of the creak of a board, the displacement of air. The first he knew was the sound of a whisper in the warm air.

"Jimmy!"

He swung round, startled.

"Who is it?"

"Quiet! Not so loud!"

"Who is it?" he said again, but more softly. "Is it – Sarah?"

She came closer.

"Yes." Stretching out a hand, she touched his shoulder. A car came down the hill road. The distant headlights blazed briefly as they made contact with the open window. The room lightened a fraction, then the beam swung away. She giggled. "Why are you standing there?"

He stood awkwardly, not knowing what to do. He couldn't remember where he had thrown his clothes. He could have dived for the bed, but she was standing there, barring the way. Confused, he stood still, his arms hanging loosely at his sides. Another car sent its beam across the valley. The hand on his shoulder moved, slid down to his chest, made a small circle of caress.

"Jimmy," she said. "Why aren't you in bed?"

He felt his muscles tightening. He didn't like being questioned. Not directly, like that. He had always shied away from giving an answer to any direct question. At West Star, that had been another reason why he had been clouted so often. Her hand moved on, down to his navel.

"Why are you naked?"

He still didn't answer. The movement of her hand on his body fascinated him. It was small and soft, not hard like Chicka's. It moved in unexpected directions, as a small questing animal moves. His mind followed it as though it was tied to it by a cord; like a tail behind a swooping kite, never quite catching up.

"Jimmy," she said. "I like you."

She went on caressing him, clumsily at first, for she was as inexpert as when she had kissed him earlier in the evening. But he didn't care. He didn't try to touch her. Not then. He simply stood there. And suddenly he was aware of more whispering, more giggling in the darkness. Then there were more hands. The room seemed suddenly full of hands. Small, cool hands in constant fluid motion, running, questing, hunting, caressing. But he knew that there could be no more than four. Giggling together in the almost-darkness were Sarah and Janey. And now, at last, he reached out with his own coarse hands. Flesh gave before him. Firm flesh, but different, even to his clumsy touch. Flesh in cool incipient curves. Clumsily, he tried to seize them. Skilfully they eluded him. It was a game played *pianissimo*, at the top of the sleeping house. If he stumbled, let out a gasp or a small cry, instantly they froze.

"Sssh!" they said, in urgent whispers. And: "Quiet! They'll hear you!" And as instantly they unfroze, and the game went on. After a while he gave up his clumsy attempts to seize them. He was too slow, and their constant "*Sssh!*" and "*Quiet!*" unsettled him. He went suddenly cunning, stood quite still, let them come close, so close that their quick, excited breath was warm against his skin. And then, instead of the clumsy grab that sent them quicksilvering away through his grasp, he edged his hands gently forward, felt them touch, felt only a momentary flinching, then the strange exciting flesh stayed firm and tense, as, gently now, gently, he ran his big work-coarsened hands over the unfamiliar contours that had so far existed only in his muddled imagination. Never, at West Star, had he ever touched a girl. Only rarely, indeed, had he ever seen one. Now, like a blind man suddenly confronted with a tactile experience hitherto unknown, he drank in the strangeness and the terror of it through trembling fingertips. The faint glow from the sky, the occasional flicker of summer lightning, the distant blaze of a car on the hill road; little enough of all this penetrated the small dormer window. Outside, the world was touched and laced with jewels of bright light. But in the odd-shaped attic room it was too dark to distinguish anything but a vague movement. Blindly, his hands gathered their unfamiliar impressions, transmitted them overwhelmingly to the incredulous control-centre of his mind.

He didn't know if it was Janey or Sal standing firm under his curious hands. He didn't care. He knew that he was on the brink of disaster. But he didn't care about that, either. He floundered drunkenly in the sudden, unexpected eroticism of the moment. It could have been one of the dreams that had constantly plagued him at West Star, dreams where he had wallowed in situations equally bizarre. He stood there, as at the point of awakening, and in that poised instant, at the very tip of the wave before it creamed and broke in thunder, the light came on, swift, cold and pitiless. In the doorway was Ted Modley, in his pyjamas. The two girls shrieked. Ted looked dishevelled, cross and bewildered. He didn't say anything: he simply stood there. They all stood there, under the cruel light, with nowhere to hide.

CHAPTER TWO

ON THE morning after his first night at home, Jimmy Roberts awoke in his attic room and stared about him for a while without any idea at all where he was. He saw the steeply sloping ceiling, close over his head, and a small square of pale-blue sky through the dormer window. He looked for Chicka and Jed and all the others, but saw only blank walls. The tank, beyond the flimsy boards behind his head, was thundering wildly, as though it couldn't take in its new load fast enough in case the deep dark reservoir in the hills should run gaspingly dry before the morning needs of Parrott Lane were satisfied. For half a minute, perhaps longer, he lay there, terrified by the strangeness. And then, to add to his fear, the memories of the night, confused and terrible, crowded in on his waking mind, and with a little animal whimper he turned over in bed and lay with his face deep in the warmth of his pillow, as though by that simple physical act he could hide from the fears that surrounded him.

The girls had shrieked, at the sight of their father in the doorway. Their shrill cries had added to his own confusion, savaging the raw edges of his slow-moving brain. It had seemed hours before he realised suddenly that they had gone. But Ted Modley was still in the doorway. He had stood there a moment or two longer, then he had lifted a hand to his throat and had made a single cutting movement with the edge of it. Then he had reached out suddenly and had turned off the light. Jimmy had heard the door close, and had listened for the sound of footsteps on the stairs. But he had heard nothing. Either Ted moved naturally as silently as the disembodied ghost he often seemed to be; or he was in his stockinged feet; or he had had his slippers on, or a pair of rubber sneakers; or maybe he had simply flown like a small grey sinister bat, silently down the stairs, back into the big double bed that he shared with Madame Joseph.

In all the confusion, through all the shrill squealing of the girls, Ted Modley had said nothing. Nothing at all. There had only been that one, final, meaningful gesture. The hand drawn knife-like across the throat.

Jimmy didn't dare go down to breakfast. He heard movements below, and the running of water seemed to go on endlessly. But at last the house quietened. He heard the church clock strike nine, then the quarter, then the half. And by then, frightened as he was, he was hungry. He climbed out of bed, dressed slowly, then pulled open the door of his room. Below him the house stood silent, and surely empty. It had the feel of emptiness. Of a house deserted. They had gone, and had left him to fend or to starve, they didn't care which. What had been decided? Undoubtedly it had all been settled while they ate. But what had been settled? Would he be sent back to West Star? Back to the jeers of the boys and the hasty fists of the staff . . .

At this stage he didn't care much, either way. But if he alone was to be in trouble, it was monstrously unfair. If those stupid little bitches had only stayed away from his room. . . . He remembered again the movement of Ted Modley's hand. The silent throat-cutting gesture that could only mean – what? But what could Ted Modley do, anyway. He wasn't his father . . .

Alternating between terror and false courage, he crept down to the first landing. Still the house stayed quiet. Bedroom doors were open. The rooms beyond them were empty. He looked inside each, saw beds unmade, clothes scattered about. Down the next flight to the ground floor. The room at the front of the house, next to the front door, was the séance room. He had been told that the night before. He had also been told never to go in there unless his mother sent for him. What he didn't know at this stage was that this forbidden room also had a door into the narrow passage that separated the house from its neighbour. This door had been specially made, so that clients who were shy of being seen entering the house at the front, could, by special appointment, see Madame in something approaching secrecy.

The door of this room was closed, and he moved on from the foot of the stairs, past the small room that was used as a waiting-room by the less shy clients, and so to the big cluttered kitchen at the back, where the family lived, ate, quarrelled, and watched television. It looked as though a warning of some disaster; a flood perhaps, or a tidal wave; had been received, and the family had acted upon it in a split second, dropping everything and rushing out in a frantic effort at escape. Plates with the remains of food still on them stood on the table in a litter of cereal packets, marmalade, a slab of butter, half a loaf, dirty cups, and the pages of a newspaper. On the stove was a frying-pan, solid with grease. In the sink were more dishes, stacked haphazardly. A half-empty milk-bottle stood on the draining-board. Over everything, a handful of flies moved in a random sampling flight-pattern.

Sitting at the table, clearing a space by pushing everything in front of him to one side, he cut a slice of bread, buttered it, and piled it high with marmalade. He ate fast, as though fearful of discovery, preparing a second slice before the first was finished. He reached back to the draining-board, and drank the remainder of the milk, tipping it straight from the bottle into his mouth, which was still full of bread and marmalade. Then, his hunger momentarily stilled, he wandered back to the front of the house, to the closed door of the séance room. For a long time he stood outside it, listening. There was no sound from inside. At last he stretched out an arm, turned the handle, pushed open the door, and took a step across the threshold.

Inside, it was quite dark, except for a faint lightness from the window of the passage behind him; a tall thin window, this, with panes of coloured glass, dark red, dark blue, dark dirty yellow. He took another step forward, released the door, and with a faint sigh it closed behind him, the latch clicking home with the sound of a safety catch on a gun, being released for action.

And now the darkness was absolute, and his panic returned. He had no idea why he had entered the room, except out of idle curiosity. Confused now, by the closing of the door and by the darkness, he stood whimpering. It was in situations like this that his limited wits deserted him. At West Star, there had been no need ever to take a decision. The routine of each day was a carefully planned repetition of an already established pattern. Such minor variations as there were between one day and another recurred in a predictable order. You knew with a comfortable certainty what you would be expected to do in an hour's time, or tomorrow, or next week – that is, if you ever thought that far ahead. Mostly, you lived for the moment, knowing that someone else would take care of the future.

In the darkness, he moved back a step, felt for the light-switch. But it eluded him. He groped for the door-handle, but in his panic he couldn't find that either. There seemed only to be a smooth, featureless barrier, shutting him in. With a little cry, he lurched forward towards where he thought the window must be. There was a crash, and a sharp stab of pain, as he collided with something that fell over under the impact. And then he felt himself seized, and held, and his fear came up like a black cloud, and he went down amongst the debris like a young pole-axed bull . . .

When his wits returned, he was staring into the eye of a white light. He closed his eyes, opened them again, lifted a hand to brush away the glare. But the light stayed firm, as fixed as a white-hot rod piercing the sensitive quick-flesh behind his dazzled retinas. He was lying on the floor still, and the light was above him. He had no idea how long he had been lying there. When he had first felt himself seized, the sheer terror of it had stopped his mind. He didn't remember falling, even. There was a dim memory of the sudden darkness when the door had closed behind him, and the pain and the din of his collision with whatever it was that had been in his way. Then something – God alone knew what – had gripped him in the darkness. And now he was lying on the floor, and the eye of God was staring down at him as it had stared down in the big coloured print in the Chapel at West Star – a single eye, huge and coldly probing, with a white searchlight coming out of the middle of it, and all the cowering sinners at the other end. He'd hated that picture; hated and feared it. But twice a day on Sundays he hadn't been able to take his eyes off it, and some nights, even in the week, he had dreamed about it, waking as he struggled and shouted and fought to free himself of that cold and critical Eye.

Now he lay on the littered floor, with all his strength drained; lacking even the will to struggle to his feet and to make a run for it, away from the hostile room and from whatever it was that it contained. There was no sound, except for his own quick breathing. If anyone else was there, was also breathing, he was not aware of it. The light beat down, steadily, pitilessly. With a sudden little whimpering cry he flung out an arm, caught the edge of something metallic, and the white rod was deflected, swinging up to the high ceiling. And half-blinded though he was, as it swung it showed him a sight that turned his bowels to water. Beyond the source of the light was a monstrous figure with the head of a goat, crowned by a pair of horns. The figure was crouched a little, its shoulders forward, as if it was about to leap, and at the sight of it his terror provided its own avenue of safety. Strength returned, and in an instant he was on his feet. Small anguished cries came from him as he hurled himself at the door. In the reflected light from the ceiling he found the handle, dragged it open, and fell into the hall. On all fours, he crawled to the foot of the stairs, and there his strength deserted him again. Against the bottom-most steps, he crumpled into a small sobbing heap, not caring in the least what should happen to him next.

Ted Modley said: "What the hell do you think you're doing?"

How long he had lain there, at the foot of the stairs, he didn't know. He felt a blow from something hard, and from the store of his experience he recognised the toe of a boot. But he didn't dare look up. Not at first. He crouched, head down, and Modley kicked him again.

"Get up!"

A third kick brought him to his knees. Slowly he lifted his eyes, forcing them up over the slack, ill-fitting suit, the pathetic string-tie, the off-white collar that stood out from the ropy neck. At last the small grey muzzle came in to focus, the sharp little features, the slightly protruding teeth; then the cold eyes, the tangle of thinning hair. His father, yet not his father. He had never understood how this could be, but when he remembered it, he was glad. He had never liked Ted Modley, and he didn't want him as his father.

Slowly, he stood up. He was a head taller than the little grey man, but Modley was still Authority.

"Did you go in to *that* room?"

Jimmy said nothing.

"Answer me, blast you!"

It was no good. Much as he resented being questioned, he knew it was no good. There was the table, or whatever it was that he had knocked over. Ted had only to open the door, and he'd see for himself. It didn't occur to him to wonder what Ted Modley was doing at home anyway, at such an hour. Newly back, he hadn't yet latched himself on to the rhythm of the house.

His eyes swivelled to the door of the séance room, now shut. He nodded, awkwardly. And with the movement there came back the memory of that brief glimpse of the creature with the goat's head. Fear clutched at him again. *Had* he seen it? He couldn't have done. It was impossible. But his memory told him that it was true. He *had* seen it, quite clearly, in the light from the spot-lamp, and he knew a goat's head when he saw one. There had been a dozen of the bastards at West Star; cunning brutes that got their own way whatever you did to them. But this thing hadn't had a goat's body. From the neck down it was more like a man. A man with a goat's head, and horns.

He was aware that Ted Modley was talking, but his attention had wandered. He stared stupidly down at the moving mouth with its yellow teeth.

"What?" he said, and Ted stopped whatever it was that he was saying, and went as coldly quiet as he had been in the bedroom the night before.

"Do you mean to say," he said at last, very carefully and very quietly, "that you haven't been listening?"

Jimmy stood waiting for the next blow, prepared to roll with it. That way, he had learned to lessen the punishment in a thousand similar situations at the school on the Madawaska.

Still quietly, Modley said: "You bloody bastard!" And: "I'll take you back in the séance room –"

Instantly Jimmy cried: "No! No – !" And Modley said: "What the bloody hell do you mean, no? You were in there, weren't you? Where you didn't ought to have been –"

"I thought you were all out –"

"So we were. But I came back. I'm taking a day off. I'm not well. And, anyway, what difference does it make, whether we're in or out? Your mother told you last night –"

Had she told him only last night? He didn't exactly remember, one way or the other. Last night had been an avalanche of new impressions, of trying to recall what they all seemed to think he should remember. His room. His bed. His family, such as it was. What made them think he would remember anyway? Good bloody grief, hadn't he had to ask the way from the station to Parrott Lane . . .

His attention had wandered again. Ted Modley's mouth was still opening and shutting, but he didn't register the words. Guiltily he braced himself, tried to get back into the stream of words heard, succeeded at last.

Modley was shouting again, as though he had decided that the only way through this barrier of non-attention was by sheer force of sound.

"– I had to go out, and when I came in, you were lying at the bottom of the stairs. What were you doing? I said, what were you doing?"

"There was – someone in there –"

"In there? In where? In the front room? Don't be bloody stupid, boy! How could there be? Everyone's out."

With an effort, Jimmy said: "There was a – a goat –"

Ted Modley's sharp little muzzle pointed up like a fox's mask.

"You're crazy!"

The contempt in his voice was meant to sting, but Jimmy was used to contempt. And he was still terrified.

"There was! I saw it –" A fine spray was flung from his lips, and he stammered a little in his fear and his excitement.

"A m-man – with a g-goat's head –"

Modley said: "You big crazy bastard!" And: "I'll show you if there's anything in there!"

He seized Jimmy by the arm, began to drag him towards the door of the séance room.

"No! No, I won't! I won't go in there –"

"You bloody well will," Modley said. And such was the power of his authority that though Jimmy was nearly twice his size, and half crazy with fright at the idea of going back in there again, he couldn't resist. Ted Modley opened the door of the séance room, reached inside to switch on the light, all without letting go of Jimmy's arm. And when Jimmy could bring himself to look at last, he saw that the room was just a room, except that it had no window.

There was no goat-headed creature waiting to leap at him. No tables were overturned, their loads thrown to the floor. There *was* a table, with unfamiliar objects on it, but it was still upright. Round it was a scattering of chairs. A bookcase and a handful of charts stood close against the walls, and there was a green-baized door on the other side. But there was no sign at all of whatever it was that had seized him, and had sent him more than half-way out of his simple wits.

Modley said: "Tell me again what you saw."

"A g-goat. Or a man with a g-goat's head –"

Modley said: "It's not here now. So I don't know whether you saw it or not. But if you *did* –" He broke off, and stared up at Jimmy. "If you *did*, I'll tell you something. You're in trouble. You're in dead trouble, that's for sure."

Jimmy shrank back.

"Why?"

"*Why?* Bloody hell, you ask me why? Do you want me to tell you why?"

Jimmy stared at him, incapable of answering, and Ted Modley said viciously: "If you can't say nothing, then I'll have to make up your mind for you, won't I? Shall I tell you why you're in dead trouble? All right, I *will* tell you. It's because *if* you saw what you say you saw, then that wasn't a man. It wasn't even a goat. It was a devil. Do you understand what that means?" And as Jimmy still forced himself back against the edge of the door, and still said nothing: "A devil! Come to get you. For what you did last night."

"No," Jimmy said at last. "No –"

"Found your tongue, boy? It won't do you no good. Not just saying *no*, like that." Suddenly he dropped his voice, glanced furtively over his shoulder. "I'll tell you something else. It's not the first time a devil's been conjured up in this room. That I do know. But usually you've got to conjure 'em. They don't just come. If it just come, just like that, then there's nothing else for it. It'd come for you. Specially."

Later, in the kitchen, Modley said: "I didn't tell your mother about last night. I only told her the girls was up there teasing you. Just fooling about. If she knew . . ." He stopped, put down the cup he was holding, and again he made that cutting movement of his hand across his throat. "If she knew, she'd have your hide, boy. I don't know *what* might happen to you, honest I don't. She's a powerful woman, your mother. She can conjure spirits. Good ones and bad ones. And they do what she tells them. That devil you saw in there, now. He nearly had you, didn't he? But he didn't. He let you go. Now why do you think he did that? Eh?"

Jimmy had no idea. He had only half-followed Ted Modley's insistent monologue. But he had heard enough to get the general drift of it.

Modley was making coffee, spooning the grains out of a jar that was almost empty. He said: "It was a warning. That's what it was. Now I think of it, that's what it must have been. Otherwise it would have had you. You'd be roasting in the flames of torment by now, boy. They meant it as a first warning. But a second warning – God, boy, if you ever get that, you'll know it!" Another furtive glance at the door of the kitchen, beyond which lay the hall and the other door that concealed the square of absolute darkness they all referred to as the séance room. "A mate of mine, he had a warning, just like yours. And he didn't do nothing about it. So they sent a second warning." He dropped his voice, and Jimmy, now hooked on the quiet words, had to lean forward to catch the barely whispered sounds. "The trouble is, you never know how they're going to come. Come in any shape, they can. This mate of mine, his demon come in the shape of his own mother. But you should have seen what it done to him. He's still up there, in the hospital, boy. When the doctor saw him, he dropped in a dead faint. I'm not telling you a word of a lie. Never seen nothing like it before, he said afterwards. Never in forty years. There's some say they may never let him out again."

The words faded, drifted away, and Jimmy felt himself drifting after them. He gripped the edge of the table, forcing himself back. Ted Modley shoved a cup in front of him, and he seized it and drank the scalding sugary mixture.

"There's only one way to keep clear of them, boy. And that's to make sure you don't ever cross them again. Don't you give no trouble to your mother and me, and maybe they'll lay off you. But you can't be sure of nothing. They could come for you tonight, if they was so minded, and you'd never know, not until it was too late. You'll have to watch it, all the time. But you do as we tell you, and maybe there'll be no second warning." A pause, then: "You got to work, boy, if you're going to stay here, and keep out of trouble. You understand?"

Jimmy nodded. He had still only absorbed the general drift of it all. But the thought of what might lie in wait for him if he didn't agree, was unbearable.

"Right, then. You finish up your coffee, and we'll get started. I'll show you what to do. You know how to wash dishes?"

He nodded again. Regular turns at it for six years at West Star had accustomed him to greasy plates and dirty cups. Nothing that Parrott Lane could produce was ever likely to prove too much for him.

"Right, then. Get started."

Jimmy drained his cup, and carried it across to the littered sink. A simple act, but symbolic. Though he could not possibly have known it, he was at the very beginning of a period of subjugation, of slavery, of exploitation. A period in which he was to lie with demons, and to pledge his soul. In which the house at Parrott Lane was to become a focus of evil, a power-house of forces that like his own strong body were imperfectly and insufficiently controlled. A period that was to end in disaster.

Ted Modley sat like a small grey weasel, watching him as he worked.

CHAPTER THREE

(1)

THAT NIGHT, his second night at home, Jimmy lay in the darkness, waiting. He didn't know whether he wanted the girls to come again, or not. In a way, he did. But he was terrified of the consequences, if they should be caught again.

But caught by whom? It had been Ted who had switched on the light and had revealed them, not only to his own sharp little weasel-eyes but also to each other. But his fear of Modley was nothing compared with his terror at the thought of the goat-headed monster in the séance room. The moment when the light had swung up and away under the impact of his hand to reveal that one brief glimpse of the creature, with its great bearded head and sneering lips under the upswept horns; that moment was etched as clearly on his shrinking mind as though it had been cut with an acid straight from the burning cauldrons of Hell.

During the day, Ted Modley had kept him busy, working around the house. At tea-time, the girls had returned from school, and afterwards they had watched television, with a break for supper. There had been no time for dwelling on what might still lie behind the door of the séance room. But now, alone in his small attic, with the quarter-bells chiming monotonously in the church outside, and the headlights of the distant cars swinging like searchlights across the window, he saw again in his memory the creature that was part man, part goat; the leering animal mouth half open to reveal the lines of yellowing teeth; the body crouched for the spring.

"No!" he said aloud, up there in the troubled darkness.

But the image would not go.

It stayed there, burning against the darkness; even when he screwed his eyes into tight painful folds of trembling skin, covering them with his shaking hands. It would not go, even though he curled like a small terrified animal into the warm black womb-like shelter of his bed, under the sheet and the single heavy blanket that was all he had.

It wasn't Ted that he feared. It was the demon who had been sent to warn him, and who next time . . .

He felt something touch his shoulder, through the blanket, and horribly, soundlessly, as in a nightmare, he began to scream.

"Jimmy! Jimmy!" His name was being whispered urgently into the darkness.

Terrified, he crouched in the small dark space under the bedclothes. He felt something – hands, or paws, or even *hooves* it could have been – scrabbling at the blanket that was his only protection. Naked, curled like a foetus in its sac, he fought to make himself small, to retreat into the oblivion from which one of Skipper Roberts' wriggling nautical sperms had summoned him nineteen years earlier.

"Jimmy!"

He felt the blanket being pulled away, and seized it in both his hands, holding it in place.

"Go away! Go away!" he shouted in his mind. But no sound came.

And then whatever it was out there ceased its restless motions of attack, abandoned its urgent whispering. For a moment there was silence. He didn't know whether it had gone away or not; or whether this also was a trap, set to catch him. He lay listening, not daring to make a slit in the bedclothes through which to peer, still terrified of what he might see.

And then, at last, he heard his name spoken again, quietly, but no longer in that urgent frightening whisper. It was the voice of Sarah, saying: "Jimmy, what's the matter? Open up, *Jimmy* –"

But still he didn't know what to do. It was her voice, he was sure of that. But was even that a part of the trap? Would he fling back the bedclothes, only to find the goat's head leering at him in the occasional light from the distant cars; the demon crouched there for the spring? Was that voice, the voice he knew, issuing in fact, quietly as poisoned honey, from the great ugly mouth with its rows of yellowing teeth?

"No," he said. "No –" And forced himself into an even smaller compass, pressing his big muscular thighs against his chest, creating in his mind the illusion that he was no more than a shrinking handful of tender child-flesh, safe in the body of its creator.

But then he felt again the movement of hands or hooves, he didn't know which, furtively against the blanket. But this time they were at his feet. He gripped the bedclothes even tighter, but suddenly blanket and sheet were whipped away from him, jerked up and away so that he was left with only his two small handfuls pulling against the strength of his adversary. The rest of him, and there was a great deal of his big naked muscular body despite his delusion of smallness, was left unprotected, vulnerable as the soft flesh of a hermit crab ejected from its shell. And in the same instant, the beast sprang . . .

He saw it, as his eyes opened, already in motion. It was between the bed and the lighter square of the window, a darker shape against the patch of troubled sky. He was too late to move out of its path. He released his grip on the bedclothes, flung up his hands, and then the demon was in his arms, and they were wrestling together on the bed, silently except for a quick excited breathing that was not his, and the pounding of his own frightened heart.

The demon had come to him, not only with the voice of Sarah, but with her body.

Deep in his limited, slow-moving mind, Jimmy remembered the man to whom the demon had come disguised as his own mother. He remembered Ted Modley's words: *The trouble is, you never know how they're going to come.* Somewhere in the shadows of his mind was a terrifying vision. That of a demon in the form of a little old lady, smashing her own son deliberately into a mess of bloody flesh and broken bone, so that even the doctor had fainted at the sight of it.

But the voice of Sarah was sweet in his ear, and the smooth, exciting, unfamiliar shape of Sarah was sweeter still against his unfolded body. The image of the old lady – what *exactly* had she done, and with what? – was forced into the shadows. Sarah said: "Jimmy, what are you afraid of? It's all right, if we don't make a noise. He's asleep. I could hear him snoring –" She giggled, and he felt a little excited tremor pass through her. "Jimmy, I'm sorry about last night. But it was funny, really. When he switched on the light, I could have died."

He moved uneasily. To be reminded of last night, was to bring back the memory of the séance room. Instinctively, his hands moved up to feel her hair, the top of her head, her face. Clumsily, like a newly blinded man, he explored her, searching for horns, for muzzle, for any sign there might be of the true nature of this phantom that lay close against him in his narrow bed, shamelessly rousing him, whispering and giggling into his ear. He wondered once if the real Sarah was asleep on the floor below, in one of the beds in the room she shared with Janey; one of the big cluttered rooms that he had first glanced into on his way downstairs that morning; in which he had later made the two untidy beds. But after a while he ceased to care. There was no room in his mind for anything but the sensations of the moment; for anything but the feel of her hands, her lips, her hair, her small sharp teeth, and the wonderful softness of her naked flesh.

"Sal," he said, and instantly her lips sought his. She seemed far less clumsy than she had been that first time, but he had no previous experience against which to measure the quality of her expertise. It was all new, all wonderfully strange after the hard male flesh that was all he had known at West Star. It was like another of his night-dreams, a fragment from the fantasy-world into which they had all from time to time escaped. Bewildered still, he let her take the lead; let her lead him through a pattern of experiment and exploration that he followed blindly, until it led him inevitably to the final shattering moment. But even then she didn't leave him. She knelt above him, and her hands never ceased their restless wandering.

He made no attempt to stop her. Reaching up into the near-darkness, he felt her still there, taut as a bowstring. But his passion had gone; leaving him spent and afraid again. Whether this was a demon, or not, the events of the previous night had been repeated. In a different form, it was true; but fundamentally, it was the same. Had the coming of Sarah, his mind nagged at him, been not the warning, but only the temptation, as before? Would the second warning – in the form of the Beast – come with daylight, as the first had done?

These thoughts, clearly set out, were anything but clear as they were tossed, panic-stricken, around the slow chambers of his mind.

"Sal!" he said suddenly, loudly, and clutched at her, drawing her down. "Sal, are you real?"

She closed his mouth with her own. Then she whispered: "Sh! Not so loud!" And with a tiny giggle, instantly suppressed: "What do you mean, real?"

"You're not a demon?"

Instantly she went quiet, withdrew from the clumsiness of his embrace.

"What has he been telling you?"

"He?"

She gripped his arms, sinking her nails into his flesh.

"You know who I mean!" Her grip tightened so that he almost cried out. "What has he been saying?"

Her sudden change of mood increased his fears. He could only stammer that she was hurting him, that he couldn't answer her if she gripped his arms like that, that he didn't know anything about anything, that –

Abruptly, she released him, but for what seemed an age she still knelt above him. Then slowly she bent forward until her face was only an inch away from his. Then in that hateful whisper he heard the words: "I am a succubus. A demon in female shape. If you were a girl, I should come to you as a male. Then I would be an incubus. Inside, I would be the same. But outwardly I would be different. Do you understand?"

He shook his head in the darkness, and suddenly she struck him across the face with the back of her hand.

"Do you understand?"

"No."

He felt her relax again, and faintly he heard her whisper. "It doesn't matter. Next time –"

He was hardly aware of the moment of her going. But as the lights of a car flashed suddenly across the window, he realised that the room was empty. He was cold, and instinctively he groped about on the floor for his blanket, drawing it over his shivering limbs, and up over his head. Back in the small dark world of his substitute womb he lay and trembled with the cold, and with fear, and with passion spent. He fell asleep at last, and dreamed of the Eye of God. And when morning came, he awoke confused, not knowing which of the events of the night had been real, and which had been only of the substance of his dreams.

(2)

He didn't dare say anything to Ted Modley, and, as it happened, there was no opportunity. At breakfast, Sal looked up briefly as he came down, but she said nothing. He ate in silence, and when they had all gone out he washed the dishes at the sink. The house around him was completely empty. In summer, Ted worked on a curious shift system that included evenings and week-ends; so sometimes he was at home on a weekday; sometimes he was out half the night, returning cross and tired in the small hours; after dawn, even, when there had been a late-night dance at the Pavilion.

The dishes stacked, he opened the door into the hall. And there he stopped. Ahead of him was the long passage, lit only by the coloured glass in the tall, thin window at the end; yellow and blue and red, with the sea-grime of years trapping most of the light from the sky outside before it could struggle through into the house. Coming down to breakfast, with the others racing about and the cheerful clatter from the kitchen, he had passed the door of the séance room without giving it a thought. But now, in the silence, the room lay, as it were, in ambush. If he were to pass the door again – as he must if he was to regain the stairs so that he could clean the bathroom and make the beds as Ted had told him to do – then surely he would be putting himself in a position of grave peril. If the beast was lying in wait – if the door was to be flung open as he reached the foot of the stairs, and he was to be dragged inside – if what had happened in his room last night –

"No," he said aloud. And the word seemed to echo back along the empty passage. Suddenly panic seized him. He retreated into the kitchen and closed the door into the hall. For a moment he stood undecided, then a further wave of panic sent him out through the back door, down the side passage as though the beast was already at his heels, and so into the sunlit safety of Parrott Lane. But he didn't stop running until he was well into the Jubilee Gardens, halfway along the main walk, between the Floral Clock and the Chinese Tea Pavilion. Even then, he might have gone on running until his breath failed him, or his panic died, but a green-keeper in the Council's uniform stood with his arms outstretched to stop him.

"What's the hurry, son?"

This was Authority again. Jimmy stopped.

"Where's the fire?" the fellow said. And as Jimmy still didn't answer, Authority grew suspicious. "Where you heading for, then, son?"

"The Pier," Jimmy said at last. It was the first name that he thought of.

"Ah!" A slow and ponderous nodding. "And you've got to get there first, in case they pull it down. Is that it?"

Jimmy stood still, waiting for Authority to have its say. This was the old familiar routine. He saw the stupid sun-burned face under its uniform cap, saw the opening and shutting of the mouth under its nicotine-stained moustache. But he no longer heard the words. He stood passively, waiting for the moment when the words would cease, and he would feel the back of the fellow's hand, or the toe of his boot. But after a while the old fool's attention was distracted by a child with a ball near the monstrous Clock that was the darling of the Parks Department. Authority turned to face this potentially graver threat, and Jimmy was left alone. For a moment, he could hardly believe his luck, then he walked slowly away, expecting every moment to hear a cry from behind him. But he reached the end of the Gardens, and exactly opposite, across the Promenade, was the entrance to the Pier, on which Madame Joseph spent her summer days, listening.

He had not consciously headed for the Pier. Until his meeting with the old fool in the uniform cap, he had been running blindly. But the first word to enter his mind, when he had been asked where he was going, was *Pier*. Now, still without any more clear-cut reason, he crossed the Promenade, paid his fee at the turnstiles, and began the long quarter-mile walk to the cluster of wooden buildings at the seaward end; where, under the shadow of the Pavilion itself, was the small cell, with the name *Madame Joseph* in flamboyant lettering outside.

When he reached it, the tide was already high, fretting

between the iron legs of the pier and throwing up small handfuls of spray, like flung pebbles, to rattle against the underside of the boards. Was it familiar to him, this almost oriental complex of painted domes and naively decorated booths? He thought he remembered it, unchanged, from the years before he had gone to West Star; but he couldn't be sure. And what did it matter, anyway? He knew that inside the small painted box he would find what he was looking for.

She glanced up, startled, as he thrust his big head and shoulders through the curtains. A woman sitting opposite her screamed and clutched a black handbag tightly against her chest. Madame Joseph said sharply: "What do you think you're doing? Get out! Stay outside until I tell you to come in!"

Awkwardly, he retreated, stood near the rail watching the heave and thrust of the sea. And a few moments later the woman emerged, scuttled off across the boards, her white face turned momentarily towards him. Then Madame Joseph was at his side, swathed in a purple cloak, with veils about her impossibly black hair. Out in the bright light, she looked almost obscene. A creature of the dark, suddenly exposed. Seizing him in a grip that hurt his arm, she drew him back into the little hut, let the curtains swing shut behind them. Thrusting him into the chair that the white-faced woman had occupied a moment earlier, she leaned across the little bamboo table on which was a small silk cushion and nothing else.

"I'll ask you again, what do you think you're doing? Don't you know better than to come pushing your way in like that? When I have a *client*!"

Small, dark, intense, her little black polished eyes stared at him in the rippled darkness. Now that he was there, he didn't know what to say, or why he had come. Still sharply, she said: "For God's sake, boy, *say* something!"

But still he sat there, listening to the tiny fretting sounds as the water played with the iron legs of the pier.

"You'll have to tell me," she said, a trifle less sharply. "I can't hear for my own family. Only for strangers. *They* won't tell me why you're here."

He stared back at her, not knowing who *they* were, or why they shouldn't talk to her about her own son. But suddenly speech came. He said: "A succubus? What is a succubus?"

Instantly, Madame Joseph's eyes were hooded. She seemed to grow even smaller.

"Where did you get that word from?"

"I want to know what it is."

"I said where did you get it from?"

"I don't know." The old reaction to a direct question. Evasion. Her hand shot out and gripped his arm. "I don't know," he said again, and tried to draw away. Already he was regretting the impulse that had sent him flying out of the house, straight into this trap-door spider's lair.

Suddenly she released him, straightened the cushion on the frail little bamboo table.

"How can I help you, if you won't answer me?"

He said nothing, but even with his limited awareness of his surroundings, he could not avoid registering the uneasiness of her reaction. And something of that unease inevitably transferred itself, so that his own fears increased. More and more he regretted that the impulse of the moment had driven him into this false haven. He sat there, looking down at her thin white jewelled fingers as they pulled at the small silk square of the cushion. And suddenly he knew that whatever happened he could never tell her of the succubus; of its strange exciting beauty, and of the strange, exciting way in which it had drawn up his manhood. The hands that kneaded the small gold cushion were the hands of a stranger. The succubus, demon though it might be, was, he realised with a sudden shock of surprise, dearer to him than this sharp, bejewelled mother-figure could ever be. He hung his head still further, to avoid the bright black probing eyes that he knew would try to wrest the secret of the succubus from him.

Over and over he asked, deep inside himself, why he had come. He had fled from the empty house with no fixed plan in his panic-stricken mind. Only when Authority in the form of the green-keeper had threatened him, had he thought of the Pier, and of the little box in which his memory had told him he would find his mother. But now that he had found her, he wanted only to escape again, to keep inviolate the secret that he had so nearly betrayed.

Peering up at last under his lowered eyebrows he realised that she was still talking. He was aware of a succession of shrill sounds, and of her mouth opening and closing, but his mind had retreated into its usual defensive position of non-reception. He no longer registered the meaning of the words that were flung at him, the sounds that surged and fretted around him just as the restless tide surged and fretted about the iron legs of the pier beneath his feet.

He moved abruptly. In one powerful, awkward thrust of his leg-muscles, he was out of the chair, and through the curtains, out into the glare of the sea-light. Behind him he heard the clatter of the falling table, and a shrill cry from Madame Joseph. Then he was off at full speed, back along the quarter of a mile of ancient boards at a fast run that made idling visitors turn and stare after him. He ran easily. At West Star, it was the only thing he had ever done really well. At games involving a ball of any kind, he had been quite useless. His reactions were too slow. But in the annual sports he had won the mile, and the five miles, four years in a row. He ran naturally, without thinking of the principles of movement. And at the end of a mile, he would be breathing only a shade faster than at the beginning.

He paused to negotiate the turnstile, then he ran again, along the promenade and down the slope at the far end onto the beach. The tide was high, but not at the spring, and there was a narrow strip of dry sand with small waves licking and sucking at his right hand. On his left was a waste of dunes and salt-flats that stretched away to the estuary of the little river. After a while he struck inland, slowed to a walk, first in the loose sand of the dunes and then on the flaking crust of the flats. By a circuit that took him almost to the edge of the river, he regained the town at the landward side, and, hungry and thirsty, he bought tea and a sandwich at a fly-blown transport café at the foot of the hill road. Then he went back into the waste-land, almost to the sea's edge, and lay on the sand under the lee of one of the dunes. It was a little after noon, and the sun, beating down, drew a shimmering heat-haze from the flats so that all the distant land across the river appeared to float in air as insubstantially as a dream. Gulls and terns flew idly overhead, keeping their place in the little wind from the sea. A plane, so high as to be almost invisible, left a white trail across the blue; a snail crawling across the bright blue dome of infinity. A pair of golden lizards flickered against the shifting sand, and were gone in a flash. Slowly, his eyes closed. It grew steadily hotter, and thoughts of the succubus began to plague him unbearably.

The sun made a golden screen of his closed eyelids, a screen on which the image of the succubus appeared, as elusive and insubstantial as the land across the river in the mirage-haze. On this golden screen the demon came, in the form of Sal. Infinitely desirable, it hovered over him. In his mind, he stretched out his arms for her, but she remained always just beyond his reach. Tantalisingly, she advanced and retreated. Once he opened his eyes, but the sun exploded into a million fiery fragments, and the image vanished. Whimpering a little, he lowered his eyelids and waited for the pain to go, and with it the sudden blackness that had followed the fire. Slowly the blackness faded, was replaced by the gold. And with it the image of the succubus returned, closer now. Closer. Closer.

Hands moved over his suddenly trembling body.

Pattern of Evil

'. . . call not upon the powers of darkness, for if you call them they will assuredly come . . .'

OCTAVIUS GIBBER

*

'. . . they are always calling you, and you have only to step down to their level and fraternise with them . . .'

ALEISTER CROWLEY

CHAPTER ONE

(1)

TED MODLEY was on his way home at the end of the day. Almost dark, it was a month before the festival of the Holy Innocents, and already winter had seized the seaward end of the little town in a grip that had drained the life from its body, leaving only an icy skeleton against whose frozen bones the footsteps of the few who still went about their daily business rang like blows on a metal frame. He put down his head against the force of the sea-wind as he rounded the barricaded shop-fronts at the corner of the Esplanade and the Arcade, heard the roar of the flood-tide as it hurled itself against the waste of empty concrete. In the fading light, great curtains of black water were flung high against the grey of the sky, hung trembling for an instant, then thundered down with a blind destructive fury that sent him running like a scared black bettle into the echoing tunnel of the deserted Arcade. It was a route that he followed regularly in such weather, and this being known, waiting for him on this day among the empty shops, was a tall figure in shapeless black, with a pair of large myopic eyes peering through a tangle of fine fair beard and hair.

He was almost past when the creature stretched out a hand, seized him by the sleeve of his overcoat and stopped him in mid-flight.

"Ted Modley –"

The voice was remote, the words neither a question nor a statement, but something of each. Modley tried to pull himself free, but the grip was maintained. Before and behind them, the Arcade, lit only by a single lamp in the centre, was empty. The fronts of the shops were boarded over against the aimless bands of wreckers who wandered every night about the ill-lit winter streets. Only in summer, when the visitors came, would they open for a few short weeks with their tinsel stocks. Beyond the mouth of the tunnel, the great curtains of grey-black water were still being flung high against the evening sky, but now the thunder of the sea was curiously muted. At the far end, the Arcade debouched into the Jubilee Gardens, now a deserted strip of frozen earth with here and there a leafless tree, a circle of railings, an empty pool. For five months of the year this section of the town stood desolate and windswept along the edge of the threatening sea. A few employees of the municipality, men like Ted Modley himself, occasionally fought their way along the deserted ways, under the boarded shops and the empty hotels. But the true life of the town was reduced to a small flame that burned only in the sheltered back streets, away from the ceaseless wind and the pounding water.

"Ted Modley –" the figure said again, and behind their powerful lenses his eyes swam disconcertingly, as though they were afloat in some pale fluid that was trapped inside the pebble-curves of glass.

Modley, halted in his scuttling dash for home, said: "Who the hell are you, for Christ's sake?" And in the dark deserted tunnel, the answer came back, magnified a little by the echoing emptiness: "Barry Simpson."

Ted Modley's sharp little face peered up at the tangle of fine fair hair that was like the first fluff on a fledgling bird, concealing the true shape of the creature; hiding, but at the same time displaying, its fundamental immaturity.

"So?"

"I know your daughter."

Ted let himself go slack in the stranger's grip. So which was this one? When you had daughters, it seemed that the entire neighbourhood was haunted by creatures like this, most of them indistinguishable one from another, like gulls around a fishing-boat.

"Which daughter?" As if it mattered.

"Janey."

Momentarily, Ted Modley registered a faint feeling of surprise. Janey was the dark and neat one; quietly intense, more like her mother. Such men as he had noticed around her had tended to be a shade older, a shade less unkempt, than those that fluttered about the brighter flame of her younger sister.

"Come and have a drink," Simpson said, and Modley answered peevishly: "I'm going home, for God's sake. Home for my tea. What do I want with a drink?"

"I'd like to talk to you."

"About what?" Suddenly suspicious. "If it's about you and Janey –"

Simpson's eyes swam alarmingly in the light from the single lamp in the roof of the tunnel.

"It's not about Janey. It's about you, Mr. Modley. You, and Skipper Roberts."

If anything can truly be said to have marked the beginning of the final phase, it must surely have been that meeting in the empty Arcade, a month before the Day of the Holy Innocents, nearly two and a half years after Jimmy Roberts' return from West Star. In that time, little had changed in the house at Parrott Lane. Jimmy was now twenty-one, but as so often happens to those of slower intellect, outwardly he had aged scarcely at all. He looked, and acted, almost exactly as on the day of his return. Every day, he washed the dishes, scrubbed, polished, and made the beds for the entire family; ran errands into the town for Ted Modley; and in the summer he sometimes worked for the Corporation, picking up deck-chairs from the beach and carrying them back to the lock-up store under the Promenade.

The demon still came to him in the form of Sarah, creeping in to his bed, riding him to destruction; but it came infrequently, and to no set pattern.

He had never entered the séance room again. Not once in all that time. And this was the only part of the house he had never been told to clean. Neither had he ever again seen the monster with the head of a goat. The closed door of the front room still filled him with blind unreasoning panic when he was left alone in the house. But when the girls had finished school, this happened far less frequently. Each had a job, but like most of the other girls in the town they were employed only seasonally, and for odd hours; Sal in the cash desk at the Chinese Tea Pavilion, and Janey in the hairdressing salon of the Royal Hotel. Never once did he mention the succubus to Sarah, and never by any look, or chance word, or touch, did she ever so much as hint that she knew of its visits to his room. Twice only in that period had it come to him in daylight, when the house was empty, and Sarah was working. The first time, he found it sitting on the stairs, waiting for him; the second, it surprised him on a hot, hot day of late July when he was asleep in his room after lunch. Each time, he asked Sarah when she came home what time she had left the Tea Pavilion, and each time she had lifted an eyebrow in mild surprise, but had confirmed that she had been working when the succubus was with him.

In some ways it was almost a relief that the succubus was his, and his alone. For the real Sarah was increasingly besieged, all the year round, by a rackety collection of the boys of the town, and by a succession of summer visitors in the season. Janey, too, was the target of almost as much male attention; though in general this was of a soberer kind, which accounted for Ted Modley's feeling of faint surprise when he learned that the tall and whiskered oddity in the Arcade was interested in dark Janey, not, as he might have assumed, in the lighter-headed Sal.

At the mention of Skipper Roberts, Ted Modley seemed

to shrink into a small core of watchfulness, a tiny defensive position from which he peered up at the stranger who had suddenly accosted him.

"Skipper's dead," he said. "Years ago."

"I know that. What I'm interested in is how he died."

"Oh, for Christ's sake!" But as an explosive comment it lacked force. Even Ted seemed aware of it. He tried to turn it into an expression of weary disinterest by adding: "The whole bloody town was in on it. There was an inquiry –"

"I've read the reports."

"So?" Still warily.

"I'd like to talk to you about it."

"Why me, for God's sake?"

"You married his widow. If Skipper hadn't died, Janey wouldn't be your daughter. Yours and hers. *Or would she?*"

Ted Modley's sharp little weasel-face grew even sharper.

"Just what the hell are you implying, Mr. Bloody Simpson?"

"Anything you like, Mr. Bloody Modley."

For a moment they tried to stare each other out; Simpson, with his head thrust out and down, like a vulture on a thorn-tree; Modley, the ferret, the weasel, the fox, looking up, his muzzle raised. At last, Modley said: "I don't know you, and I don't want to talk to you. Is that clear?"

"If I marry Janey –"

"Marry?" The word came out in a shrill falsetto, startled prematurely out of the small man's tightened throat. "Who said marry?"

"I said *if*."

"There won't even be an if, not if I have anything to do with it!"

The tall man shook him gently, then suddenly released him.

"What will you do to stop it, Mr. Modley? You and her mother? Will you do what you did before? Will you whistle up another storm?"

Ted Modley stood quite still. He was suddenly calmer,

released from the grip that had held him immobile. Deliberately he glanced both ways along the dark tunnel. Then he said viciously: "We might do just that, Mr. Bloody Simpson. So watch it."

The tall man laughed.

"I'll watch it. Don't you worry about that – *dad*!"

Modley flushed.

"Stop that!"

"Well?" Simpson said. "Do we have that drink?"

"No."

"You really can't afford not to."

Modley said: "You don't tell *me* what I can do!"

"I will one day, *dad*!"

"I said stop that –"

"I know you did. Why don't we go and have that drink, as I said?"

"No."

"All right, then. But I'll be seeing you again. You'd better get it sorted out, in your twisted little mind. I want to know why Skipper died –"

"He was drowned, for God's sake! Everyone knows that."

"I didn't say how, this time. I said why. Why, on a dead calm day? If I'm going to marry Janey, I shall want to know, shan't I? I wouldn't want to marry her, not knowing that. Now would I?"

(2)

At home, at tea, Ted Modley suddenly said: "Who the hell is Barry Simpson?" And Janey flushed scarlet.

Sal giggled, sat watching the rest of them over her teacup.

Madame Joseph said: "Who is *who*?" And Ted Modley repeated the name.

"Barry Simpson?" she said vaguely. "Is that Boatyard Simpson's son?"

"Ask Janey."

"Why Janey?" Madame Joseph turned her black eyes on her daughter, saw the confusion that still lingered. "Oh, I see. Well, is it?"

"No. That's his uncle."

"Then who is his father?"

"Jack Simpson. At the garage on the top road."

Madame Joseph gave a small cry, and turned back to stare tragically at Ted Modley.

"*Jack* Simpson? Then –"

He said roughly: "It's a long time ago."

"Then his mother must be – *that girl* –"

"That's right. Kathy Adeay."

"Who's Kathy Adeay?" It was Sal, bright and curious.

"Someone we once knew."

Janey, suddenly quiet and pale, said: "Someone your first husband knew, you mean."

"You know about that?"

"Yes, mother."

Sal said: "Know about what? Won't somebody tell me?"

"It's nothing." Janey reached for the jam, spooned out a bloody gobbet on to her plate.

"Nothing?" her mother exclaimed. "Nothing? Is that all you can call it?"

"Steady," Ted Modley urged her. "The girl's right. It was nothing. And all over and done with."

"You started it!" Madame Joseph's black eyes looked enormous against the pallor of her cheeks that were suddenly as white as her daughter's. "You mentioned his name –"

"I didn't know then that he was Kathy's son –"

"Why bring him up at all?"

"I met him on my way home."

"You mean he met you," Janey said. "In the Arcade."

"You knew he was going to meet me?"

"He told me he was. But I didn't know it would be tonight."

"*Why* did he meet you?" Madame Joseph demanded.

"He wanted me to have a drink with him."

Janey gave a short, sharp mirthless laugh.

"That's good. What the hell would he want to drink with *you* for? He wanted some information. That's what he wanted."

"About – Kathy?" Madame Joseph spoke with an effort. "About Kathy and –?" She broke off, stared helplessly at Ted Modley.

"That's right." He pushed his plate away, felt for a cigarette. "I told him I was on my way home. I told him to fuck off."

Janey said: "*You* told *him* to fuck off! That's a likely one. He could eat you –"

"He said he wanted to marry you."

Madame Joseph cried out again. "No! No, I forbid it!"

Janey stirred the jam, that still looked like a mess of coagulated blood on her plate.

"I haven't said I'm going to."

"But you're – on *those* terms?"

Coolly, she stared across at the mother she so closely resembled.

"I don't quite know what that is supposed to mean. But if it means what I think it means, the answer is yes. And there's not a blind thing you can do about it. Either of you." Her glance flickered towards Ted Modley. "Except tell us the truth about Skipper Roberts."

Jimmy was the only one still eating. The rest sat in a frozen little tableau around the table. Sal was turning her eyes from one to the other, but keeping quiet and watchful. Madame Joseph winced at the name, but recovered. Ted Modley's left hand paused half-way up to the cigarette that hung from the corner of his mouth. Jimmy tried to eat silently, and almost choked with the effort.

At last Ted Modley said out of the opposite corner of his cruel little mouth. "I told your boy friend, and I'll tell you the same, Miss Clever-pants. Everyone knows what happened to Skipper. There was a public inquiry –"

"With an open verdict," Janey said. "Which means they didn't know, and they weren't prepared to give anyone the benefit of the doubt."

"What I don't understand," Madame Joseph said, "is why now? Why rake all this up now? It's twenty years ago –"

Janey said: "I'd never thought about it. I knew the boat was lost. But boats do get lost. It was Barry who –" she paused, shrugged her shoulders, and touched her knife again to the mess on her plate, "– he's a schoolmaster."

"What in Christ's name," Ted exploded, "has that to do with it?" The words were forced out between a fit of coughing and a long pull on his cigarette.

"He's an educated man –"

"What you can see of him! He's all hair and bloody whiskers."

"He writes for the literary magazines in his spare time. And he reads a lot. He read up all the old back copies of the *Gazette*."

Sal said: "Do you mean there was trouble? That it wasn't just bad weather?"

"It was dead calm."

"That's what they said," Ted Modley interposed. "It was a sudden squall. You get them out in the bay. Come up out of nothing. I've seen them often."

Madame Joseph stood up.

"Can't you see how painful all this is to me? There are some things that it is far kinder to leave buried in the past."

Janey looked up at her.

"Such as how you and dad murdered Skipper, because he was having an affair with Kathy Adeay?"

There was a long spinning silence. Madame Joseph stood with a hand under her left breast. Ted Modley seemed to retreat behind the line of blue smoke that spiralled up from his cigarette. Sal gave a little gasp, then sat tense and expectant. Only Jimmy, who didn't understand what it was all about, though he knew in a dimly groping fashion that it concerned someone who in some wholly incomprehensible way was his father, went on eating, but still as silently as he could, sensing the atmosphere.

"And not only Skipper," Janey said at last, "but Kathy's young brother, and five others, strangers, who happened to be in the boat."

Madame Joseph said: "Ted –" and began to sway, holding on to the back of her chair. Ted Modley's eyes were screwed up against the heat from the hanging cigarette. He said: "Is this what your boy-friend told you?"

"I've seen the *Gazette*, too. And Kathy –"

"Have you been up there? Up to his house?" Madame Joseph stopped her swaying, stood small and hard. "Talking about *us*, with *her*?"

"I like her."

"She was the town whore when she was still at school. Did she tell you that?"

"No, and I don't believe it!"

"Where do you think Jack Simpson got the money to open the garage? *She* bought that place. And some of the money she used came from Skipper. From me, if you like to trace it back far enough, I dare say –"

"That's a lie!"

"It isn't. Everyone in the town knew about it. That boy. Her brother. He was only a year older than she was. He used to hawk her around like they do in Egypt, taking a cut for himself –"

"Shut your face," Ted Modley said. "You'll say too much, and be sorry for it."

"I won't have my daughter marrying the son of that girl! How do we know he isn't Skipper's son?"

"What difference would it make?" Janey demanded. "I'm not Skipper's daughter."

"Are you *really* thinking of getting *married*?" Sal said uncertainly. "Surely not, J –"

"I don't know. I might. Why shouldn't I? I'm a year older than you. And you're as good as hooked with Mel –"

"I forbid it!" Madame Joseph exclaimed dramatically. "I absolutely forbid it!"

"You can't."

Ted Modley said: "She's right. You can't, Jo. She's supposed to be old enough to know her own mind –"

"Then I shall stop it!"

"How, for God's sake?" Janey demanded. "A shot-gun at the altar? Talk bloody sense, ma!"

Madame Joseph said: "I have the power. Make no mistake about that. And if it proves necessary, I shan't hesitate to use it."

Ted Modley stubbed out the end of his cigarette, pushed back his chair, and stood up.

"Now, Jo –"

"Tell her!" Madame Joseph said. "Tell her what I did to *Seamew*! Tell her everything I've done! Then perhaps she'll listen –"

"Jo!" he said sharply. And: "For Christ's sake shut your stupid trap, woman!"

CHAPTER TWO

(1)

ANOTHER summer passed; another winter. Another thousand tides had licked with their rough wet tongues at the shrinking land. Now it was spring again, and Janey and Sal were married; no longer living in the house at Parrott Lane.

Despite her mother's opposition, Janey had married Kathy Adeay's son. Three months earlier, on her eighteenth birthday, Sal had married Melvin Williams. Both girls, like most of the young marrieds in the town, had kept on their seasonal jobs; *to give them something to do*, they always said. But like everyone else in a town that regularly staggered from one season to the next along the knife-edge of threatened bankruptcy, it was only the money they really wanted.

Mel had his own business, such as it was; while Barry, with a second-class History degree, and literary ambitions on the side, had long ago drifted into teaching. If it had been left to Mel, things might possibly have stayed that way for all of them. But Barry had other ideas. Big ideas. Dangerous ideas. He wanted out. Out of Westport, and the dull treadmill of provincial wage-earning. Out in a big way. And because he needed the others, he persuaded them that that was what they wanted, too. Out, at any price.

In the Marine Bar, behind the Skating Rink, Barry Simpson and Mel Williams sat at a small table in an empty corner, each with a glass in front of him. Mel said: "I told you the old fool wouldn't come. You scared him off."

Barry's eyes swam alarmingly behind the magnifying lenses of his spectacles.

"He'd better come."

"What's that supposed to mean? What can you do if he doesn't, for Christ's sake?"

"I can beat him up," Barry said. "That's what I can do to the little bastard."

"And what would Janey say if you did? Talk sense, for Christ's sake!"

"Janey hates his guts –"

"He's her father, for Christ's sake!"

"So he says."

Mel Williams moved impatiently.

"That bloody hare running again! Who else would it be?"

Barry's mouth was like the predatory gape of a young bird, a raw red hole in his downy fuzz of beard.

"I wouldn't trust the old woman. She knew what was what in those days."

"But, Christ, I thought it was Ted Modley that –"

"Sure, he married her. After they'd got rid of Skipper Roberts. But that doesn't mean he was the only one."

"Does it matter?"

"It might. But it probably doesn't. It doesn't make Janey hate his guts any more, or any less. She just hates them."

Mel glanced over towards the door. Except for a group at the far end, the Bar was empty. He said: "You seem pretty certain about Skipper."

"I'm as certain as I need be."

"But *how*, for Christ's sake? How'd they do it? You don't believe in that other crap?"

Barry said: "I believe they tried it."

"And it worked? Sinking a boat two miles off-shore, on a clear day?"

"Keep your voice down! Or do you want to share it with all the rest of the town?"

"What difference does it make?" But he lowered it a fraction. "You said yourself that's what most people thought at the time –"

"That was twenty years ago. The rest of the town's mostly forgotten it. Keep this to ourselves, and maybe we can use it. Spread it, and it'll be useless. Remember that."

Melvin said: "I'll remember it." And: "The old fool's here. I was wrong."

Barry turned his head, saw Ted Modley standing just inside the door.

"I'd've killed him if he hadn't come." And waving across the dimly-lit Bar, with its stuffed fish and glass floats and plastic seaweed and blown-up photographs of mermaids with blown-up breasts and silver-paper tails, he shouted: "Hey, dad!" And only a shade less loudly: "Over here, you silly old bugger. Can't you see your own two loving sons-in-law?"

"Don't rattle the old fool. He scares easy."

"I'd like to do more than scare him. Get the drinks, Mel. Make his two doubles and a dash of soda in the same glass. He may want softening up."

Melvin moved over to the counter, nodding to Ted Modley as he passed. When he returned to the table, Ted was sitting sullenly, his arms folded. He took the glass, tasted it, said: "For God's sake, what's this? Dynamite?"

"We're ahead of you," Barry said. "Drink up."

Ted Modley drank, wiped his mouth, closed his eyes for a second as the fire of the whisky went down his throat like a flaming sword. Then he drank again, and relaxed.

"All right," he said. "What do you want?" He held the glass up to what underwater light there was in the Bar, squinted at the handful of bubbles that rose through the pale amber. "You didn't get me here just to give me this."

"Drink up," Barry said again. He lifted his own drink, said: "Cheers!" and automatically Ted Modley drained his glass. "Get the same again," Barry said. "Here's the money." He passed a fiver across to Melvin, who pushed back his chair, and went over again to the counter. It didn't occur to him to say: "Get it yourself." He deferred in most things to the tall, hairy, half-blind Barry.

When he returned with the drinks, and a plate of crisps, Ted Modley was sitting loosely, as though the whisky had slackened the tight strings that had held his body rigid.

Modley said: "Is that the other half of the dynamite?" He tasted it, giggled, and said: "Christ, it's a bloody atom bomb." Then he said again: "What do you want?"

"Information."

Ted Modley looked up at Barry, his small eyes suddenly shifty.

"You've asked me before for information. Time after bloody time. Even before you were married. Is this the same?"

"The same, dad."

Modley put down his glass, hauled himself to his feet, stood swaying a little.

"How many more times, then? I've told you –"

"This is different now. Your old woman's been talking."

Ted sat down again, picked up his glass and drained it. He had to close his eyes again as the fire burned, but he said clearly enough: "She's always talking. You don't want to take no notice of anything she says. She still thinks she's on a direct line to the spooks."

"She doesn't do so badly out of it."

"They're born every minute." His eyes were open again, still shifty, moving about the shadowy clutter of the Bar. Mel eased himself out of his seat, came back with another glass of almost neat whisky, slid it unobtrusively in front of the old man. Barry was still pressing him, but he didn't seem to have made much progress in the minute or two that Mel had been away.

"But that's exactly it," he was saying, still on the subject of Madame Joseph and her voices. "The suckers pay good money for that sort of crap. So why not for something bigger?"

Ted Modley seemed suddenly to notice that his glass had been filled. He took a drink, leaned forward across the table. "What sort of something?"

"Tell me," Barry said. "Did the Jo-bird really whistle up a storm that day?"

And now the old man was at last beginning to show that he had downed four double whiskies in the same number of minutes, and was already nibbling into the next powerful pair. He hit the top of the table with the flat of his hand, and as solemn as a pussycat, as Mel said afterwards, he put his face close to Barry's and said: "She whistled it. Sure she did. She went through all the bloody pantomime –" He broke off abruptly, turned his head towards Mel. "Who the hell are you?"

"I'm nobody. I just married your other daughter. Remember?"

The old fool took another drink, then he said to no-one in particular. "All the bloody pantomime –" And: "Which other daughter?"

"Sal."

Ted Modley seemed to be trying to remember who Sal was. Either he remembered, or he gave up the attempt, for when he spoke again it was about the storm. "Christ, what a bloody pantomime." And: "It's a long time ago."

"Twenty years. Give or take."

"Is it? Is it that long?"

"So I'm told, dad. And the *Gazette* wouldn't lie, would it?"

Something like a tear ran down out of one shifty eye.

Mel said: "Maybe that last drink was a mistake."

"He'll do. I'm hopeful." And then Ted Modley's fist hit the table again.

"She thought she'd done it. She still thinks she done it. Whistled it up, with all the bloody trimmings. And down it went in deep water. Did you know it was in deep water? They never got her up."

"I know that." Patiently. "It was all in the *Gazette*."

"This week?"

"No, you stupid old bugger! Twenty years ago!"

"Twenty years ago?" Ted Modley was fast losing control of his wits. "What do you know about what happened twenty years ago?" He sounded frightened.

Barry said: "We've got him rattled. Any moment now he'll talk."

"He, or the whisky."

"What's it matter, so long as it's the truth?"

Ted Modley said: "What's she been telling you?"

"What's who been telling us?"

"The old lady –"

"Oh, you remember that, do you? She's been telling us how she did it."

"Did what?" But his eyes were wild with what certainly looked like fear.

"Killed Skipper Roberts, of course. What else?"

"She didn't kill him."

"Someone did."

"She didn't raise no bloody storm! That was all for the birds."

"But she tried to."

"Sure, I told you that. She went through it, and she thought she'd conjured up a spirit –"

"What sort of a spirit?"

"A demon. One that raises storms and causes shipwrecks."

Mel said: "*Crap!*" and Barry reached out a hand, held it rigid, brought it down hard on his wrist. Mel jerked his arm away, and tipped over his glass. "What's that for, for Christ's sake?"

Barry ignored him. To Ted Modley, he said: "Go on, dad. She raised this spirit –"

The old man almost spat at him.

"You don't bloody listen! She didn't raise no bloody spirit. She only thought she did."

"How did she come to think she had?" Barry said quietly. "Did she see it?"

"She thought she did."

"What *did* she see?"

"Never you mind."

"She saw you, dad. Didn't she?"

"You can't prove that –"

"I don't have to. You've told me. That's good enough for me."

"I never told you –"

"Yes, you did!"

"I never –" The old man – they always called him the *old man*, or the *old fool*, though he wasn't much over fifty; it was just that he was old to them, small and grey and desiccated – swung his head like a beast before its slaughterer, bemused by the whisky and by the turn of the argument. "I never said that."

"But you don't deny it? Do you, dad?"

"You've no right –" the old fool began. But Barry said suddenly: "Forget it. What we want to know is how you fixed Skipper's boat."

The swinging of the old man's head stopped. It was as though he had been fighting his way through the tangle of question and answer, and had suddenly come up against a plate-glass wall. It brought him up short, held him suspended, his drooling mouth half-open, his eyes fixed on the reflections in Barry's pebble-lenses.

"What was that you said?"

"You heard me, dad."

"That's right," Mel said encouragingly. "Tell us how you fixed it so it went down, and no-one got away to tell how it happened."

Skipper Roberts, the boat-boy, and the five holiday-makers had set out soon after breakfast to spend the day on Sanctuary Island, a narrow, rocky, bird-haunted strip of land that unexpectedly reared itself out of the open sea, ten miles off-shore, and five miles or more to the north of the little town. No-one lived on the island, which was a protected breeding ground for sea-birds, but there was an automatic light at each end to warn shipping. Only with permission from the local Protection Society were tourists allowed to land there, but bird-watchers and photographers used the place from time to time, when landing conditions were favourable. There was only one rocky inlet, on the leeward side, and Skipper Roberts was one of the few local boatmen who cared to risk what could be a hazardous exercise even in a halcyon calm. On this day, July the eleventh, the sea was like a flat blue field that had been lightly scored by a celestial harrow. There was a morning haze, as Skipper took *Seamew* out of the little harbour and headed her into the misty blue. Later, the sun would draw the mist off the sea, like a great curtain slowly raised from a vast proscenium arch, but for the moment, visibility was no more than a quarter of a mile, and there was no other vessel in sight.

Skipper waved to the harbourmaster, George Pullen, as *Seamew* passed the end of the breakwater, and shouted something that George didn't catch. But it seemed unimportant, from the relaxed fashion in which Skipper lounged at the helm. George waved back, and thought no more about it. *Seamew* chugged on across the lightly furrowed blue field, disappeared at last into the bright mist. And no-one ever saw her again.

The alarm was raised by the master of a Norwegian timber ship, towards evening. Off the Sanctuary, he had found a water-can, with the name and port of origin of *Seamew*, floating in a scattering of other items of ship's gear. Arrived in the harbour, he showed the few things that he had picked up, and George Pullen immediately organised a search. The town lifeboat was launched, and a growing number of volunteer craft went out into the westering light. The air-sea rescue station at Cranes Head sent a fast launch and a pair of helicopters. A few more articles were found, floating peacefully enough in the evening calm, and a small patch of oil. But no sign of the seven people who had been on board – five men and two women – or of the boat's life-saving gear.

The news spread fast in the little town. A small crowd waited all night on the harbour wall, while the work continued with the aid of searchlights from the rescue launch and from a corvette that had been ordered up from the base at Calston. At dawn, three more aircraft joined in, and though, as on the previous day, the morning was hazy, the choppers quartered the ocean only a few feet above the heads of the volunteers in the boats, working on a precisely charted flight pattern that made it unlikely that anything still on the surface could have been missed. On the Sanctuary itself, a landing-party found no sign that *Seamew* had ever reached her destination.

What could have happened to such a craft – old, it is true, but sound enough – under an experienced skipper like Bob Roberts, in such weather? A collision? Some other vessel, looming out of the mist? Hit and run, and the little *Seamew* left to sink? But, if so, why had the skipper and his passengers not seized the life-jackets that the boat was required to carry under government regulations, and stayed afloat in the halcyon sea until the alarm was raised? No time, perhaps. But if the collision, or whatever it was, had been sudden and violent, surely parts of the hull, or of the superstructure, would have been found? There was nothing, except a few items of gear, including the half-empty water-can.

The first body was sighted, floating at the edge of the tide near the estuary, eight days later. It was one of the women, an artist and ornithologist of some repute. Later the same day, the cabin-boy, young Johnny Adeay, was washed ashore near the same place. And during the next few days, the bodies of three other passengers, and of Skipper himself, were recovered. All bore marks of injuries; of contusions and abrasions that could have been caused at or after the moment of death. Some even had what one pathologist described as scorch-marks. But after anything up to two weeks in the water, it was difficult to be sure. One body, that of a young man named Charles Fletcher, a professional bird photographer, was never found.

"Tell us," Mel said. "It must have been a damn clever trick."

Ted Modley still seemed hypnotised by the reflections in Barry's powerful glasses. But he stared at them in a curiously unfocussed way; as though, perhaps, he was looking right through them back into the past.

"Tell us," Barry said, very quietly. "Tell us, dad. We want to know."

"They all wanted to know."

"But you didn't tell them, did you, dad? You didn't even tell Madame Jo."

"No, I didn't tell no-one."

"It's a long time ago, dad. You can tell us."

"Why should I?"

"Because we want to help you."

"Help me?" the old man repeated, as though in a trance. "Why should I need help?"

"Because they're going to reopen the inquiry. That's why."

The old man seemed to shrink still further into his loose-fitting blue suit. His eyes came back into focus with an effort that seemed at one stage to be almost more than his frail strength could achieve. Whether through the whisky he had drunk, or through fear, or from a combination of the two, he seemed incapable of closing his mouth. With difficulty, he whispered: "*What* did you say, boy?"

"You heard me, dad."

"*Reopen?* But they can't –"

"They can, dad. One of the passengers was a man named Charles Fletcher. His body was never found. He was a young man, about twenty-eight, and he was a damned good photographer. He was also married, with a child. His wife and child stayed behind. He went out in *Seamew* to get some pictures of the birds on Sanctuary Island. Remember?"

The old man nodded. His frail neck looked as though it might snap under the movement. He said: "I remember."

"Fletcher's child was only six at the time. A boy. His mother had a hell of a wait before she could establish legally that her husband was dead. She also had a hell of a fight to get her insurance money. In all, she had a hell of a fight. The boy is now twenty-six. He's a journalist and a photographer, like his father, and he's organising an expedition to raise *Seamew* to try to find out just what happened."

"They can't raise her. She's in deep water."

"So it was assumed at the time, because of the place where the oil-slick and the water-can and the other bits were found. But there's a new theory. That there's a tidal drift. They've been out there studying it. The boat is assumed never to have reached the island, because the record book in the Society's hut there had no entry. So it must have gone down on the way there. But if it did, and the oil and the other tacker were caught in this drift and carried to where they were found by the Norwegian skipper, then it could be that *Seamew* had already crossed the deep channel, and was over the rock-shelf that surrounds Sanctuary –"

Ted Modley looked as though he was about to collapse. He said almost inaudibly: "They tried to find her before. All round the island. They couldn't locate her then, so why should they now?"

"Things've moved in the last twenty years, dad. They don't use guess-work and grappling-hooks any more. They can dive a hell of a lot deeper, and they'll use echo-sounders, metal detectors, under-water television, the lot. And the main thing is, they'll know just *where* to look."

Mel said: "Drink up, dad, you're going to need it." But the old man didn't seem to hear him. He sat at the table, seeming to grow smaller and frailer with every word that oozed out of the pink, wet, hair-fringed baby-mouth of his daughter Janey's husband.

"They'll use computers. They'll calculate the speed from the harbour, the time, the course, the tidal drift. And from that they'll get a fix that'll take them right to it. And if it's on the shelf, not in the deep, they'll find it."

(2)

In bed, that night, Barry said: "I think we've got the old man."

"Did he talk?"

"Not a lot. But he's dead scared."

Janey ran her hands over the fine fair hair of his body. He lay relaxed, absorbed in his thoughts, staring at the ceiling. As a lover, he was unsatisfactory, and there were times when she wished that she had married Melvin instead. But Barry had the brains, there was no doubt about that. He'd make enough for the four of them, if she played along with him.

"Did he tell you how he did it?"

"No. But it's obvious he did. The old lady conjured up a demon to do the job, but the demon was her own boyfriend!" He began to laugh, deep down inside himself. "I'd've given my right hand to have seen it. Honest, I would. The stupid old cow still thinks it was old Nick, or Duke Focalor –"

Janey withdrew her hands abruptly.

"Duke *who*, for God's sake?"

"He's one of the spirits that are supposed to cause death by shipwreck and drowning."

Janey giggled.

"I still can't believe it! Even though I lived with her for long enough. I know she's cracked as a cob-nut. But *that* old story!"

"The old man says she still thinks she did it. But for my bet it was Ted himself. I wish I knew how, though."

"It was a bit wholesale, wasn't it? However they did it.

All those passengers –" She gave a little shiver. "Did he have to drown them all, just to get rid of Skipper?"

"It had to look like an accident. With no clear motive. There was the insurance to be claimed –"

Janey said: "I still can't think of dad and mam –" She leaned across and kissed him. "Hell, lover-boy, they aren't exactly Romeo and Juliet, are they? Do you think they were on the cock and pullet themselves before it happened, like Skipper and Kathy?"

"I should think it's more than likely. Otherwise, why would the old man risk a murder rap for her? And would he have appeared as Duke Focalor outside her magic circle, naked as a coot and with a pair of home-made wings –"

At the thought of it, Janey began to laugh, and he held her to him, laughing himself at the absurdity of the image. But suddenly she stopped her laughter, raised herself on her elbows, and said: "How do you know about this Duke, for God's sake? And his wings? Did he tell you?"

"No."

"Then how do you know?"

"I've been reading. It's all in the books."

"Barry," she said, "I know what you and Mel want. And, Christ, lover, we can do with the money. But –" She broke off, and shivered again. "I'm cold. Pull the blankets up."

"What's the matter?" he teased her. "Frightened of the spooks?" But he covered her gently enough. "Don't worry, love. I'll look after them."

"Barry, do you think we ought to go on with this? I *am* frightened. Just a bit. If you push dad too far –"

"Do you think he might try something on us? On Mel and me? He better hadn't –"

But he sounded less sure of himself. Janey said: "I still can't believe it of him. But if he *did* fix the boat –"

"Of course he fixed it! There's no other explanation. And if you'd seen the old fool tonight in the Bar –"

"Did he believe the story about the Fletchers?"

"He hadn't any option. And he isn't likely to go about

asking questions, in case it *is* true. He won't risk drawing attention to himself."

"And what about Mam?"

"That's *his* job, to fix it with her. The longer she goes on thinking she can raise spooks, the better."

In bed at the same time, Mel was saying: "It'll work, Sal. Leave it to Barry. He'll fix it. All we have to do is go along with him."

In bed a few hours later, Ted Modley awoke with a suddenness that was alarming. Madame Joseph lay asleep beside him. The face of the luminous alarm-clock, when he could draw it into focus, said four a.m. His head ached, and his mouth and throat felt like blotting-paper. He had only a muddled recollection of what had happened in the Marine Bar, but it was enough to make him sweat with sudden fear. He'd got out of the habit of drinking, and the unaccustomed whisky had softened his wits. What had he given away? That was the problem. Somewhere in the fragments of his memory was the name Fletcher. Fletcher was presumed dead in *Seamew*, but his body had never been found. What had they told him about Fletcher? He couldn't remember. But the name sent him back to the days after the sinking. The little town had waited with a shocked incredulity for the seven bodies to be delivered up from the drowning sea, but only six had ever been found. Then had followed the inquiry. Even then, he'd been terrified that Madame Joseph would boast about what she thought she had done. But she had had sense enough to keep quiet at the inquest, and at the inquiry they hadn't called her. As for him, he hadn't dared ever to get drunk since. Not once in twenty years. Not until last night, in the fish and mermaid gloom of the Marine Bar.

Madame Joseph stirred.

"Ted?" she said sharply. "Why are you awake? What time is it?"

How the hell did she know he was awake? he thought savagely. He wasn't tossing around. He was just lying there, sweating a little, trying to remember. She was a curious creature. Sometimes she put the shutters up, and then she didn't know if it was Christmas Day or half-past bloody tea-time, and you could have stolen her fat black purse right out of her hand, and she wouldn't have known. But other times she was like a precision microphone, picking up vibrations with the sensitivity of a moth's antennae. You daren't even *think* when she was tuned in like that, never mind do or say anything. That was how she was when she scared the scepticism and the self-esteem out of the holiday-makers on the Pier. And that was how she was now, he realised. He tried to put his own shutters up against her, but it was no good.

"What's the matter, Ted?"

"Nothing."

"You're worrying about something. It's that old business. *Seamew* –"

"Let it rest."

"What time did you come in last night?"

"I don't know. You were asleep."

Sharply: "You'd been drinking."

"Only one."

He felt her sitting up in the big bed.

"You fool! Who were you drinking with? Barry – and Mel –"

How did she know that? But there was no point in denying it. He kept quiet, and she said sharply: "You're a fool, Ted Modley. You should keep away from that Barry Simpson. He's dangerous. He's got bad blood in him –"

"I know he's dangerous. But you'll be a bigger fool if you cross him. He knows too much."

"Too much about what? About *Seamew*?"

"What else? He told me that someone's going to salvage her – reopen the inquiry –" That much, at least, he unexpectedly remembered.

There was a sudden catch of her breath in the darkness. Then: "How can they? She's in deep water."

Suddenly it all came back.

"That's what I said. But they think she might be on the island shelf."

A long silence. Then Madame Joseph said: "It was the only way. What I did was deserved. I had the power, and I used it. The others who died were incidental. One cannot always direct power with absolute precision."

Ted Modley tried to keep his thoughts from going back to that night, twenty years earlier, but he couldn't stop the images crowding back. He was afraid that Madame Jo would see into the chaos of his mind, but as she went on talking, he realised that she had withdrawn the antennae, that she was no longer the ultra-sensitive receiver. She was concerned only with her own memories.

"Even if they find her, there'll be no means of knowing. Focalor wouldn't leave any traces. When I ordered him to do it, I told him specifically it was to look like an accident...."

Barry said: "At a guess, she used the *Lemegeton*, the *Little Key*, and the *Grimorium Verum*. She's got both in her séance room."

Janey had given up trying to rouse him. She had fallen asleep at last, waking to find the light still on. He was lying on his back, his eyes without their glasses staring unfocussedly at the bedroom ceiling.

"What are those, for Jeez' sake?" She yawned and stretched her long legs in the warmth of the bed.

"Grimoires. Text-books of magic."

"The ones you've been reading? About the Duke?"

He said: "There's more than the Duke in them."

She said sleepily: "Christ, lover-boy, surely *you* don't take them seriously?"

He didn't answer, and she pulled at his arm. "Did you hear what I said?"

"I heard you." And after a long pause: "No," he said. "No, of course not."

"Then why, for Jeez' sake, are you lying awake at – what the hell time is it, anyway?"

"Four o'clock. Give or take a thousand years."

She sat up at that.

"Barry, what's the matter with you? You're all hooked up on this business –"

"It fascinates me."

"What's so fascinating? The spooks, or the mugs who think they raise them?"

"Both, maybe. Go to sleep."

"I like that! What about you?"

Still with his eyes fixed blindly on the ceiling, he murmured: "I shall repeat the seventy-two names of God. And then I shall fall asleep."

Uncertainly, she said: "Christ, Bar, I've got a spook-raiser for a mother, and maybe a killer for a father. I don't want a crazy spook-raising bastard of a husband."

"Not to worry," he said. And at last he took her in his arms.

When I ordered him ... Ted Modley repeated the words in his mind. All these years the stupid old cow had clung to the idea that she had ordered a demon to sink *Seamew*, and that her orders had been carried out. She'd been young then, of course, only twenty-eight; dark, intense, passionate. Odd, even then, with her voices; but strong-willed, and with the hot southern blood of her gipsy mother. Ted was already a rake, a gambler, a heavy drinker. Like Josephine, he was small and dark, wholly unlike the big blond extrovert that Madame Jo had married, and had grown to hate with a fierce intensity that was like a core of fire, nursed in darkness, waiting for release. The aura of dissolution, of petty evil, that clothed the young Ted Modley was an aura that she recognised instantly, the first time he came to Parrott Lane to see Skipper about some work he was to do on *Seamew* in his spare time. For when he wasn't gambling or drinking, or working in the Entertainments Office, Ted Modley could turn his hand to almost anything if there was money in it. Skipper did most of his own maintenance on *Seamew*, which meant that he hired jobbers like Modley to do the work while he applied himself to wenching, or to fishing from the harbour wall, according to the time of the year.

In Ted Modley, she saw a tool; a multi-purpose item of equipment. A means of satisfying the itch of passion that could no longer be eased against the man she had married. A way of revenge against that blond unfeeling giant. A source of help in the running of the house; help which Skipper had never given. And finally a channel, conditioned by petty evil, for the greater forces that she was already attempting to conjure. She saw a man hopelessly in debt, harassed by the rules of the world, weak as a kitten in moral strength, but cunning as a jackal when it suited him; still with something of the attraction of the handsome young boy who had once sung in the choir at St. Luke's for the sake of the small sums that it earned him, and that even then he had gambled away in the vestry or behind the tombstones in the churchyard.

Madame Joseph said: "I still can't think why they want to reopen it. After all this time."

"Barry told me you've been talking –"

"Not me! He's a liar if he said that."

"You've come damn close to it a good many times –"

"Close is not the same. At a guess he was trying to trick you. What else did he tell you? Why are they suddenly so interested in it again?"

"It's Fletcher. The one they never found. His son –"

"I never understood what happened to Fletcher. All the others were accounted for. Duke Focalor must have taken him."

Duke Focalor, he repeated again contemptuously in his

mind. This woman, lying beside him, that he had once found attractive, who had paid his debts, who had taken him into her bed, who had sucked the manhood out of him like a female mantis who starts to eat her mate even in the act of copulation – this woman whom he had once deceived into thinking she had raised a demon ... He was still not altogether sure what had actually happened on that particular night. But he remembered how it had all started. They had been in bed in Parrott Lane, one day at noon, for he had been on late shift the night before, and Skipper was out with his boat. He'd lain back, drifting in the warm euphoria of passion spent, and he'd heard her say: "Before the Moon is out of Cancer, he could be dead." And: "If you will help me, all your debts can be paid." She had told him how, and he'd said *no*. Confidently she had said: "You *will* help me. And he *will* die. Before the Moon is in Leo, he will be dead."

Over and over, in the next two weeks, he had said: *No!* And: *For Christ's sake!* And: *Don't be a fool, Jo!* And at the end of the two weeks, the thugs from the chain of betting-shops to which he owned the most had set on him as he came away from yet another late-night dance on the Pier. On the following day, waking bruised and frightened, he had telephoned the house in Parrott Lane to say that he would do anything she asked.

"Tell me," Janey said. "How would she have done it?"

Barry's eyes went out of focus again.

"Done what? Raised the Duke?"

Janey said: "As a lover, you're improving. Yes. Tell me that."

"The old man said she went through what he called the whole bloody pantomime. So maybe she did."

"Tell me, Bar."

"It'd take all night," he said. "And more. Some time when I've a thousand years to spare."

And in a sharp little voice that she hardly recognised

she snapped at him: "Oh, for Jeez' sake! You and your thousand years. . . ."

He'd helped her with all her preparations, crazy though they had seemed. He'd stolen holy water from the Church in Westburne, bringing it home in a couple of empty vinegar bottles. He'd stood by while she had said her conjurations over the knife, the salt, the ink, the pen, and God knows how many other bits and pieces. He'd borrowed a van, and together they had gone out beyond Westburne to Compton Morva, to a drunken old woman who kept a herd of half-wild goats. They'd brought back a young kid in a sack, and had taken it down to the cellar under number forty-three, where he'd knocked up an altar for her out of some timber he'd taken from the boatyard. And if ever he had seriously thought she was crazy, it was then. With Skipper safely on his way out to the island in *Seamew*, she had made him strip, and, naked herself, she'd told him to hold the struggling kid on its back in front of the altar. She'd taken the sacrificial knife that he had himself sharpened until he could have shaved with it; a wicked blade a full fifteen inches long with a heavy six-inch handle. All the words had been said over it; holy water had been sprinkled on it; it had been fumigated with herbs. Now she stood in the harsh light of the single lamp in the ceiling over the altar, small and dark and intense, her arms raised high over her head, the knife in her left hand. Firmly, her voice echoing a little in the confined space of the little cellar, she had said: "I kill you in the name and to the honour of Focalor!" Then with a single blow she had sent the long razor-sharp blade through the throat of the little animal, almost severing the head. It had made one convulsive movement, and blood had fountained out over their naked limbs. Then, warm as it still was, its heart still fluttering in its small white body, she had set about skinning it, hacking at it cruelly with the sacrificial blade. She had been covered in blood before she had finished, coot-crazy and trembling.

And he had had to gather up all the warm slippery entrails and gobbets of flesh that she had torn away from the cruelly mangled skin that was to be the basis of her virgin parchment. At least, he had comforted himself, it had been only a kid; not, as some of the books said, a male child. . . .

Mel and Sarah were also, unaccountably, awake again.

Sarah said: "What do *you* think, Mel? Is there really money in it? Big money?"

"Barry says –"

"*Barry says!*" she mocked him. "Just for once, let's hear what Melvin Williams thinks."

"It's Barry's scheme. All we have to do is go along with him."

"That's what you said before. What I want to know is –"

"All right!" he said. "All right. I know what you want to know! That's all I'm interested in, too. I don't give a damn whether anyone's ever raised a spook or not."

"Does Barry?"

"He nearly turned the old man inside out last night. The poor old sod didn't know if he was on his head or his arse when we took him back to Spookville."

"But isn't that just –"

Mel yawned and turned over. "I don't know what's in his tiny mind. Honest, I don't, love. Sure, we want to get the old man in, and we want to know what's what. But it seemed to me –" He broke off, and yawned again. "Christ, I'll never get to work in the morning if I don't get some bloody sleep. Just leave it to Barry, love. He'll fix it, if anyone can."

CHAPTER THREE

(1)

THE Chapel did not exist in daylight. It was a place conjured out of darkness and illusion.

Five miles out of town, towards the Moor, a wilderness of broken concrete and thistles and gaunt buildings that had been a service air-field in the war had been partly cleared and re-opened as an industrial estate. A few firms had been persuaded to rent space there, and either to build their own small factories, or to take over and adapt part of the existing ramshackle collection of admin blocks, stores and small hangars that had lain idle for over a quarter of a century.

Mel Williams, after four years at the local College of Technology, which was shortly to become the new University, had set himself up with a diploma in electronics, insufficient capital, and almost no knowledge at all of the cut-throat world of modern business. As Melvill Electric, he had taken a twenty-year lease of a one-acre plot that included a former vehicle repair-shop; an echoing metal-framed building with a high roof, and with sliding doors that had rusted solid over the years. He had borrowed more than he could afford, installed adequate heating, and had turned the place into a workshop and store. It was too big for a one-man business, merely to house the few stores that he carried, and the small bench area, which between them occupied no more than a tenth of the available space; but when the doors were freed of their accumulation of rust, at least he could run the van inside, lock it safely away, and ride back home in the small white convertible that he and Sarah used. Once locked, the place was a fortress, safe against the marauding motor-cycle gangs that occasionally plagued the rest of the estate.

The wartime repair-shop had been built with double walls and roof, so that it was really a building within a building. This had been done so that work could go on all through the night, with no risk of light escaping to give away the location of the airfield to enemy raiders. It meant now that, with the sliding doors locked and black-out curtains lowered over the entrance to the inner shell, the Chapel and all its conjurations were equally unlikely to attract attention from outside.

It was Barry Simpson who had found the place, who had talked Mel into moving out there from the shed behind the Skating Rink where he had first set up his largely unprofitable establishment. For six months, time and materials that Mel could ill afford were taken from the business, until they were satisfied that they could improve no further on the performance they could offer. The two girls, Janey and Sarah, were schooled in their own parts. Initial reluctance once overcome, they stripped and went through their routine, over and over again, under Barry's critical and short-sighted eyes, while Mel worked his tapes and his electronic flashes from the space behind the altar.

At last, one night, Barry said: "This is it. The first."

It was nearly eight weeks after the evening with Ted Modley in the Marine Bar. He and Mel and Janey and Sal were sitting on the grass on the Headland, watching the night crawl slowly in from the sea. Behind them, a small green van stood patiently; an unobtrusive vehicle with removable plates on either side which said simply *Melvill Electric*. It was Mel's new service vehicle, not yet paid for. And it was planned to use this, without the trade name, or with something far less traceable, for any transport that might be needed.

With a little tremor of excitement, Sarah said: "Well, tell us, for Jeez sake!"

Barry said: "I saw Madame Jo tonight. He's coming to see her tomorrow at ten p.m. At twenty-two hundred."

"And she'll tell him what?" Mel's voice was as uncertain as Sarah's.

"What we told her to tell him."

"And do you think he'll be there?"

"He'll be there. He's got problems. Big problems. He can't afford not to be there."

"What sort of problems?" Janey asked.

"Business problems."

"And what the hell are we going to do about those?" Sal demanded. "Christ, we can't even solve our own! Mel's got –"

"Shut that sweet little bloody trap," Mel said viciously. "Barry knows what he's doing."

"Sure he does," Janey said. "He's going to raise a Duke or something, who knows all about Business Methods." She giggled, and put her head on Barry's shoulder. "Isn't that right, lover? There's a Duke for every purpose, most of them with wings on."

Barry pushed her away.

"We've got to do better than this It's no good being flippant –"

"Take it seriously, and we'll all be in the bin together!"

Mel said: "We've put a lot of work into this, and a hell of a lot of cash we haven't got. Other people's cash. If it doesn't come off –"

"It'll come off," Barry said. "But only if –" He stopped, and spread out his hands. "One false move, and we're out of business for good. Play it straight, and maybe we can retire in five years. Go and live in the Bahamas, or Spain, or some place."

"I'll believe it when I see it," Sarah said. "But, Jeez, I sure would like just that. You and Janey and Mel and me. Lying on a coral beach in the sun."

Barry stood up, stretched out his arms towards the dark that was crawling in faster now from the sea.

"Just that and more, we might well do. But only if we work for it. Don't kid yourself it'll come without that."

(2)

Robert Cargrove's telephone had rung at precisely midnight. Mingled with the shrill summons of the bell was the striking of the long-case clock in the hall downstairs. Grumbling, he reached out a hand, murmured sleepily, then came suddenly awake. Beside him, his wife stirred, turned over, said something that he did not catch. His whole attention was focussed on the voice in his ear.

Three minutes later, he replaced the telephone, lay tense and sleepless while the clock downstairs struck one, then two, then three. When daylight came, he had slept only fitfully.

His wife said: "Did I hear the telephone? In the night?"

"What? Oh, yes. It was –" he thought desperately, "– the watchman at the factory. He thought he'd heard prowlers."

"Why disturb you? Couldn't he have got on to the police?"

"That's what I told him."

But all that day, and the day that followed, he thought of little else but the quiet voice that had dropped words like poisoned nectar out of the darkness into his troubled mind.

Cargrove was desperate. Or he would not have gone at all to the house in Parrott Lane. He would have dismissed the telephone call as the ravings of a madman; or at best the work of a joker. But the caller had known too much for it to have been either.

In the late afternoon of the second day, momentarily alone in the big house on the edge of the Moor, he had telephoned to Parrott Lane, and had arranged to see Madame Joseph at ten o'clock on the following evening. When the time came, he was admitted through the side door. Madame Joseph sat opposite him, with the big crystal ball that she used for effect in the centre of the table between them. In its base was a microphone, and in the cellar under their feet

Mel's tapes revolved slowly, adding to their store of knowledge.

She sat in her usual attitude of listening watchfulness. She listened, not only to the vibrations of trouble from the white-faced man on the other side of the table, but to the remembered voices of her own sons-in-law, threatening her with exposure unless she did exactly as she had been told. When she had talked of Duke Focalor, and of the impossibility of any proof being found even if *Seamew* were to be raised, Barry had laughed in her face. He'd said: "Duke Focalor was Ted Modley. Ask *him* how he fixed *Seamew*." And Ted at last had broken, had told her what he had done, had said for Christ's sake don't cross them, especially Barry – can't you see he's dangerous – he's Kathy Adeay's son –

Had Madame Joseph ever seriously believed that she had raised the Duke? That was what none of her family could agree upon, even now. But did she, even now, truly accept that Ted, and Ted alone, had tampered with *Seamew*'s gas cylinders, linking them to a time-operated battery lighter, so that they had blown an irreparable hole in the bilge? Did she, even now, believe that it was Ted Modley who had emptied *Seamew*'s safety-locker, carrying the heavy life-jackets and the inflatable raft well out to sea in the small outboard dinghy that he borrowed from time to time from Boatyard Simpson to fish in the early morning out in the bay. Lashed hard to lumps of broken concrete filched from the Corporation yard, they had gone overboard with barely a sound, the lips of the deep water sealing over them. It was common knowledge that Skipper never checked his boat before setting out. If the engine started at first kick, that was all that mattered.

Above all, did she truly believe that the indistinct figure that she had glimpsed in the near-darkness out on the salt-flats was Duke Focalor himself, or, as Barry maintained, and Ted now admitted, the same Ted Modley, naked as a coot, with a stocking-mask on his face, and a pair of home-made wings strapped to his bare shoulders?

She was a deep one, was Madame Joseph. That was what most of the town had said twenty years earlier. And now she did nothing to destroy that reputation. All she said was: "The Duke has his own way of working. If he used Ted Modley as his instrument . . ."

She gave nothing away, and what she really believed remained the subject of conjecture. But she seemed to accept the fact that she was vulnerable.

"Very well," she had said, her black eyes fixed on Barry's myopic stare. "I'll do as you tell me, within reason. I can see that I haven't much option. But I warn you most solemnly, you are playing with fire. Don't you realise that?"

"We know what we're doing," Barry had answered her. And she had replied, quietly but clearly: "I doubt if you do. But you must learn for yourself."

So to Robert Cargrove, of Cargrove and Fisk Associates, she said: "I know that you are in desperate trouble. I could give you the kind of general advice that I normally give to my clients, but this would be wholly inadequate in your case. I have reserves of power, but they need to be directed with precision. I must know exactly what you are seeking from me, so that I can help you to the full . . ."

Three times, Robert Cargrove came to the house in Parrott Lane. Each time, he stayed for about an hour. At the end of the third visit, Madame Joseph said: "I can help you. But you must do exactly as I tell you. And you must not tell another soul of it. Not even your wife. I repeat that. Not even your wife. If you do –" She broke off, and from somewhere far away Cargrove thought he heard the beating of powerful wings. Madame Joseph sat with her head on one side, listening. The sound of the great wings grew louder, then faded. "There are forces in the universe," she intoned, "that may be harnessed. There are sources of untold power that may be tapped. But only with the exercise of the utmost care. Electricity is the perfect analogy. With care, power that can destroy in a flash may be channelled and tamed. But neglect the rules, and – *pfft!* Do I make myself clear?"

Cargrove sat tense, still only half-convinced.

"Quite clear."

"Very well, then. Listen carefully. Do you know the point at which the upper road crosses the old green road, near the ford at Axel Heath?"

Cargrove nodded.

"I know it."

"Go there alone, at midnight on Friday next. The midnight between Friday and Saturday. Check your watch carefully. Arrive there with exactly five minutes of Friday still to go. Leave your car under the trees, down by the water, and walk to the cross-roads. You will carry with you a crucifix, which you will hold reversed in your left hand –"

Cargrove moved impatiently.

"Oh, for God's *sake* –!"

Madame Joseph froze.

"And what is that supposed to mean?"

Another impatient movement.

"Is all this – necessary?"

"Insulation, earth-wires, fuses. Are they necessary? The forces we invoke are the other face of God. The reversed crucifix will serve as a protection, and also as a means of identification. At midnight you will be met by a messenger, who will take you to a certain place, a clearing-house of power. You will obey this messenger implicitly. If you do not, you could be in grave danger. But if you do, no harm will come to you. Are you prepared to do this?"

Cargrove hesitated only for a moment. Then he said: "There is only one thing. I am in deep financial trouble, as you know. What will all this cost me?"

Madame Joseph named a sum, non-returnable and payable before Friday, to be a token of good faith. When the operation was successfully concluded, and only then, the balance would be due; payable, if desired, over a period of twelve months. A large enough sum, but not exorbitant under the circumstances.

"And if I don't pay?"

Madame Joseph's eyes hooded. The effect was disconcerting; as though a light had been extinguished, leaving him groping in darkness.

"You will pay."

"I could refuse," Cargrove persisted. "There will be no written contract, and in any case you wouldn't want it known that –"

Madame Joseph re-opened her jet-black eyes. The light returned.

"If the powers we control can help you out of your present difficulties, do you think they would hesitate to bring pressure on you to honour your debt? Or to destroy you, if you failed?"

*

So it was that with precisely three hundred seconds of Friday still to slide past from the infinite reservoir of time future into the bottomless pit of time past, Robert Cargrove stopped his grey Jaguar among the floodlit aisles of beech trees by the ford at Axel Heath. For a moment he hesitated, then he switched off the lights, flinched as the darkness pounced back. Recovering himself, he took a small silver crucifix from his jacket pocket, held it reversed in his left hand. Then he opened the door of the grey car, and stepped out into the body of the night.

He felt foolish, but afraid. A countryman still at heart, he had gone into his father's smithy and wrought-iron workshop at the age of fifteen. When he was eighteen, Joseph Cargrove had died, and Robert had carried on the business, at first in partnership with his mother, and then with Ray Fisk, another westcountryman, who had come out of his technical college with big ideas and who wanted a practical man to do the work. The partnership became Cargrove and Fisk, Engineers; then Fiskrove Fabrications.

Later still, when Fisk developed his own version of *cire-perdue*, the lost-wax method of casting in rare metals, together with a new process involving the use of a dimensionally stable ceramic mould, they had concentrated their entire resources on this new, and potentially limitless field. A loan was negotiated through the Coast Development Board, part of it secured on the new factory, the balance guaranteed by Fisk and Cargrove personally. A group of associated companies, for marketing and research and export and God knows what else, was set up to fool the taxman – all of this Fisk's idea. Cargrove bought a seven-bedroomed house up on the Moor, an Aston Martin for his wife, and a fast grey Jaguar for himself. All was set for the boom.

But the boom had not materialised. There were others already in the same field, and the market was not as limitless as it had at first seemed. Everything was on borrowed money, even the house on the Moor and the two cars. And after a moratorium of two years, the first repayment instalment of the big C.D.B. loan was now imminent. Fisk had been sensible. He had rented a small cottage near the factory, where he lived modestly. He was a co-guarantor of the loan with Cargrove, but what he had to back it with was problematical. Unmarried, he had only to skip and run, and Cargrove would be left. . . .

The night was fine, with a gibbous moon sailing fast through high banks of cloud. Or so it seemed to Cargrove, as holding the crucifix before him like a shield he climbed the slope to the ancient cross-roads. His reason told him that the moon's flight was an illusion. That it was the clouds, carried on some secret river of wind, that were being swept across the high dome of heaven, and over the moon's face. But as he climbed to the point where the track made by prehistoric men to the ford by the beech grove, crossed the newer road, he was uneasily aware of the ceaseless flight of the pregnant moon, now hidden, now showing its white face momentarily in the valleys between.

Axel Heath was ten miles from the sea, high up on a limestone plateau that had itself once been under the water, countless millions of years before. All over its wild surface were signs that primitive man had hunted, warred, and worshipped among its outcroppings of weathered rock. Deep down were caves, honey-combing through the heart of the hills; with black lakes of ice-cold water that had never seen the light of the sun; caverns the size of a parish church sculptured with curtains and pillars of bright colour; passages that were littered with the fossilised bones of those early men, and of the beasts they had hunted, long extinct. If the old gods still lived, it was surely in places like this, on such a night.

All around, the plateau stretched emptily away into the deceitful light of the fugitive moon. Hummocks of tortured rock quivered in the half-dark, half-light; appearing to move a fraction, then freezing again into watchful immobility.

Robert Cargrove's fear mounted. Ahead of him were the cross-roads. Shadowy and indefinite the ancient track lay under the later one that led nowhere but over the plateau to join the inland road at Roddon. A signpost stood like a white gallows, pointing either way. Cargrove, despite himself, murmured: "Our Father which art in Heaven . . ." and held up the silver crucifix. But then he remembered that it was reversed, pointing down into the complex world under his feet. He began to turn it, but before it had moved through more than twenty degrees he heard again the beating of wings, the same distant sound that he had heard in the séance room at Parrott Lane; powerful pinions that beat rhythmically at the air, torturing it into giving tongue. Instinctively, he looked up. The sound of the wings grew louder. A line of swans it could have been, flighting across the plateau down to the distant estuary. His eyes searched through the shifting light, but saw nothing. As the sound swelled, he turned the crucifix back to its original reversed position, came to a halt a dozen paces from the white post.

The great wings faded. Then suddenly, terrifyingly, a bell began to strike the hour of midnight.

The sound of the bell appeared to be all around him. It was a thin, cracked sound, like that contained in some ancient country steeple. But there was no church within a radius of miles. Such wind as there was, came from the sea. The wind that drove the clouds was another force altogether, high up in the dome of the sky. But the sea and the town were ten miles distant at least, away to the south-west, and this small cracked bell was close at hand. Rigid, he stood there and counted the strokes. The twelfth stroke died into the silence, and from behind him he heard his own name spoken.

"Robert Cargrove."

It was less of a question than a statement, underlying his presence there. Instantly, he swung to face the speaker.

"Yes?"

The figure was all in black, immensely tall. Only the shape of it, the outline of its blackness against the less black night had substance. It's face was a paler blur, without features. Cargrove held out the reversed crucifix, saw that the figure held a similar, larger crucifix in its left hand, the head pointing down.

"You are alone."

Again, it seemed a statement of fact. But Cargrove answered: "Yes, I am alone."

"I am the Messenger, sent to conduct you to those whose help you crave." The voice had an unreal, almost an unclear, quality. It was like the voice of a man speaking through a barrier that trapped certain vibrations, altering the pitch and structure of the sound. "In a few moments transport will arrive. Unremarkable, unobtrusive, ordinary to the point of banality. This is deliberate. We do not wish to draw attention . . ." The voice from behind the barrier faded. The figure stood listening. From the east, over the moor, came the sound of a vehicle, travelling fast.

(3)

A million stars rushed headlong past; a million points of brilliant light, flowing in the form of a river that had no beginning and no end. Over and round and through them drifted diaphanous clouds of purest colour, azure and amber and berylline and damask, changing almost imperceptibly to lapis lazuli and carmine, saffron and orpiment. And now the stars became precious stones. Diamonds the size of a turreted castle sparkled from a thousand facets. A turreted castle, brilliant as a diamond, appeared, grew nearer. Borne along by the hurrying stream, and by the drifting clouds, it sailed majestic as a bright-lit ship through the phosphorescence of a tropic night. From somewhere near at hand, voices were chanting in unison. The sound of the beating of wings swelled, became almost unbearable, screaming at the sensitive quickflesh of his hearing, drowning the chanting voices. As they faded, a single voice repeated over and over: *Come Béelzébuth, Lucifer, Astaroth ... Astaroth, Lucifer, Béelzébuth, come mighty Lords! I conjure thee by the other face of God; and by the seventy-two Names of God, each reversed, each the other name of God, who is at the same time the Prince of all Evil, Lord of all Good....*

Cargrove was intensely aware of his surroundings. All his senses seemed sharpened to a quivering pitch of almost unbearable receptivity. Slowly, solemnly, the seventy-two Names of God, each reversed as in a satanic mirror, swept past him, borne on the river of light.... *SATINIRT, REHTOS, SAISSEM, LEUNAMME, TOHABAS....* Each sound had its own colour. Every colour sang richly. *YANODA, SUSEJ, NOTAMMARGARTET, SUNGA, ARTEP, SIVO....*

He remembered with crystal clarity the earlier events of the night The bell that had struck the hour at the cross-roads, the tall Messenger, the arrival of the small van. Locked in the body of the thing, he had had no idea how far they had travelled, but at last it had stopped, there had been the sound of heavy doors opening, the van had been driven inside, the doors relocked. A key had turned, and he had climbed stiffly out into a blackness unrelieved. Hands had seized him, he had been led through heavy curtains that had brushed against him in the darkness. And on the far side he had found himself in what appeared to be a chapel, before an altar on which black candles burned with a golden flame, sending thin spirals of grey smoke up to the almost invisible roof.

SUCIDEM, SUTRIV, ROTAVLAS, RETAP, ROTAIDEM ... the single voice continued its reading of the Names. With his sharpened awareness, Cargrove felt a gathering of the forces of evil. Around the altar swirled a multitude of bright colours. Through them, and down the steps, came the girl, young, fair-haired, naked, her arms outstretched. The girl he had seen when he had first entered the Chapel....

... He had been led through the heavy curtains, had stood before the altar, and the girl had appeared, naked as now, but bearing in her hands a metal cup. The Messenger had said: "Drink," and when he had hesitated the word had been repeated, more sharply. "Drink! You were contemplating suicide, were you not? What have you to lose, even if the cup is poisoned?" And he had seized it, had held it while his eyes travelled over the beauty of the girl's nakedness in the light from the black candles. Her features were indistinct, but every detail of her body was clear. Watching her, he had lifted the cup, and had tasted the liquid it contained. It was a bitter brew, and he had hesitated once more. But then he had tipped the cup and had drained it in a single harsh draught. A stool had been brought for him, and he had sat facing the altar. Glancing behind him a moment later he had realised that the Driver and the Messenger had disappeared. The girl took the empty cup, placed it on the altar and slipped away into the shadows. He was alone, staring at the great image of the Horned Beast that he now realised dominated the space above the altar, only half-seen in the darkness beyond the smoking candles.

Suddenly a voice spoke from high up where the Beast's head leered under its monstrous horns.

"Robert James Livingstone Cargrove, why have you come here?"

He felt the bitterness of the strange drink still on his tongue, the fire of it in his throat At the same time he felt as though a corner of a dark cloth had been raised from his mind, revealing a small area of ultra-sensitive awareness. So far it was only a corner, a glimpse, a promise. But the sensation was there.

He forced himself to answer.

"To seek help."

"Are you aware of the nature of the help you seek?"

"I am."

"Say it. What manner of help do you require of us?"

The dark cloth shifted a fraction more. His awareness sharpened. The edges of the indeterminate shadows in the Chapel began to harden. The flames of the candles crystallised, seemed brighter, more concentrated. The voice from the Beast grew more insistent, seeming to be focussed along a narrow beam so that as with a diffused brilliance that is collected and channelled into the rod of a searchlight, it probed deep.

"Say it," the voice repeated. "You must say it. What manner of help do you require of us?"

Humming through the vibrant darkness into his memory came the words that Madame Joseph had used. His awareness, not only of his surroundings, but of himself, increased still further. He seemed to be withdrawing rapidly to a high vantage-point from which he could survey not only the scene in the Chapel, but also its place in the complex tangle of his affairs. He heard himself say: "I require you to raise the powers of evil, to help me out of my business troubles."

Faintly, but clearly, he heard again the beating of the powerful wings. The Voice said: "Well spoken. So shall it be. Are you ready now to take the Oath?"

And again, from the new height of his awareness, he heard himself answer: "I am ready."

Instantly, the wings sounded louder, as though they were immediately overhead. Distant thunder rolled, and a blinding flash of white light seared his eyes. The Chapel vanished in a blood-red thrust of stabbing pain. He cried out, and his hands flew to his face. The chanting voices returned, and when he dared again to open his eyes, still holding his hands close to guard them from any further pain, he saw that a masked and robed figure was standing by the altar. Lying on the altar itself, between the candles, was another girl, naked like the first, but dark-haired, darker-skinned in the golden light of the candles. She lay on her back, her head on a golden cushion, and again he saw how indistinct her features were. There was the outline of a face, but it was blurred, as though the details had yet to be finished. But her body was perfect. Her arms were raised, her hands clasped under her head, so that her breasts were pulled taut, the nipples hard and clear. Her legs were wide apart, and as he still stared at her, the black-robed figure said: "Come! Approach the altar."

In his new awareness, everything seemed full of meaning. The simplest words were of the utmost significance. The candle flames were living, vital creations; a part of the vast empire of evil that was the other face of God. He took a dozen paces forward, realised that he was still grasping the inverted crucifix. And suddenly the bright colours began to play about the Altar. Soft clouds of palest pink and amethyst formed and re-formed, insubstantial as the smoke from the golden flames.

The masked figure seized his right hand, laid it palm downwards on the body of the girl. He felt a tremor pass through her, but then she lay still again.

"Repeat after me: *I, Robert James Livingstone Cargrove –*"

In a loud and clear voice, Cargrove heard himself repeating the words.

"I, Robert James Livingstone Cargrove –"

– do hereby swear by the Living God –

"– do hereby swear by the Living God –"

– by the true God, by the blessed and omnipotent God –

Cargrove repeated the sonorous phrases.

– he who created the Heavens, the Earth, the Sea, and all the things that are in them, both good and evil, from out of nothing –

The girl's body moved again, a small tremor that was no more than the impression made by the stirring of a summer wind on a field of ripe corn.

– that I am desirous of accomplishing by the aid of demons that which my heart desires, namely the restoration of my worldly fortunes, whenever and by whatever means this may be done –

Cargrove felt again that he was standing apart from the group at the altar, looking down from a high vantage-point. But he followed the words clearly, repeating them faithfully. And he was acutely aware of the warmth and the softness and the unusual beauty of the faceless girl under his hand.

– and by the same token I do solemnly swear that however and wherever this may be accomplished, I will not reveal to a living soul that I have so requested and received the aid of the powers of darkness. I accept that should I break this my oath, the same powers will destroy me utterly, and with me all that I hold dear in this life. For theirs is the Kingdom, the Kingdom of Evil; theirs is the Power, the Power of Evil; and theirs is the Glory, the Glory of Evil;

of that same Evil which is the Other Face of the True God, who created all things, and in whom is all power, and glory and kingdom.

". . . and glory and kingdom," Cargrove repeated obediently, and for a moment there was silence. Then the Voice from the Beast said: "So be it. Return to your place."

He withdrew his hand, turned, and retraced his steps to the stool. As he reached it, the thunder sounded again, and there was another brilliant, searing flash that took him unawares. Again, the shadowy Chapel vanished as he instinctively thrust his hands against his eyes. The thunder faded into distance, and when he turned again to face the Altar, the girl and the black-robed figure had disappeared. He groped his way to the seat on the stool, and gradually his eyes accustomed themselves again to the candle-flames and the shadows. But now, the colours that surrounded the Altar were even brighter. It was as though the golden light of the candles was transmuted into these delicate evanescent clouds of colour. The chanting began again, and suddenly the stars began to swing into his line of vision, rushing forward from the shadows, racing past him to disappear again into oblivion. Faster and faster. It was as though the entire Milky Way had been drawn down, had been channelled into a racing torrent of stars. And then the stars had become jewels, and the Voice had begun the conjuration. *Come, Béelzébuth, Lucifer, Astaroth. . . .* And then had followed the recital of the seventy-two Names. And down the steps of the altar had come the fair-haired girl, naked as before, her arms outstretched.

She stopped before him, and again he saw the perfection of her body, but only the indeterminate outline of her face. And now the recital of the Names was complete. The Voice said: "Robert James Livingstone Cargrove, do you accept that the utmost power of evil shall be invoked in the solution of your problems, or are there any lengths to which you will not go in the pursuit of your ambitions?"

The girl's hands were slowly lowered, began to move over her body. Bright birds and animals appeared from the shadows and gathered round them. A black and yellow snake coiled itself into a pattern of death at their feet. The girl's movements grew faster. The Voice said: "Answer!" And he heard himself saying: "I accept the invocation of the uttermost power of evil."

Distantly, the thunder rolled again. Lightning flashed. The animals and birds vanished. Only the snake remained. It reared its head, swaying slightly. Its eyes were bright points of orange fire. The bell that he had heard on the open plateau began to toll again. Thirteen times the cracked note of it troubled the air of the Chapel. Then the Voice said again: "Béelzébuth, Lucifer, Astaroth –"

(4)

Looking back, his memories of the night were clear, but fragmented. He had only to close his eyes, and he could see again the shadowy Chapel, the black candles, the unformed faces; the body of the girl that had quivered under his touch as he had repeated the words of the oath; the bright visions that had surrounded him. In the cold light of morning he asked himself how much of what he had witnessed had been real, and how much had been hallucination, induced by the atmosphere that had been created, and by the bitter hell-brew that he had drunk. There was no answer to this question. All his memories were equally vivid. As he lay in his own bed, staring up at the ceiling of his room, he could hear again the words of the conjuration, endlessly repeated, and the beating of the invisible wings. Only the true sequence of events eluded him. At one stage it had seemed that the Beast had descended from the altar and had stood before him in the form of a hairy man with the head of a goat. The two girls, one so dark and one so fair, had floated in and out of his fantasies, as real and as unreal as the bright birds and animals, and as the unwinking eyes of the zig-zag snake. Hands had stripped him of his jacket, had ripped his shirt from his left shoulder. Over his heart, the Messenger had drawn a pentagram in what had seemed to be blood, using the middle finger of his left hand, the rest of the hand clenched into a tight fist.

Flinging off the bedclothes, he opened the jacket of his pyjamas. The pentagram was still there, outlined faintly against his skin. A reddish-brown five-point star, irregular, fading, but still recognisable for what it was. It had been almost daylight when they had opened the door of the small green van at the crossroads. He had climbed out into the last of the night, with the sky already paling to the east. He was still in the same state of heightened awareness. The signpost that was like a white gallows stood out with a startling clarity. He tried to find some mark on the van, some means of identification, but there was no name, and the number had been covered over. It disappeared, scuttling obscenely away, its belly close to the ground, like a scared green beetle afraid of discovery. As the sound of it faded, the silence folded back. On all the wide plateau, nothing stirred. He could see where the shape of the ancient track cut through the rocky surface, and still holding his crucifix he had stumbled down it to where he had left his car. It was still there, safely in the shelter of the beech grove. Only when he was inside, with the lights blazing and the engine running did he slip the crucifix back into his pocket. He drove home, undressed in the pale dawn-light, and climbed into his own bed without disturbing his wife. And now it was ten o'clock, and he was awake, and it was Saturday, when the factory was closed, and he was lying there with his pyjamas open and the five-pointed star in fading blood still over his heart.

"Robert?"

It was his wife, carrying a tray.

Hurriedly, he drew the sides of his jacket together. But she had already seen it. The tray tipped dangerously, was recovered. White-faced, she set it down on the table by his bed. Then she said: "What is that? On your chest?"

He said: "It's nothing. It'll wash off."

She stood there, tense, her hands clasped tightly.

"Where did you go?"

"Go?" he said harshly. "When? Last night? I went out on business. I told you."

Not even your wife, they had said. *Or the powers of darkness will destroy you utterly; and with you all that you hold dear. . . .*

"You weren't back by midnight."

"No. It was very late." He couldn't meet her anxious gaze. "There was a lot to talk about. Some people who might be able to help."

"And what was the outcome?"

"Too early to tell."

"Robert," she said, "why are you lying to me? Where did you go?"

He stared back at her, helplessly, not at her anxious, tired eyes, but at her mouth, her kind, generous mouth that had comforted him so often. "Mary – don't ask me. I don't know if they can help us or not. If they do –" He broke off, shrugged. "I wouldn't count on it, if I were you."

Leaning forward suddenly, she pulled open his jacket, revealing the pentacle. He put up his hands to stop her, but then he lay back, his eyes fixed now on the white ceiling.

"What else did they do to you?"

In his mind he saw again the altar, and the body of the faceless girl. He felt the trembling of the girl's body under his hand, and his own voice repeating the words of the oath.

Mary's voice sharpened.

"What did they do to you?" She seized him by the shoulders, shook him blindly. "Where did you go? Tell me! Tell me! What have they done to you?"

Do you accept, they had said, *that the utmost power of evil shall be invoked* . . .? And his own voice: *I accept. . . .* Then the conjuration, and the appearance of the man with the head of the Goat, with hair in thick matted swathes all over his body, like an animal's fur. And finally, the release into the pre-dawn on the plateau; the small green van scuttling rapidly away to the east.

"Tell me!" she flung at him. "Tell me! For God's sake!"

"No," he said.

She stared at the fading mark on his skin. "Why did they put that on you?"

"I can't tell you," he said miserably. "Believe me when I say that. I can't tell you. Not now, or ever. It would be dangerous. Nothing may come of it, anyway. They said they will help. But I still don't know what they can do."

To himself, he said: "There's only one thing they *can* do." But that one thing would be unthinkable. Desperate as he was, he would never agree to that. But to what had he already agreed, in the candle-lit Chapel, in the presence of the Beast?

The utmost power of evil....

He dragged himself out of bed at last, scrubbed off the pentagram. For six days, he went about like a man under sentence of death. And on the seventh day, Friday, at seven in the morning, the police came to his house.

CHAPTER FOUR

IT WAS Mel who first heard the news. He was repairing the closed-circuit security television in Greenall's, in Broad Street, when Jack Carter, the furnishing manager, said: "Did you know Ray Fisk? Of Fisk and Cargrove –"

Mel went suddenly tense.

"No," he managed to say. "No, I don't think so. Why?"

"Found dead this morning."

It was the Friday after Robert Cargrove's visit to the Chapel. Mel reached for a screwdriver, found that he could scarcely hold it.

"Dead?" he repeated. "How?"

"Gas, they reckon. Explosion. The watchman at the factory heard a hell of a bang about four o'clock. He telephoned the police, and they sent a squad car round the area. Fisk's cottage is about a quarter of a mile from the factory, on the moorland side. He rented it from old Mrs. Geeson who used to keep the *Feathers* at Maulbury. Not much of a place; not even on the main road. Right up a farm track. No main services. Make your own electricity, with an engine in a shed at the back. That sort of place. Daph and I looked at it when we got engaged, but one look was enough. Picturesque, if that's what you want. But give me the mod cons, and you can stuff the roses round the door."

Mel said: "Gas? There's gas up there?"

"Not mains. Only the stuff you buy in tanks, or cylinders, or whatever you call them. There's a couple of them stand outside the kitchen. They use it for the cooker and the hot water. The rest's electric from the engine. They reckon it must have leaked. Blew half the place to bits. And poor old Ray went with it. Mother Geeson'll have kittens.

Knowing her, I doubt if she's insured. You said you didn't know Ray?"

"No, I don't think so."

"No interest to you, then. I'm interested because Daph and I might've been living there, instead of Ray. Not that we ever would have, not from choice. Same as I told you, it's too bloody primitive. But we did take a look at it. And if we hadn't been lucky, and got the flat, it might've been us, blown to bits. See what I mean?"

"Yes," Mel said. "Yes, I see what you mean."

Sarah pressed the back of her right hand to her mouth. She said indistinctly: "What's it mean, Mel? What does it *mean*, for God's sake?"

"I don't know."

He had finished the job at Greenall's, then he had taken the van from the Store car park and had driven home. Now Sarah took the hand away from her mouth, put both arms round his shoulders. He could feel the trembling of her body, tight against him. With her lips close to his, she said: "Mel, why *him*? Why *Fisk*?"

"He and Cargrove were both insured by the Company against death, and against accident. It was virtually a two-man show. If either died –"

"So how much, for an accidental death?"

"Fifty thousand pounds."

"To the Company, or to Cargrove?"

"What difference does it make? To the Company – but who's left in the Company?"

"But *how*? How did it happen? How *could* it happen?"

"That's what everyone'll be asking."

Sal was breathing fast. The trembling of her body became an invitation.

"Mel, do you honestly think –"

"I don't know what to think."

"It's – strange, though, isn't it?"

"It's bloody strange." Something of her excitement was

being transferred to him. "When Barry gets back for lunch –"

"Why should Barry know, any more than you?"

"He's the one. You should know that. I'm only the engineer. I only drive the bloody engine."

Excitedly, her lips sought his, clung then broke away.

"Mel, how much do we get? If it's –"

"Ten thousand."

"Will he pay?"

"Barry'll see to that."

"It's a start –"

"It's a start," he agreed. His hands moved over her, stripping away her clothes. Outside, the morning life of the town went on as usual, except for the widening circles of transmission of the news of Ray Fisk's death. Inside, though the thought did not strike them until later, it was like the ritual intercourse that primitive people invariably engage in after an invocation of the spirits.

It was only when the excitement died, that fear came in to replace it.

Janey said: "He's not back yet. You're early." A sharper glance, then: "What's the matter, for Pete's sake?"

Sal said: "You haven't heard? About Ray Fisk?"

"Who's that?"

"Cargrove's partner –"

"Co-director," Mel said. "It's a company."

"What about him?"

"He's dead."

"How?"

"The same as *Seamew*."

Janey went to the door of the flat, opened it, looked out. Coming back, she said: "Drowned?"

"No. Gas explosion. The same kind of gas."

Janey said: "Oh, my God!" And "Come into the kitchen. I'm cooking lunch." And as they followed her through: "I thought something might happen today."

"You seem remarkably bloody calm!" Mel said. "For Christ's sake, did you *know* that was what he was going to do?"

"What who was going to do?"

"Who the hell do you think?"

"Duke Focalor," Sal said, and giggled nervously. "That's who fixed it before. He and Dad."

Mel said as nervously: "If he's brought that old fool into it –"

"Leave it to Bar," Janey said sharply. "He knows what he's doing." Dark, small and intense, she was suddenly a younger Madame Joseph. "You want the money, don't you?"

"Yes, but –"

"But what?" Barry said, and Mel swung round to face him.

"I didn't hear you come in."

"Does it matter? I gather you've heard the news?"

He stood watchfully in the open doorway. Behind his powerful glasses, his eyes swam disconcertingly.

Sal said: "Meet the Duke."

Janey was carrying a saucepan over to the sink. "If you're staying to lunch, it'll be cheese and biscuits. This is Bar's. I'm on my fruit-day diet."

Mel said: "Why did you say you thought something might happen today?"

"She felt it in her pentacles," Sal said, and began to giggle again.

"What's your trouble?" Barry asked. "Are you complaining about the service?" In a small clearing in the tangle of his facial hair, his lips showed pink and wet. Like the lips of a monstrous baby, forever sucking at some fount of evil, Mel thought, and was alarmed at the simile. "Do you want to back out? You and Sam?"

"No," Sal said. "We want the money."

"I was asking Mel."

Mel said: "What is there to connect it with us?"

"Nothing. Cargrove has got what he wanted. He won't talk. And if he did, how far would they get? As far as Madame Jo. That's all. He doesn't know who met him, or where the Chapel is."

"Jo might talk."

"There's too much at stake. She won't. And Ted certainly won't."

"Was Ted in this?"

"No."

"There'll be an inquiry –"

Barry laughed.

"There was an inquiry into *Seamew*. Remember?"

"But, Christ, man, this is for bigger stakes. Fifty thousand quid's not peanuts. The insurance company –"

"Let 'em wriggle," Barry said. "They won't find a bloody thing. They'll have to pay, in the end. And Cargrove'll pay us. We might have to wait, but we'll get our money. Now where's my lunch, Janey, love. I've got to be back in school by two-fifteen."

When Melvin and Sal had gone, Janey said: "So that was it."

She looked pale and the skin of her face was tightly drawn.

"That was it." He was eating his lunch, shovelling it in through his baby-lips.

"You could have told me where you were going. Instead of all that mystery."

"You might have tried to talk me out of it."

"I might."

He reached across the table and touched her face. She didn't shrink away. She simply sat there.

"Would you?" he said. "Would you have tried to talk me out of it?"

Her bright black eyes, so like her mother's, regarded him steadily.

"I don't know. If there was no other way –"

"There wasn't any other way. Either we do what we set out to do, or we pack it in."

"But we didn't set out to do that. Not deliberately. Or did we?"

"I knew we might have to. I was prepared for it."

"What about Mel?"

"What about him?"

"He hasn't the stomach you've got. He might crack."

"Talk to Sal. She must keep him up to it." He went back to the business of shovelling away his food. "If Sal wants to get out of where she is now – to go and live in the sun like the rest of us – she's got to do her share –"

"Yes," she said. And sat and watched him eat.

White-faced, trembling, Mary Cargrove said: "That mark on your body. I know now what it was. It was a sorcerer's mark. A pentagram –"

"Hush," he said. "For God's sake!"

"I won't hush." In her voice was already the sharp edge of hysteria. "Robert, what have you done?"

"I've done nothing. Nothing at all!" He felt his own voice rising to match the panic in hers. "Mary, I beg you – don't talk about it –"

"But I must! How did Ray Fisk die? Robert, don't you see? If you won't tell me –"

"It isn't that I won't! I can't! I mustn't!" And: "Oh, sweet God, why did I ever get involved?"

She caught him by the sleeve as he began to turn away from her, drew him back to face her.

"You can trust me Robert. But I *must know*! I must, if I'm to go on living with you –"

"I was desperate," he said. "You know how desperate I was. I even thought of suicide."

"So you hired a black magician to kill Ray Fisk instead –"

"No!" he almost shouted at her. "No, I did nothing of the kind!"

"Who put that mark on your body? Did you paint it on yourself?"

"No."

"Then who? The man who killed Ray?"

"Pity me, for God's sake," he said. "I didn't know Ray was going to die."

CHAPTER FIVE

"MR. ROBERT CARGROVE?"

"Yes."

"Jamieson. Insurance assessor. From Jones and Wylie –"

"Glad to see you."

"Are you, sir?"

Cargrove made a deprecatory gesture with one hand.

"You know what I mean. Please sit down."

"Thank you, sir." And: "Yes, sir, I think I do. But most people don't usually make me feel very welcome. You'll appreciate why I am here, I'm sure?"

"Isn't it – routine, in such cases?"

"Fairly routine, yes. Standard practice for sums as large as this one. We have to be satisfied as to what happened. And why."

Cargrove gripped the edge of his desk.

"Isn't it obvious what happened?"

"Fairly, I imagine. But that still leaves the *why*, doesn't it, sir? *Why* did it happen? That's the main question as far as I am concerned."

"The police –"

"Oh, yes, sir. The police will look at it, too. But a fresh mind – a second opinion, if you like – never does any harm. And we get a lot of experience at this sort of thing. You'd be surprised, some of the things we turn up."

Cargrove telephoned the house in Parrott Lane early on the same night. Caution had made him drive out along the road to Maulbury, to a public call-box. Madame Joseph said: "No!" to his request for an immediate appointment. And: "Make no further contact. None whatever. When the deal is satisfactorily concluded, we will contact you."

"There's an assessor here, from London. From the insurance company. Investigating –"

"Of course."

She heard the sharp hiss of indrawn breath over the wire.

"You're not – worried?"

"No. Why should I be?"

"I hadn't expected – I mean, I didn't think –"

"You didn't think what? That the solution to your problem would have come in this way?"

"Yes."

"How else? It had to be on the normal materialistic plane. You surely didn't expect to find a crock of gold at your bedside?"

There was a long, uneasy silence. Then Cargrove said unhappily: "There won't be – anything for him to find, will there? Are you quite sure of that?"

"Quite sure. Unless –" She paused, delicately, then she said: "Unless, of course, he's a magician."

*

But to Barry, Madame Joseph said: "You fool! You arrogant, stupid fool!"

Barry stared insolently back at her.

"Arrogant?" he mocked her. "Because I've done what you couldn't do? Even with your wand, and your virgin bloody parchment, and all the rest of it?"

She looked as though she was about to spit in his hairy face. Instead, she switched off the main light in the séance room, left only the spotlight, the Eye of God that had once scared the wits out of Jimmy Roberts. Sitting at the table, she rested her hands on the big crystal ball.

"I warned you. You don't know what you are doing. Did you kill this man Fisk?"

"No, it was the Duke."

"Which Duke?" Sharply.

"Any Duke. What's it matter? As long as he's on the payroll."

"Don't mock the Powers!"

"On the contrary," Barry said, "we did them proud. You should come and watch the next Conjuration –"

"I wouldn't dare!" She began to rock herself backwards and forwards, angrily, as though the physical movement gave her some tensional relief. "Do you mean you're going on with it?"

"Of course. We want the money."

"This assessor. If he finds something –"

"*If* he finds something! When *Seamew* sank, there was an inquiry, too. And what did *they* find?"

"Fisk's house isn't at the bottom of the deep channel. I'll say it again. You're not only a fool, you're an arrogant fool, which is the most dangerous sort of fool to be." Suddenly she ceased her rocking. She sat quite still, her eyes hooded against the light. "Never underestimate the Powers you are blaspheming. They can pretend to serve you, just as you pretend to honour them. And they can turn and rend you, when you least expect it."

"I'll remember that, ma. Meanwhile, cover for us, and you're in the clear. And there'll be another sucker coming up."

For a few moments longer, Madame Joseph remained immobile. Then quietly she said: "I want a share of the money –"

"Oh no! That was agreed. All you get is protection –"

"*Protection!*" The word came out with surprising force. "Don't you ever listen to anything I say? I'm not the one who needs protection!"

"No money, ma! That's final."

"Then no more cover."

"You're in no position to dictate terms –"

"Neither are you. Not any longer. You're as vulnerable as I am. More vulnerable. If I talk to the police –"

"You'd be in it as much as we are!"

"We are none of us in it as much as you are, Barry Simpson!" A pause, then: "Whatever profit comes, we'll split it three ways. One-third to you and Janey. One-third to Melvin and Sarah. One-third to Ted and me."

Tight with anger, Barry said: "You scheming old bitch! I'll see you in hell first!"

"You may well be there before me, if you go on as you're going." Suddenly her eyes opened, with that devastating bright black stare that went right through you. "One-third, or no cover."

"No."

"Very well."

The eyes hooded again, the rocking motion was resumed.

"No!" he said again. And flung himself out of the room. The door whispered shut behind him, and in an instant she had leaped to her feet, had turned the key, and had resumed her seat. With her eyes now tight-closed, and her hands clasped in a curiously complex interlocking grip, she began to intone: *Pater noster adversus, rex et imperator, deus et diabolus, venite, venite, venite, ex sepulcrum universum . . . Eia! Eia! Eia. . . .*

As the words of the Great Invocation from the Grimorium Pristinum formed their pattern in the small closed cube of the séance room, the ray of white light from the Eye of God slowly changed. From the outside, through to the centre, it turned a deep blood-red. Soundlessly the trapped air began to vibrate, as though it was composed of a million tightening strings plucked ever more rapidly. Then a low humming, like that of a distant but enormously powerful dynamo, grew almost imperceptibly out of the void that lay under the words.

Eia! Eia! Eia! Pater noster adversus . . . deus et diabolus . . .

In the blood-red light the far wall of the room dissolved into a shifting vortex of swirling mist, was funnelled into a deep inverted cone.

In the cellar below, Ted Modley stood transfixed. On an upturned box, one of Mel's tapes revolved slowly. He had been about to switch it off, after that last violent "No!"

from Barry, when his headphones had picked up the new sound from the room above; the sound of the beginning of the Invocation. Now, though he tried to tear the apparatus from his head, he had no strength in his arms. The humming increased in intensity, grew shriller more urgent. Even over the microphone circuit it drilled unbearably at the sensitive quick-flesh of his hearing. Through it, and over and beneath it, the voice of Madame Jo intoned: ... *upto in terra ... upto in inferus ... homunculus infimus non filius sed gener ...*

In a high corner of the séance room, Mel had fixed one of his seeing-eye cameras, linked in a standard security circuit to a small screen in the cellar. As the humming grew louder, and the image of the wall dissolved, Ted Modley began to whimper, clawing at the earphones. Then suddenly the whimper changed to a wordless scream. In the eye of the vortex, mirrored in the tiny screen, something appeared. Something huge and hairy and obscene, but as yet infinitely distant. Madame Joseph never ceased her intoning, in her curious ritual Latin; never relaxed for a moment the complex interwoven grip of her hands. The Beast grew nearer, moving at the speed of Evil, until at last it filled the opening in the wall. A powerful stench pervaded the room, seeped down even to the cellar below. Terrified, Modley screamed again. The Beast presented its vile rump, from which the matted hair fell away on either side. Without stirring from her chair; without opening her eyes, yet appearing to see clearly; she kissed the loathsome fundament.

Deus et diabolus ... deus et amator....

And as Ted Modley, unable to bear it an instant longer, collapsed in a small terrified heap on the brick floor of the cellar, he heard from the room above: *Mandamus in nomine Béelzébuth, Lucifer, Astaroth, Chameron* ... Then the words of the Solemn Charge, and finally the name: *Edward Charles Barry Simpson....*

Suddenly, the humming ceased. The pressure was relieved. The air lost its choking animal stench. The small screen showed only Madame Joseph, sitting quietly in her chair. Slowly, Ted Modley climbed to his feet, removed the headphones. The tapes still revolved. He put them in reverse, then switched to playback. But nothing came. Farther and farther back. Still nothing. Until at last he heard the voice of Madame Joseph.

"One-third, or no cover."

And Barry: "No."

"Very well," from Madame Jo.

And Barry's final emphatic: "No!", before he flung himself angrily out.

From then on, nothing. Nothing whatsoever on the tapes.

Barry said viciously: "I'll kill that bloody old woman!"

He was in the kitchen, with Mel and the two girls, and Jimmy Roberts; waiting for someone to come and say that supper was ready.

Mel said: "Lay off her, Bar! You don't have to give her the money, do you? Unless you slip her a hundred to keep her quiet."

Jimmy said nothing. He was staring at Sal, whom he now saw only seldom. He was trying to find some point of dissimilarity between the real Sarah, as she sat opposite him now, on her husband's right hand, and the irresistible succubus that came in Sal's own image. But he could find none. Every small sun-bleached hair at her golden temples was duplicated on the forehead of the demon. Every trick of movement or of speech belonged equally to them both. He sat at the table and stared, like a yokel at a fair, until she said sharply: "Jimmy!" and he jumped guiltily and blushed and began to stammer.

But then the door from the hall opened, and Ted Modley came in. He stood just inside the kitchen, his small sharp face pinched and grey.

Janey said: "For Jeez sake, dad, what's the matter with you?"

For a moment his jaw trembled, but the words refused to come. Then he managed to say: "Your mother –"

Barry pushed back his chair, heaved himself to his feet, stood looking down at the little grey man.

"What's up with the old woman?"

"I don't know. She's in there, but the door's locked. She won't answer –"

"How do you *know* she's in there? She could've gone out of the side door –"

"That's bolted on the inside. I tried it. And, anyway, I saw her on the screen. She's just sitting there. But she won't answer."

Barry let out an explosive: *"Christ!"* And "The stupid old bugger! What's got into her now?"

He started to move towards the door, but Sal reached out a hand, seized him by the sleeve of his jacket.

"You'd best keep out of it. Let Janey go. She can handle her if anyone can. But not you."

He hesitated, but then he said: "All right, only make it quick, for God's sake. I'm starving."

Janey said: "O.K., lover. Cut yourself a slice of something. This might be a long job. Give or take your thousand years –"

But then they heard Madame Joseph in the passage outside. Ted Modley moved away from the door with a muttered: "Save us, O lord, from the fear of Hell!" His right hand sketched a rough cross in the air of the kitchen. "Let not the devils destroy my soul –" And then she was in the kitchen with them, and was saying quietly: "Have no fear, Ted. It is not for you they will come."

Barry said: "What were you doing in there?"

She looked up at him.

"When next you raise the Lord Lucifer, why not ask him? Now let us have supper."

She sat like a queen at the head of the table, her hands folded in her lap, waiting to be served.

CHAPTER SIX

(1)

IN THE end it was Barry himself who spoke to Sal.

One afternoon, when she had finished her duty turn in the Chinese Tea Pavilion, he was waiting outside for her. They walked together through the Gardens, talking idly, along the edge of the sea, and out to the wild part where the dunes began. Here the beach was almost empty. Only a line of wading-birds scoured the edge of the retreating tide, and a few distant figures were half-lost in the hazy heat.

"Well?" she said at last. "You didn't walk me out here for nothing. What's on your mind?"

She bent swiftly, removed her sandals, let her toes curl in the wet sand.

"What about Mel?" he said.

"What about him?"

"Is he opting out?"

"No," she said. But it lacked conviction.

"He's still worried about Fisk?"

"That's an understatement."

"What about you?"

"I'm only worried if someone finds out."

"They won't," he said confidently.

"Barry," she said, "how did you fix it?"

"The Duke fixed it," he teased her. "I told the Duke what we wanted. Remember?"

"And you don't think they'll find anything?"

"Four days, and nothing's been reported yet. Not in the papers, anyway. No, the Duke knows his stuff. He and I fixed it good."

There was a small silence. Then: "Tell me something," she said. "When did you first know?"

"Know what?"

"That you had to kill him."

He stooped, scooped up a flat pebble, sent it skimming over the ebbing waves.

"Let me ask you something. How badly do you really want out?" Glancing down at her, he saw her face cloud over. "You know what I mean by that. Out of the cage. Into the sun."

"I know."

"Well?"

Suddenly she swung ahead of him, turned, stopped, and he walked forward into her arms She was carrying a leather handbag, and her sandals, but her arms went round his neck, and her body was taut against him. With her mouth an inch away from his, she said: "I want out, and I don't care what it costs."

Half mocking, half-serious, he said: "Sarah Anne Williams, born Sarah Anne Modley, do you accept that the utmost power of evil shall be invoked in the solution of your problem?" Running his hands down her back, he said: "Stop me if you've heard those words before."

A small tremor passed over her.

"I don't want to stop you. I've told you: I want out, and I want it at any price. I've always wanted it." He could feel the warmth of her breath against his lips, as she said: "I was sick of always living in the kitchen with mam and dad, and Jimmy and Janey. Living on bread and jam and fish fingers and canned fruit. So what did I do? I married Mel."

A gull flew low, riding the small wind from the sea. It turned its head to look at them, then slid obliquely away over the dunes.

"I thought that was the way out," she said bitterly. "And, God help me I ran straight into it. Straight into the bloody trap."

His hands never ceased their rhythmic movements over her back.

"Go on."

"That's it," she said. "That's the story of my life. You know Mel. What'll he ever do, or make, unless you make it for him?"

"Not me. Us. I can't handle Mel without you."

"Bar," she said. "Why the hell did you marry Janey? We'd've made a far better team –"

And he answered seriously: "I was too late. You were already tangled up with Mel. It was you I wanted. I've always wanted you. I only married Janey to get into the family."

"Would you have married me for the same reason?"

"No. But that was my reason to start with. I admit that." A pause, then: "You know who my mother is. As soon as I was old enough to realise, I've always been fascinated by the thought that Skipper might have been my father –"

"Mam suggested that once."

"It could have been. My mother was pregnant when Skipper was drowned. But only just. She didn't marry Jack Simpson till after I was born."

Sal said: "Why did you let me marry Mel?"

"Christ Jesus!" he exploded. "Didn't I try to get you away from him? You wouldn't even look at me! Except to laugh at my glasses, my whiskers, every bloody thing about me."

She rubbed herself against him.

"I was too young. I didn't realise you had brains. I wouldn't make the same mistake again."

He said: "If we make what we ought to make out of this business, in a year or two we'll have enough to go and live in the sun. Lie on a coral beach. That's what you said you wanted, wasn't it?"

"That's right. Only I said you and Janey, and Mel and me. I'm not so sure that's what I want now."

"That's not how it'll be, then. It'll be you and me. Mel and Janey can find some place else."

"Do they get half the money?"

He bent forward and kissed her.

"You're right, Sam. We do make a better team. Our minds work the same way. But for the moment we carry on as we are. We want them with us, not against us."

"Understood, Duke. But is there any reason why we shouldn't take a few minutes off, every now and again?"

"Such as now?" he said, and ran his hands over her again.

"Such as right now," she agreed.

Side by side, only their arms touching briefly, as though by accident from time to time, they walked sedately up the sloping beach, and into the shelter of the dunes. On the hot sand they made love, and it was barely over when he said quietly: "The next sucker is lined up. If he bites, there'll be a job for you. Just for you, this time. Will you do it?"

"It depends –" she began, but he stopped her mouth with the tips of his fingers.

"Are you with me? If so, there's no *depends*."

"Tell me, though."

"All right. But it's for you and me only. And I mean only. We shall want the others in the Chapel, but that's all they'll need to know. It's up to you to talk Mel into doing that much again."

"Don't worry about that. He'll do it –"

"He mightn't if he knew what it might lead to."

She was lying on her back on the hot sand, looking up at him. A little shiver of – of what? – excitement? – came and went.

"Another killing job?"

"Not for you."

"Bar," she said, "if that's what it is – if that's what it's going to be every time –"

"Yes?" he said, as she hesitated.

"If that's what it is, why do we have to go through all

the business in the Chapel? Why don't you just –?" She broke off again, frowning up at the light.

"Because," he said, and teased the hair behind her ears. "Just because."

"No, seriously –"

"It needn't be a killing job every time. There'll be other ways."

"Even so. Why don't we just *do* what has to be done? After all, they must *know*."

"But they aren't *certain*. That's the point. They can't be. The other way they *would* be certain. And, anyway, in this country, with the sort of people we want on our books, you have to go carefully. If you go to a man and say: *I'll kill your partner for ten thousand pounds*, he'll be horrified. Or he'll pretend to be. Most likely he'll go to the police. In the same way, there aren't so many that'll come to you openly and say: *There's ten thousand for you, if you'll kill my partner*. It happens sometimes but not in the circles in which we want to trade."

"The circles in which we want to trade!" she mocked him. "Christ, Bar! You sound like a high-class fishmonger or something."

"What's the difference?"

"*Simpson and Williams, Butchers to the Nobility*. That could be not so far out." Was there the merest trace of hysteria in her voice?

"Doing it my way," he said, "wraps it up. That's what people always want to do with anything unpleasant. Wrap it up, hide it, pretend it isn't there. Put the responsibility on someone else. There was only one solution to Cargrove's troubles. But Cargrove would never have faced it himself. It had to be wrapped up in the trimmings at the Chapel. That way he didn't have to make the decision. That way, he's not responsible, even though he must have known what was going to happen. He can live with it."

"He could rat on us, even now."

"If ever he feels like it, we've got him on tape and on

film – by infra-red and by your clever husband's electronic flashes. No, he won't rat. Not if he doesn't want to lose everything."

"You're the clever one," she said. "Mel wouldn't have thought it out like that."

"Mel's useful. Technically useful. That's why we still want him. The atmosphere's the thing. Everything depends on that. Those magnified swan's wings are superb. And the church-bell up at the Ford –" He teased her hair again. "Don't fall out with Mel just yet, Sammy love. He's still useful to us. To both of us. Just string him along until we're ready. Then we'll cut the string. Meanwhile, you do this little job with me."

"Tell me what it is, Bar."

"All right." He had taken off his glasses, and his face looked young and vulnerable in its fair fuzz of downy hair. His pale, half-blind eyes unfocussed, he said: "There's this solicitor. A man called Delany. Pierse Delany. And he's another who's in trouble. Big trouble. For him, there's only one way out. But like Cargrove, he'd never do it himself . . ."

As he told her what she had to do, she lay quite still. Beyond the dunes, the tide was going out rapidly. The line of wading-birds was now far down the rippled beach. The sand glistened wetly in the westering sun and on the Pier, Madame Joseph was closing and locking her tiny cell for the night.

"Will you do it?" he said at last. "Will you, Sam?"

And with another small shiver she answered: "Sure, Duke. Anything you say. If that's what has to be done –"

"There's no other way."

She reached up, and took his softly-whiskered face between her hands.

"If you say so." Then: "Where'll we go, Duke? The Caribbean? Or South America? It'll need to be some place they can't get us back from . . ."

(2)

Despite the apparent confidence of Jamieson, the assessor, nothing further emerged during the next two weeks from his investigation into the death of Ray Fisk.

Robert Cargrove drove down each working day to the factory. But he looked strained and ill, and people in the town commented on his obvious distress at the loss of his fellow-director. No-one outside his immediate circle of family and advisers – his Bank Manager, his Accountant, the Development Board – knew of the existence of the accident policy.

Jamieson still hung around the place; going off for a day; reappearing unexpectedly; sitting for long periods in Cargrove's office, staring at him while he telephoned, or taped a letter, or discussed production matters with the works manager. There were times when Cargrove came near to breaking, but somehow the two weeks passed.

At the adjourned inquest, evidence was given by the police and by the company who supplied the gas cylinders. The main control, it was stressed, was *outside* the cottage, and the instructions were that this should be turned off every night, or whenever the apparatus was to be left unused for any long period. It was simple enough. An arm through the kitchen window, and a couple of turns of a metal wheel-tap. There were ordinary taps on the kitchen stove, and a water-controlled valve on the heater for the sink and the bathroom. A pilot light had to be relit each morning. This warmed a thermostat which controlled the inflow of gas to the heater. If the pilot went out, even though the hot tap was turned on, gas would not enter the heater.

"And was the main wheel-tap found in the off position after the explosion?" the coroner asked the company engineer.

"No, sir. It was on."

"In your experience, do many people remember, or bother, to turn off the main tap at night?"

"They are clearly instructed to do so."

"That doesn't answer my question."

"We have really no means of checking whether they do, or do not. Under normal conditions, of course, it wouldn't greatly matter. If all the taps on the stove were firmly *off*, and the water-heater pilot was also switched off –"

"And were they?"

"The apparatus was severely damaged in the explosion. But as far as we can tell, the water-heater pilot *was* switched off. And so were the taps."

"Could one of them have been faulty?"

"There is no evidence of a fault."

"But such evidence might have been rendered unrecognisable in the violence of the explosion?"

"That is possible, sir."

"Does this gas smell?"

"In its natural state, no. But we add a smell to it, for safety reasons."

"And what would be needed, assuming a leak of some magnitude, to cause the gas to explode? You have said that the pilot appeared to have been turned off."

"Almost anything, with the gas at the concentration there must have been to cause that havoc. A spark, a match –"

"But who would strike that spark, or that match? The medical evidence was that Mr. Fisk would probably have been unconscious, from gas poisoning, before the actual explosion took place. The bedroom is on the ground floor, this being a bungalow type of cottage; and as it is next to the kitchen and the bathroom, the gas would not have far to travel. So who struck the spark?"

"Nothing," the company witness said, "has been found that would give us the answer to that question."

"How did you fix it, Bar? So they didn't find anything?"

"Ask no questions, and you'll get no lies."

Sarah lay back against the hot sand. It was the third time they had met and made love out on the dunes since the death of Ray Fisk, and every time she had asked the same question. Every time, his reply had been the same.

Now he said: "Never mind that one. That's all over. We've got to concentrate on the next. I've been thinking about it. This is how we'll have to do it."

CHAPTER SEVEN

(1)

MADAME JOSEPH hooded her bright black eyes.

"You are in trouble," she said. "In deep trouble. I can feel it. I can hear it. There are vibrations."

The man had come to the side door of the house in Parrott Lane. It had been late when Madame Joseph had answered the knock; deliberately late, by an appointment made earlier that day by telephone.

"I have heard," the man said, and hesitated. Then, almost apologetically: "They say you have the power to control."

"To control what?" Madame Joseph demanded sharply. "Speak out, or we cannot make progress."

The man stared at the crystal ball that stood for effect on the séance-room table. His long fingers knotted together uncomfortably; were released, then re-entangled.

"The powers of darkness."

"That's better. And do you accept that the powers of darkness *can* be so controlled? *Directed?*"

"I don't know."

Madame Joseph watched, listened, assessed. She saw the weak, tremulous mouth; the high, balding forehead. Under the expensive suit, she was aware of the meagre figure, such flesh as there was drawn tightly against the bony frame.

"Who sent you here?"

"I can't tell you."

"You must."

"Someone – telephoned. I don't know who it was."

"And have you told anyone of your visit here?"

"No. In my profession you learn to be discreet."

"You would need to be more than discreet," she said. "You would need to swear a solemn oath of absolute secrecy. Or the same powers –" She stopped, shrugged, and the man heard, very faintly, the beating of powerful wings. Startled, he looked up, but saw only the ceiling of the séance-room, painted by Ted Modley a uniform and uncompromising black.

*

The Goat looked down from between the spirals of grey smoke. On the altar, a naked girl.

"John Pierse Delany," the Voice said, "do you accept that the utmost power of evil shall be invoked in the solution of your problems, or are there any lengths to which you will not go in the pursuit of your ambition?"

On his tongue, he was still aware of the bitter taste of the hell-brew they had made him drink. The unformed face of the girl was haloed in bright shifting colours; her perfect body shone as though light was being generated deep inside her, radiating out through the milky surface of her skin. The conjuration was already complete, and the recital of the seventy-two Names. On his left breast, the pentagram was outlined in fresh blood. In the river of stars floated the heads and the severed limbs of children. There had been voices chanting, and the sound of the great wings had seemed to fill the air of the shadowy Chapel. As he stood there now, the river of stars became a river of blood, flowing sluggishly past, swirling about his feet. In this dark flood, the white faces, and the severed arms and legs and trunks of the dead children passed in an endless silent stream.

Again the Voice said: "John Pierse Delany –" and the question was repeated. As though from the farthermost depths of an echoing tunnel, he heard a voice reply, barely recognising it for his own: "There are no lengths to which I will not go . . ."

Dawn found him sitting in his own car, in the beech-grove by the ford. He felt little but a great weariness of both mind and body. With the last of his strength, he locked the doors from the inside, then he leaned back against the expensive leather, and slept. When he awoke, it was broad daylight, and for a while he had no idea where he was. Beyond the trees, the shallow river raced sparkling in the sun, and suddenly he remembered the events of the night. Abruptly, the starry water changed to blood. The eyes of a thousand dead children were fixed on him as they floated silently past. He heard the voice of the Beast, calling him by name. And he heard his own voice, repeating the oath, his hand on the body of the girl.

In the bright light of day, the Chapel, and all that it had contained, was still as vivid in his mind as it had been in the light of the smoking candles. On the passenger seat beside him lay the crucifix he had carried; a gaudy, painted thing bought hurriedly from one of those Catholic supply shops that specialise in the tools of the Faith. And opening his shirt, he saw the red-brown stain of the pentacle, covering his left breast.

"There are no lengths," he had said in reply to the Beast's question, "to which I will not go . . ." But even now he could not wholly believe that what his heart desired would be accomplished. As he felt in his pockets for the keys of the car, he told himself that nothing would come of it. That what he had experienced was no more than hallucination, induced by whatever was in the bitter-tasting brew, and by suggestive hypnosis. He had seen, in fact, in symbolic form, only what he had wanted to see. Drugged, conditioned by the atmosphere of the Chapel, clinging to his own desires that had been born out of his own fear and his own desperation, he had been an easy prey for a bunch of cranks. Or were they more than that? He had paid a not inconsiderable sum for the entertainment. And more, much more, would be payable if –

Shaking his head, he tried to put the thought to one side.

If they were indeed no more than petty crooks, small con men, putting on a show simply to get their hands on the initial payment, with no intention, and indeed no hope of ever organising the powers they claimed to dominate; then what could he ever do? He could never tell the police, for example, why he had paid money that he could ill afford to a group of strangers.

But if there *was* something in it, then he had committed not only the initial payment, but a good slice of the ultimate profits as well. He could simply refuse to pay, of course. Or he could offer them a proportion. Would they settle for half, he asked himself as he started the engine of his three-year-old Bentley, and sent the beautiful expensive car whispering across the ford, through water that was now clear again, up to the cross-roads, and over the deserted moorland road to Roddon.

The days passed, and nothing happened. Despair returned. He had been a fool ever to think . . .

But at lunch in the Conservative Club, five days later, a man named Bartram, an estate-agent, said suddenly: "Did you see the case in the local paper this week? Three youths digging up a coffin in the churchyard?"

They were at the Club table, a small group of regulars at the fireplace end. Taylor, the manager of the Midland Counties Bank, looked up with his mouth full, said: "They'll do anything. Young bastards."

Bartram said: "You're right. Anything for kicks. I wouldn't've given it a second thought, except that one of them is a clerk in one of my offices. A boy called Paul Ridley. Only seventeen. A quiet youth, good at his job."

"Then why, for God's sake?" someone else asked.

"Black Magic, they said."

"Oh, no!" Taylor took a long drink of his beer. "That was the excuse, maybe. But it's just for dirty little kicks. That's why they do these things. You said it yourself, Charles, and you're right. I doubt if any youngster of that age knows the first thing about true Black Magic."

Delany had put down his knife and fork. He sat with his hands clasped tightly on his knees, hidden by the table.

"Do *you*?" Bartram asked, and guffawed loudly. Delany felt the load of food in his stomach tilt dangerously as Taylor answered quietly: "I know a little about it. It's on the increase again, of course. You've only to read your newspapers. But not amongst kids of seventeen, I imagine."

"Amongst who, then?"

Taylor shrugged.

"In my experience, it's either a highly intellectual pursuit, cultivated by nutty dons and unfrocked priests, and maiden ladies with private incomes; or it's of the earth. And when it's of the earth, my God, is it earthy! It's just one form of witchcraft, of course, and there are said to be at least three thousand known witches in Britain today. There may be half a million others practising in secret. Who knows? And probably ten times that number in America. But I doubt if any youth of seventeen who digs up coffins with two of his young friends, is amongst them."

Someone said: "I thought witches were always female, anyway."

"Not always, though usage tends to imply so. There are male witches, but they often prefer to call themselves something else. Sorcerers, magicians . . ."

Charles Bartram guffawed again.

"For Pete's sake, Harry! Is that what you do in the Bank, when we can't get in to see you? Are you down in the basement, turning scrap-iron into gold? Oh, boy! Oh, boy! If the National Westminster could hear you now!"

Still quietly, Taylor said: "You can laugh, Charles. But if you took the trouble to find out a little more about it –"

He shrugged again, and went on eating as Bartram said loudly: "I've better things to do with my time, old man!" And there the conversation ended.

But afterwards, as they drank their coffee in the Men's Lounge, collecting it in man-sized cups from the steward at the table near the fireplace, Harry Taylor drifted across to where Delany was sitting alone by one of the windows overlooking the street, a double brandy on a small table near him.

"Mind if I join you?"

"No – no, of course not."

They sat in silence for a moment, Delany pale and nervous. Then Taylor said: "Bartram's a fool. Anything outside his immediate comprehension, he dismisses."

"Yes."

Another silence. Then Delany said suddenly: "Do *you* believe in it, Harry? What we were talking about earlier, I mean."

Taylor stirred his coffee deliberately.

"Do I believe in the fact that a great number of people practise what is commonly called magic? If that's what you mean, then the answer is yes."

Delany drank a little of the brandy. "Not only that they practise it, but that it works," he said, the glass still in his hand.

He was treading on dangerous ground, he knew that. If anything came out ... But it was suddenly important to him that he should know where Taylor stood.

"The answer again is yes. But that's probably too direct an answer for a lawyer. Let me qualify it a little. Let me say that I believe that there are two main sources of power in the universe. The power of good, that we call God. And the power of evil, *which is also God* –"

Delany opened his mouth, moved a fraction in his leather chair. But then he seemed to change his mind, and said nothing. Instead he drank a little more of the brandy. He was remembering the Voice from the Beast ... *of that same Evil which is the Other Face of the True God, who created all things....*

"Everything has its opposite," Taylor said precisely, "its other face. Top and bottom, left and right, positive and negative. So with good and evil. But none of these attributes can exist independently. There can be no top without bottom, no rich without poor. If one exists, then it must have its other face. So with God. If we accept that God is all-good, as many do, then surely it is logical to assume that he is also all-evil. Why not? If God created the entire universe, and for want of a better theory many of us still accept that, then didn't he create evil as well as good?"

"And do you believe," Delany heard himself asking, "that the power of evil can be –" He paused, and struggled with the word, his jaw suddenly locking around it, as though some inner conflict had produced its own impediment. When it came out at last, it sounded unnaturally loud, "*– invoked?*"

Taylor regarded him steadily from behind his glasses.

"Of course. Why not? For centuries we have begged with pomp and ritual for the intervention of divine power. With bell, book and candle; with holy water, incense, and the bones of martyrs, we have tried to interest God in our tiny affairs. That is, the God we like to think of as the fountain of all good. We make the sign of the cross, we ask for the assistance of saints and archangels, and we pay the priest to act as our intermediary. Is it so very different if we pay the magician, instead of the priest; if instead of invoking the aid of the Lamb, we call on the Goat? Does it really matter on which side of the ladder we climb, as long as we reach the top?"

Somehow, Delany finished his coffee and the rest of the brandy. Several times he felt the little bank manager watching him across the small mahogany table. Why had he spoken as he had, so freely? Did he *know*? Glancing up, he saw the speculative gaze behind the dark-rimmed glasses. If Taylor *knew*, then he could be in a position of the utmost peril. And with the thought came the sudden realisation of the enormity of what he had done. Who were those strangers, the faceless ones in the Chapel? They were human, of that he had no doubt at all. Which meant that in daylight they were ordinary citizens of the town. Girls like some of those on his own staff, even. Pat, or Sue, or young Kitty Steele. Men like Harry Taylor . . .

Pushing back his chair at last, he murmured something about an appointment, and walked to the door with the unsteady exaggerated caution of the newly-drunk. *I must get to them,* he thought wildly, *tell them to stop. But how, for God's sake? Through the woman? Madame Joseph?*

Outside, in the street, he hesitated. He crossed the road, turned, and glanced up at the windows of the Men's Lounge. Watching him, bland behind his glasses, was Harry Taylor.

Somehow, he reached his office. He thought of telephoning at once to Madame Joseph, but it would have meant going through his own switchboard. He should have used a public call-box. But it was too late now. His first clients were already waiting. He didn't know how he was going to face them. But he would have to go through with it, sooner or later. If he didn't –

Closing his eyes, he saw again the sleek little bank manager, watching him through the double glazing of the Club window. What *did* he know, for God's sake?

Alone in his private office, with the door locked, he sat with his head in his hands, refusing to see anyone. Until Pat, on the switchboard, rang through to say that the police had arrived, and were insisting on being admitted.

(2)

The Pierse Delany problem was not a new one. In fact it was two problems, each as old as civilisation.

Delany was a solicitor, the senior partner in an old-established firm still known as Delany, Carson, Dodds and Peters. The original Delany, now dead, was the present Delany's uncle. Dead, too, were Arnold Dodds, Philip Carson, and Ignatius Peters. The firm was now John Pierse Delany; with a handful of junior partners, assistants and clerks, who did little else but investigations of title, conveyancing, mortgage work, and a smattering of wills and county court summonses. The old-established trusts and executorships, Delany kept for himself. And a considerable portion of the money that rightfully belonged to these special clients, he had also begun to keep for himself. Or, rather, to spend for his own purposes; or to gamble with, in the hope of personal profit.

There had been an element of peril in this from the start, but at first the danger of final disaster had seemed remote. Pierse Delany was the only child of a rich enough father, Andrew Delany, who had made his small fortune from a new line in cosmetics, before selling out to one of the big combines. His money safely tucked away, the old man had settled down to living the life of a rich old fool. A widower, he had done at last what every rich old fool at some time dreams of doing. He had married a girl less than a third of his age; a half-English, half-Swedish, long-legged, wide-eyed, ruthless sex symbol, who had presented him with a son that he confidently believed to be his own. But when the child was four weeks old, she had abandoned it, and him, in favour of a young French journalist, taking only a double handful of diamonds, and the few thousands of pounds that he had settled on her, as mementos of their year together. Exhausted, disillusioned, the old man had developed a heart condition that threatened to cut short his final loneliness. Only the necessity of caring for young Andrew, his doctor said, kept him alive at all.

His father's marriage had alarmed Pierse Delany from the start. The almost certain inheritance, which had been his safety-line, had become uncertain, even unlikely. After the child was born, it disappeared entirely. Inevitably, he had gambled further, in a frantic attempt to recoup his earlier misappropriations. And, as inevitably, he had lost. When his telephone rang, at midnight on July 11th, and the strange voice told him to go to the side door of the house in Parrott Lane, he owed somewhere between eighty and one hundred thousand pounds to his clients, and from his father's latest will he could expect no more than a token ten thousand, the rest being settled in a trust fund, managed by the Bank, for the benefit of young Andrew, now aged three months.

*

The Goat looked down from between the spirals of grey smoke. On the altar, lay the naked girl.

"John Pierse Delany," the Voice said, "do you accept that the utmost power of evil shall be invoked in the solution of your problems, or are there any lengths to which you will not go in the pursuit of your ambition?"

The unformed face of the girl was haloed in bright shifting colours; her body shone as though light was being generated deep inside her. On his left breast, the pentagram was outlined in fresh blood. In the river of stars floated the heads and the severed limbs of children.

As though from the far end of an echoing tunnel, he heard a voice reply, barely recognising it for his own.

"There are no lengths to which I will not go . . ."

And now he was sitting at his desk, in his locked office, and Pat, on the switchboard, was saying with concern in her voice: "Mr. Delany, the police are here. They insist on seeing you . . ."

"Very well," he managed to reply. "Give me two minutes. I'll ring when I'm ready."

In that two minutes, he spread a pile of documents over his desk, drank a double whisky from the bottle that he kept hidden in the heavy Chippendale bureau-bookcase that towered against the inner wall. Then he unlocked the door. He returned to his desk, pressed the clients' bell. Within seconds, a young detective-inspector was sitting watchfully on the other side of the desk, brushing aside his disjointed: "So busy . . . a special case . . . You do understand. . . ."

A detective-sergeant sat by the bookcase, as though to prevent him from reaching the whisky again.

"Mr. Delany," the Inspector said, "when did you last see

your –" he consulted a small scrap of paper "– your half-brother?"

"My – half-brother?" It sounded odd, coming from this quiet stranger. "You mean – Andrew?"

"Have you another one?"

"No. No, of course not."

Delany was forty-two. Andrew was a little over three months. As he had often told himself, if he had married Eleanor Peters when he had wanted to, when they were both eighteen and full of romantic idealism, he could by now have a grandchild of Andrew's age, or more. Not that he would have cared to be a grandfather at forty-two. It would have seemed ridiculous, undignified even. A mark of premature ageing, like the grey wings at his temples that he so carefully concealed.

"Well, sir?"

"I'm sorry." A hand across his forehead, a half-gesture towards the papers on his desk. "Why do you ask, Inspector?"

"There is a very good reason, I assure you, Mr. Delany."

The whisky, on top of the lunch and the liquor he had drunk before and with it, was dulling his wits. He had to force himself to concentrate on this watchful stranger.

"Is anything the matter?"

"Can we take one thing at a time, sir?"

"Yes. Yes, of course." He looked to the right of the sergeant, to where the bottle was hidden behind its mahogany screen. Desperately, his mind scrambled around in the fumes of the alcohol. What he really needed was another one, to clear the air. "I shall have to think, Inspector. I visited my father on Sunday. I had lunch with him."

"And you saw Andrew then?"

"I must have done." Another vague gesture, behind which his panic grew. "I really can't remember. It's a big house. The baby is usually kept out of sight. There's a young woman, Miss Olliver –"

His voice trailed away. There was a small silence. Then: "This Miss Olliver." The Inspector was eyeing him warily. "How long has she been employed by your father?"

"I've no idea. Since the child was born, I imagine."

"Is she – reliable?"

"Oh, for God's sake, Inspector! How should I know that? I see my father once a week. I've seen the child on perhaps three or four occasions only, since it was born. Miss Olliver I have seen probably about the same number of times."

"You are not on good terms, then, with your father?"

"Perfectly good!"

"You approved of his re-marriage?"

Delany gripped the arms of his chair. He could feel the blood pounding at his temples. But at all costs he had to keep control.

"That was his own affair. I didn't think it would last. And it didn't, of course." He paused, and gripped the arms of his chair even more tightly. "But what exactly has happened? About Andrew?"

*

Delany Senior had lived for over twenty years in one of the few remaining Edwardian houses in The Avenue, off Marine Drive. Once a pleasant residential road, it had become more and more a part of the business area of the town. Flats and offices now stood squarely where once the lawyers and the bankers, and those of independent means had played croquet under the cedars, and had entertained each other in a somewhat stuffy atmosphere of *art nouveau* behind tall windows that were never quite free of their coating of sea-salt from the wind-blown spray.

The new shopping area of the town was just around the corner from *Cedar Lodge*. And most mornings, Frances Olliver took the perambulator into the pedestrian precinct, with a small list of groceries and other oddments that were needed in the kitchen. A housekeeper came in by the day, to cook and to clean, and the garden was kept in some sort of order by a contractor. Only Miss Olliver slept in, she and young Andrew sharing the guest wing at the back of the house, divided from the old man's quarters by a double sound-proof door.

At first, this door had been kept locked, but after a while they no longer bothered. The old man had had his fill of young women. His heart was now concerned only with its own dull ache that had nothing to do with his emotions. And Miss Olliver in any case was a plain, worthy creature, interested only in doing her job, and in the mediaeval history in which she hoped one day to take an external degree. Young Andrew slept a great deal, so there was plenty of time for study. But she was a willing creature, as well as a dull one, and she shopped for the house without complaint.

In this, as in most of her life, she was a being of regular and easily observable habits. Once out of the small gate in the south wall of the *Lodge*, she would turn right along the Avenue, past *Tidesreach*, and *Neptune Court*, the two latest blocks of holiday apartments. At the corner, now dominated by an ugly insurance building, she turned right again, into Broad Street, off which lay the new shopping precinct, with its tiny fountain and the tables of the ice-cream parlour that were supposed to make it seem almost continental when the sun shone. There was a double layer of shops, linked by a complicated spiral of concrete, and on three or four mornings a week Miss Olliver pushed the undistinguished-looking black perambulator uncomplainingly about this dull little backwater; all among the boarding-house keepers, and the young wives, and the slow-moving files of holiday-makers who could find nothing better to do than stare aimlessly at shop-fronts that were identical with those in their local High Streets at home.

On the morning of July the eighteenth, the pattern was repeated. Outside the gate, she turned to the right, pushing the perambulator ahead of her. Andrew lay on his back and stared at the underside of the canopy that was there to keep off the harmful rays of the summer sun. He was a silent, contemplative child. At *Neptune Court* a strange dog came bounding up, but Miss Olliver spoke to it sharply, and it kept its distance. She walked on to the corner, turned right again into Broad Street. A small green van that had been parked for some time in the Avenue, swung after her, passed her, and turned into East Lane, which brought it to a car park at the far side of the shopping precinct. From it a bearded man took a black perambulator, with a canopy. When it was clear of the van, a woman in a white dress, with a pale blue headscarf and large white-rimmed sunglasses concealing most of her face, climbed out of the passenger seat, and without a word to the man, pushed the empty perambulator in the direction of the precinct.

Miss Olliver went first to the post office; then to the supermarket where there were already half a dozen perambulators parked outside, some with babies, some containing only the morning's purchases. A handful of dogs, also forbidden in the store, sat disconsolately chained to the low railings that surrounded the central flower bed.

Miss Olliver saw that the brake was on, touched Andrew briefly on the forehead, took one of the little wheeled supermarket carts and disappeared into the store. A minute later, the woman with the sunglasses left the market with a small jar of coffee, stowed it away in Andrew's pram, released the brake, and pushed it carefully down the spiral walk to the car park. Two minutes more, and the green van was threading its way through the traffic into Station Road, and so to Leas Avenue, where Sal and Melvin lived. It stopped, and a girl alighted who appeared to be dressed in a dark navy sweater worn over a white skirt. Her blue eyes were unencumbered, and her fair hair fell in a light gold shower about her shoulders. She turned to speak to the man in the car.

"How –?"

But he was already about to move off.

"Leave it to me," he said, and she gave a small shiver of mingled excitement and fear and revulsion.

In the back of the van, sharing his perambulator with the forgotten jar of coffee, Andrew Delany stared philosophically up at the underside of the canopy that was there only to protect him from the harmful sun.

Miss Olliver came out of the store, pushing her wire trolley, and headed for the undistinguished black perambulator with its cream canopy. Drawing up alongside, she had a pound of cheese in one hand, and a bottle of sauce in the other, preparatory to stowing them away, when realisation hit her.

At first she simply did not accept the evidence of her senses. She put the cheese and the sauce back on the trolley, felt with one hand the emptiness of the perambulator as though she thought that Andrew might still be there, though invisible. Then she looked carefully around the assembled baby-cars and chained dogs. Only then did she begin to scream, standing there in the warm, potentially dangerous summer sun, her hands clenched into two hard white-knuckled fists at her sides, her plain face unlovely with horror and grief and with the physical effort of screaming. The chained dogs leaped up and down, barking furiously. Sunburned faces turned towards her. Shops around the precinct emptied. Miss Olliver went on screaming, screaming, until she had no more strength left in her. Then she collapsed in a small untidy heap on the concrete-covered way.

*

"Andrew Delany," the Inspector said, "has been reported to us as missing, believed kidnapped."

Suddenly, the room was a spinning void. The heavy desk tipped dangerously.

"Kidnapped?"

"Believed kidnapped," the Inspector corrected him.

Behind the heavy mahogany drop-front, under the shelves of law-books most of which had stood there undisturbed since the days of the original Delany, was the bottle, and with it the glass he had used for the double shot. Suddenly the craving for a second drink dominated all other emotion. Even fear took second place to this terrible desire to quieten his nerves with the only means at hand.

The Inspector was still talking.

"We've got road-blocks out, and we're searching all the likely spots. But the town's full of strangers; and if the child is no longer in the area, then God help us, unless we get a lead. It was cleverly done, substituting an almost similar perambulator, which indicates forward planning, not a random snatch. Tell us what you know about the child's mother."

He was already half-way out of the chair, on his way to the bookcase, when the words penetrated his awareness. He kept moving, while his mind played with this new thought.

"I'm sorry," he said. "The shock . . ." He took out the bottle and the glass. "Inspector? Sergeant?" Anticipating their refusal, he poured a couple of inches of the whisky into the glass, and carried it back to the desk.

"The child's mother . . ." the Inspector prompted him. "You were going to tell us about her. . . ."

*

Mel's van was returned to him soon after lunch. Barry came in warily; avoided looking at Sal.

"You took long enough," Mel complained. "I thought you said an hour."

"It took longer than I thought."

"What did you want it for, anyway? I thought you'd finished at school."

"The little bastards have finished. The staff have to clear the decks, ready for next term."

And now he couldn't resist a swift glance at Sal. Their

eyes met briefly, slid apart. She murmured something, and went out, a high flush burning suddenly in the pale-gold skin under her sun-bleached hair. Mel saw it. He couldn't avoid seeing it. He said: "What goes on?"

"Nothing."

But Mel wasn't satisfied. "What have you two –?"

And suddenly he was on his feet. "What the bloody hell have you been doing? You and Sal? What did you want the van for?"

*

Delany said: "I know nothing about her, except that she took anything she could from my father, and left him the baby in return. Where she is now, I have no idea. But I suppose it's possible she came back for it –"

"It's possible," the Inspector agreed. "We're not discounting it. But there are other possibilities, too. So you don't know where Mrs. Selma Delany might be at this moment?"

"No. She went abroad, I understand, with a young Frenchman. If you want to trace her, why not ask my father – though I doubt if he knows any more than I do."

The Inspector examined the palms of his hands.

"So you haven't been told? I thought you had."

"Told what?" Delany's fingers tightened about the glass.

"Your father died suddenly this morning. The news of the baby's disappearance . . . I understand his heart. . . ." A pause, then: "It only happened an hour or two ago. When the baby was reported missing, a thorough search was made before telling him. Miss Olliver told us of his heart condition. But when it appeared certain that –" He stopped again, and spread his hands as though to say what else could they have done?

Delany thought: *You sleek official bastard. You knew damn well I couldn't have known of my father's death. You simply wanted to see my reaction to young Andrew's disappearance first.*

But all he said was: "I should have been told at once."

"I'm sorry. I thought you knew."

You bloody liar, was Delany's second thought. *You gave yourself away when you said: "You are not on good terms, then, with your father?" Are, you said, not were. . . It was a deliberate trap. But what good has it done you?*

"Just for the record, sir, where were you between ten o'clock and noon this morning?"

"Here, of course! Where else would I be? My secretary can confirm –" He reached out a hand for the internal telephone, but the Inspector rose to his feet and said: "No need, sir. We have already asked her." He motioned to the sergeant, who moved towards the door. "Thank you for being so helpful, sir. We'll keep you posted, naturally."

The door was open, and they were almost through when the Inspector took a couple of steps back into the room.

"Oh, just one other thing, sir. Do you happen to know the terms of your father's will?"

Delany clung to his chair. He said: "No, Inspector. At least, only in general outline. I gather he made provision for the child."

"Did he? That's interesting. You didn't draw up the will, then?"

"No. My father had his own solicitor. Gordon Wakeling –"

"Oh, yes, sir, I know Mr. Wakeling. I'll have to see him later today in any case." The Inspector nodded, turned away, with a "Thank you, again," and at last Delany was alone.

On his way back to the desk from re-locking his door, he picked up the bottle, and when the telephone rang and rang and rang he didn't answer it for a long time. Just as Pat was about to raise the alarm, she heard him say: "No calls. No clients. My father has died, and my step-brother has been kidnapped."

She said afterwards that she thought perhaps he was drunk. Everyone in the office knew that he kept the bottle in the bureau, and that it had to be renewed every few days.

She didn't for a moment believe the bit about his father, and his step-brother; thinking it was only the maudlin ramblings of the whisky. His voice sounded odd, too, as though it was coming from a long way away. And in the background was a curious high-pitched humming sound through which she could barely hear the words.

But that was afterwards, when she said all that, when the storm had already broken.

(3)

Mel said: "He's mad! He's stark bloody mad!" And: "Sal! Come here!" His voice was shrill. Barry had gone, pushing his way out through Mel's detaining hands and stammering words. Sal came back to the living-room, saying for God's sake don't shout. The neighbours, for Christ's sake! Do you want the whole town to know what we're doing?

Mel was sitting at the table, still littered with the empty plates and dishes from the mid-day meal. Now he looked up at her, his face lined by his growing fear. "*Did* you go out with him this morning?"

"Yes."

"To do what?"

"I can't tell you. You'll find out fast enough."

"You'll tell me now!"

"No."

Before she could move, he was on his feet, the chair falling backwards, the table rocking dangerously. A swift lunge forward, and he had seized her by the arms.

"You bloody well will! What has he made you do?"

"He didn't *make* me do anything! Stop it, Mel! Stop it! You're hurting me!"

He shook her until her mane of light-brown hair was scattered in a wild tangle over her eyes. Then suddenly he quietened, but he still kept his hurting grip on the soft flesh of her upper arms.

"The kid! My God, you took the kid! Is that it?"

She looked as wild as a cornered lynx.

"What if we did? What else could we do?"

"Why *you*? Why not Janey, for God's sake? She's his wife –"

"Janey works mornings. It had to be done then."

"Was that all?"

"That was all," she answered defiantly. "Now let me go, or so help me I'll do you an injury."

"You'll do *me* an injury! Haven't you done enough?" But he released her at last. She stood there rubbing her arms, breathing hard, her full lips thrust mutinously forward.

"Don't you dare do that again, Mel Williams!"

"That and more," he flung back at her, "if you don't tell me. Where's the kid now?"

"How should I know? Barry took it away in the van. He dropped me off here –"

Word by word, he dragged it out of her. At the end, he said: "For Christ's sake, love, don't you see where it's leading us?"

"I know where it *could* lead! A life in the sun."

"There's no sun where we'll land up! Only concrete floors and iron bars –"

"Barry's playing for big stakes. We've got to take a risk –"

"A risk! Christ, I was prepared for a risk. But not this sort of risk!"

"What else could we have done? The baby was the key to the whole problem –"

"Stop quoting Barry, for Christ's sake! You sound like a bloody text-book –"

"It's true! Just tell me what else we could have done. All that stuff at the Chapel. Then what? Nothing? Where's the money in that? Barry knows what he's doing."

"You've said that all along. *Leave it to Barry. He'll fix it. All we have to do is go along with him . . .*"

"It was you who said that. Not me!"

"Well, I don't say it now!"

"What's wrong with it anyway?" she demanded. "Leave it to you, and where would we be?"

"We wouldn't be facing a double murder-rap, for a start –"

"How do you know what he's done with the child?"

"Use your common-sense. Is he feeding it out of a bloody bottle, right now? Is he changing its bloody nappies? Don't act the sweet little innocent! You know damn well what's happened to it."

Barry said: "Sure, I got rid of it. What did you expect me to do. Bring it home?"

Det.-Inspector Ken Roper said: "It adds. Every bit of it adds. That smooth lawyer stands to make something like a quarter of a million, less duty, give or take a pound or two. Either way, it's money, not peanuts. The only thing is, how'd he do it? He didn't do it himself, that's for sure."

Janey said: "Why didn't you let the Duke do it? What's the good of conjuring them up, and then doing the work yourself?"

She tried to make it sound like a joke, but it was a dismal failure. She looked pale and nerve-ridden, a shadow of the dark confident gipsy-creature she had been for the first nineteen years of her life.

"Next time, maybe I will."

"But why Sal? Why didn't you ask me?"

"It might have caused talk if you'd asked for time off in the morning. Sal was free anyway."

"Was that all?"

"That was all."

"You could have told me –"

"You said that last time. Remember what I told you then? I said you might have tried to talk me out of it." He reached out for her, unexpectedly, began to run his hands over her. She could feel the trembling excitement that possessed him. "Remember what else I said? That there was no other way."

She stood passively, under the movement of his hands. Now their usual roles were reversed. How many times had he lain unresponsive while she had tried with hands and lips to rouse his ardour?

"There are times," she said, "when I think Mel may be right."

His hands stopped.

"About what?"

"About you."

"What about me?"

"He says you're mad."

CHAPTER EIGHT

"Is your name Henry Arthur Taylor, of 3, Moorland Terrace, Westport?"

"Yes."

"And were you, until October seventeenth last, manager of the Westport branch of the Midland Counties Bank at 174, High Street, with a sub-branch at Roddon?"

"I was."

"Will you tell the court why you are no longer employed by the Bank?"

"I am under suspension. That is my correct position."

"But are you performing any duties for the Bank?"

"No."

"Or receiving any salary?"

"No."

"Then the distinction is not of any great value, surely?"

Harry Taylor shrugged, and counsel for the prosecution repeated his original question: ". . . why you are no longer employed by the Bank?"

"Because I gave confidential information about our clients' affairs to an outsider for profit."

"That is very frank, Mr. Taylor. When you say to an outsider, will you please specify to whom you gave this confidential information."

"To Barry Simpson."

"For gain, you said? No, profit; that was the word you used. Let us be careful in our use of words. Was this a monetary profit? Did he actually pay you cash for this information?"

"No."

"What form did this profit take, then?"

Harry Taylor stared straight ahead of him.

"A regular supply of heroin."

*

Out near the estuary, a small wind was whipping the fine sand from the tops of the dunes. The tide was high, and clouds of screaming gulls fought and wheeled over the incoming boats that were bringing the day's catch up to the old town.

Barry Simpson sat on a high ridge of sand, watching the approach of the little bank manager. Taylor was still dressed in his Bank clothes; a dark blue-grey suit, with a grey and blue striped tie. In his unsuitable black shoes, he walked awkwardly over the salt-flats to the point where the wilderness of the dunes gave way suddenly to the cracked and crumbling edge of drying mud that held the estuary of the river. The evening light flooded in from the sea, and he kept his head down against the wind and the glare, glancing up only when he reached the end of the sea-wall. He saw Barry, stopped, looked carefully round at the wind-swept desolation of the flats, then turned towards the dunes, picking his way fastidiously among the debris that the last spring tides had flung up on the edge of the sand.

Barry didn't move towards him. He sat quite still, until Harry Taylor had climbed the shifting slope of the dune, and was standing by him, breathing hard. Then he said: "Why don't you wear something a little less conspicuous, for God's sake? Out here, you look as well camouflaged as St. Peter in all his robes walking in hell."

"I only left the Bank a quarter of an hour ago. I didn't want to risk missing you."

Barry said: "What's the info? It'd better be good."

"First the stuff. I'm right out."

"I don't believe you. You're better organised than that."

Harry Taylor looked out over the dunes to the sea. A

fine spray was being whipped from the crests of the waves by the same small wind that was troubling the sand.

"I have friends," he said at last, "whose need is as great as mine. When we have it, we share. I've had nothing since early morning."

Barry said: "First the info."

"No," Taylor said. "One shot. You can keep the rest until you have it."

He held out a hand, and Barry saw how it trembled. He hesitated for a moment, then he drew a sealed package from his inside pocket, broke it open. Taylor produced a small leather case, opened it, revealed a needle, a measuring glass, a small phial of liquid. Carefully, he went through the ritual, removing his jacket and inserting the needle in a vein near his left elbow. Barry saw with a small sense of shock the scar tissue, the discoloration, the fading marks of a hundred previous injections.

*

"How long," Taylor was asked in court, "have you been addicted to heroin?"

"Three years. Nearly four."

"You are a registered addict?"

"Yes, I am now. But not then."

"Why not?"

"Because of my position at the Bank. If it had ever been known . . ."

"But now it is known."

"Yes. But it wasn't then. I had to be extremely careful."

"What I cannot understand," counsel said, "is how a man in your position, a man with all the advantages of a liberal education, a man in a well-paid and honoured profession –"

With the tattered remnants of the respectability of his office flying like a shot-torn ensign, Harry Taylor lifted both hands.

"Spare me the clichés, please," he said. "I was a fool.

but there were what seemed to be good reasons at the time. My work, which had become too demanding. The loss of my wife. My son was in trouble at his university. These are not excuses, they are reasons. Or they seemed to be then." Turning to the judge, he said: "I will give my evidence to the best of my ability, my Lord, but may I please be spared the moralising?"

The judge removed and polished his glasses.

"I am inclined to sympathise with the witness's request, Mr. Arlingfold. This is not a court of morals. Will you please confine your questioning to the matters on hand?"

"As your Lordship pleases."

*

"Well?" Barry said.

Taylor had replaced his jacket, had repacked the needle and the rest of the kit. Now he sat with his eyes closed, looking relaxed and calm. Without opening his eyes, he murmured: "What happened to the Delany child?"

"That's my side of the business. You stick to yours, and maybe you'll keep out of trouble."

"I agree it's no direct concern of mine. But I'd like to know if the operation was a hundred per cent successful. I still have an interest in it, don't forget. You promised me another consignment, on successful conclusion. Incidentally, I haven't had the second one for Cargrove yet."

"You'll get it, when we are quite certain."

"You've had no money yet?"

"Not yet. But it'll come."

Taylor said reasonably: "You can't go on with this. Not indefinitely."

"We don't want to."

"What you need is one big one. Then stop, before they catch up with you."

"That could be the answer. But it'd have to be big."

"I might be able to put you on to something." Taylor paused again. He ran the tips of his fingers over his closed eyes, savouring the almost instant euphoria induced by the drug. "Though, mark you, it would have to be worth my while. In advising you to go for the big chap, and then stop, I could be cutting the props from under my own feet."

"We'd arrange something."

"You'd have to. I should want –" He opened his eyes, glanced slyly at Barry, "– ten years' supply –"

Barry laughed.

"You'd be lucky! Ten *years*? Talk bloody sense, man! What's that worth in hard cash on the black market?"

"But presumably you don't pay black market prices?"

"I pay enough."

"Or promise enough."

"I keep my promises."

"I hope so. Indeed I hope so."

*

"Where," Mr. Arlingfold asked the witness, "was this vast amount of heroin – this ten years' supply – to come from?"

"He said he had contacts."

Mr. Arlingfold raised his eyebrows.

"Oh, come now, Mr. Taylor! Was *he* – I presume by that pronoun you mean Barry Simpson, by the way?"

"That's right," Taylor agreed.

"Was he not more specific? Did he not tell you where he obtained his supplies?"

"No. And I didn't want to know. As long as he supplied me."

"Precisely, Mr. Taylor. As long as you had your supplies of this terrible drug, to which you had become addicted, you didn't want to know anything. You didn't even want to know to what use the information you supplied was put. The information that you were paid to keep as secret as is the doctor's knowledge of his patient; as is the priest's knowledge of the deeds and thoughts of the penitent."

"That is so," Taylor agreed reasonably; and with another shrug of his eyebrows directed this time at the jury, Mr. Arlingfold suddenly said: "Do you believe in what is popularly known as Black Magic, Mr. Taylor?"

And Taylor answered readily enough: "Yes. Yes, I do. Indeed I do."

*

Barry said: "At that price, it would have to be more than just good."

Taylor picked up a splinter of bleached driftwood that could have been a fragment of bone, long-drowned and cast up on the shore by the violence of the murdering sea.

"Do you know Sir James Prynne?"

"No."

"He's chairman of Mowdell Publishing."

"I still don't know him."

"It's a pretty wide empire."

"Local?"

"No. London-based. But with interests all over the world. They're currently the subject of a take-over fight. They've had offers from T.W.P., and from Parian-Laing, but at the moment there's stalemate."

"So?"

"You sound unimpressed. But Mowdell has an equity of sixty-five millions. T.W.P. are currently offering the equivalent of seventy-eight, and Parian-Laing are reconsidering their last bid, which worked out at only a fraction less." He turned the fragment of bone, or wood, or whatever it was, between his fingers. "The vice-chairman of Mowdell is Alan Horton-Crawley, who used to be with Parian-Laing, and who is still Parian-orientated. If Parian-Laing win the take-over, Horton-Crawley will probably be made Chairman in place of Prynne, who is openly backing T.W.P. I gather Prynne has big ideas for a North American link-up, which Parian-Laing don't favour."

"Wait a minute," Barry said. "This is high-level stuff.

How are you involved? Big boys like that don't keep their bank accounts down here."

"I told you. I have friends."

"In London?"

"Why not?"

"The friends you were talking about? The ones with the same needs?"

"That's right," Taylor said. "We're a widely scattered lot, but our lines of communication are often quite good. Don't you think it's time you began to widen your own sphere of operations? If there are too many strange happenings in a small area like this, someone, and soon, is going to start asking questions."

"What the hell can *we* do?" Barry demanded. "We don't play in that sort of league."

"The rules are the same, whatever league you're in. I happen to know, from one of my friends in the London branch where Mowdell keep their main account, that Horton-Crawley and Prynne's wife ..." And, later: "Prynne will be in New York for ten days immediately before the Special Meeting at which the take-over question will probably be decided. He has to be over there for the International Book Expo, but he's flying back in time for the Special Meeting. Unless something happens to prevent him –"

Barry ran a hand through the fine fair hair that surrounded his baby-mouth.

"Hell, he'll have fixed it so someone else –"

Taylor said: "This is very much a clash of personalities. And publishing is a curiously emotional profession. If Prynne is at the meeting, he may well sway enough of the shareholders into saying *no* to Parian-Laing. If he isn't there, Horton-Crawley may well swing them over to his side by sheer persuasive talk and personal magnetism."

Barry said: "I still say this is outside our league. What the hell can *we* do from here to trip up a man who's probably a millionaire, staying at the Waldorf-Astoria in New York, a little matter of three thousand bloody miles away? Talk sense for Christ's sake!"

Harry Taylor looked startled.

"How do you know where he's staying?"

Barry pulled impatiently at his whiskers.

"You said it yourself. New York, you said. For the Book Expo."

"I didn't say which hotel. I didn't say the Waldorf-Astoria."

"Is that where he's staying?"

"Yes."

"A guess. That's all it was. It's like saying the Ritz, or the Savoy, if you think of London."

"It was a damn good guess."

"Forget it."

"Why couldn't you do it? If the price was right?"

"In *New York*?"

"Why not? What's the difference?"

"I don't know my way about, that's what. I'm on my home ground here."

"He'd pay fifty thousand pounds –"

Barry froze into a watchful immobility, sitting with his shoulders hunched and his whiskered head thrust forward. Like a vulture on a dead branch, Taylor described him later, waiting to feed on death. After a long pause, he said quietly: "Fifty thousand? How do you know that?"

"My friend –"

"Your *friend*!" Barry said, still quietly. "What have you told your *friends*?"

"Nothing. Nothing that matters."

"How the hell do *you* know what matters?" And now he spoke less quietly, spitting out the words with a savage venom. "You stupid bloody junkie! If you've been talking –" He took the package in his hands, the seal now broken, one shot removed. "What did you tell them?" He began to take the inner packing from the outer cover. "Tell me, or I swear by all the names of God, I'll scatter this lot over the beach so you won't find a single bloody grain of it!"

Climate of Evil

'... they will assuredly come, and no prayers of yours will turn them whence they came.'

OCTAVIUS GIBBER

*

'... fraternise with them. They will then tear you in pieces at their leisure.'

ALEISTER CROWLEY

CHAPTER ONE

(1)

THE big man came, like Cargrove and Pierse Delany before him, to the side door of the house in Parrott Lane.

He was a big man in every way. Six feet four, Madame Joseph estimated; with upwards of two hundred pounds, none of which looked at all like soft flesh. He came in through the double door, from the side passage, like one of the big cats, a Bengal tiger perhaps, coming into the show-cage from the narrow tunnel that leads to the circus ring. He came in soft-footed, wary, prepared to do what was required of him, but ready to turn, to hurl those two hundred hard pounds into instant attack rather than defence, should the need arise.

In the cellar under the séance-room, the tapes revolved, and Mel's monitor screen showed Horton-Crawley and Madame Joseph together, with the crystal ball between them.

Mel had been persuaded into taking part in this one last venture. No, not persuaded. Bludgeoned. Terrified out of his small-town mind. Barry had quoted the Homicide Act: *where two or more persons* ... And: "For Christ's sake," he'd said, "face up to reality! We're all in it. Do you want out, in the sun, or gaol for life? You *and* Sal? Have you forgotten who took the Delany child? Your wife, chum!" And: "After this," he'd said, "we pack it in. It's too dangerous." But he had said it without conviction. So far, luck had been with them. Luck or the devil. So was there any reason why it shouldn't stay that way? Privately, in the dark places of his mind, he didn't believe that this would be the end. But Mel was persuaded at last. Or bludgeoned.

"At midnight tonight," Madame Joseph said, "you will go to the place where the upper road crosses the old green road, near the ford at Axel Heath . . ."

For Alan Horton-Crawley, the drill had been streamlined. There was no point, Barry felt, in expecting one of the big boys – one of the very big boys – to travel down from London more than once. The problem was already clear; the price had already been fixed. He had brought the first instalment with him, in five-pound notes, neatly bundled with elastic and stuffed into a leather brief-case. A map had been prepared. He was even to be lent a crucifix.

*

"Were you not afraid," counsel for the prosecution was to ask him at the trial, "of the possible consequences? Did you not realise that you would almost certainly have been filmed, possibly in the house in Parrott Lane, and later, by infra-red, in the Chapel – filmed, recorded and subsequently blackmailed? This is a not uncommon practice, as I am sure you are aware."

"It had crossed my mind. It was a risk, but I never hesitate to take a risk if there is a possible advantage to be gained. The stakes were high on this occasion."

"You believed in what these people said that they could do?"

"I was prepared to gamble on the possibility that they could produce results."

"By supernatural means?"

"I had no interest in *how* the results might be achieved."

"Did you, in fact, when you visited the house in Parrott Lane, believe in what is popularly known as Black Magic?"

"No."

"You are quite certain about that?"

"Quite certain."

"Then let me ask you another question, and I want you to consider your answer very carefully. Do you *at this moment* believe in Black Magic?"

There was a long, expectant pause in the courtroom. Then counsel said: "You must answer the question. Do you wish me to repeat it, or did you understand me the first time?"

Horton-Crawley took a deep breath.

"I understood you perfectly," he said.

*

"Alan Sebastian Horton-Crawley," the Voice intoned, "do you accept that the utmost power of evil shall be invoked in the solution of your problems, or are there any lengths to which you will not go in the pursuit of your ambition?"

He had been a difficult subject from the start, refusing to drink from the Cup that the fair-haired girl had offered him. She had stood there, naked in front of him in the flickering light of the two black candles, holding the Cup towards him. The Voice from the altar had said: "Drink! We cannot invoke the Powers of Evil unless you drink from the Cup of Evil."

"No," he had said.

"Have no fear. It will do you no harm. We want you alive, and we want you to achieve your ambition. It is to our advantage as well as yours that you remain unharmed. You must have faith. Faith in us. Faith in yourself. Faith in the Power you seek. You *must* drink."

He had swallowed the bitter-tasting brew at last, and then had come the Invocation, and the Oath. He had rapidly begun to experience hallucinations of colour. Rainbows had arced about the body of the girl on the altar. A different girl, this. Dark, not fair. The Messenger had taken his hand to lay it on the girl's body, but he had shaken him off, and instead had placed both his spread hands on the girl's breasts. She had shivered once, then she had lain still. But while he repeated the words of the Oath, he had let his hands wander over her, caressing, probing, insulting, knowing by all the familiar reactions that he was rousing her – this beautiful, vulnerable, faceless stranger – knowing this, and experiencing a sudden fierce pleasure, not so much in the arousal itself, but from the knowledge that in this small way he was asserting himself against those who were forcing him step by step through this outrageous pantomime.

The effects of the drug grew more bizarre. The colours were stronger, and suddenly the figure of the girl changed to that of a rotting corpse. His probing hands broke through putrescent skin, were plunged into the gaseous liquids of decay. With a cry of horror he flung himself back from the altar, shaking his outstretched hands to rid them of the contamination. But then, just as abruptly, the girl was a girl again, dark-haired, dark-skinned, beautiful.

The Voice was repeating its question.

"Alan Horton-Crawley, do you accept that the utmost power of evil –"

Loudly, clearly then, the words echoing a little under the shadowy roof, Horton-Crawley said: "I do not accept the existence of the power of evil. I do not accept that what I seem to be seeing in front of me at the moment is any more than a drug-induced fantasy. I want help in the plan I have in mind, but that help must be practical, in and of this material world. For God's sake, let us stop this nonsense and talk things over sensibly."

The words, so confidently uttered, trailed away into the shadows, as did the rising smoke from the black candles. The body of the girl on the altar moved convulsively once, then lay still again. In the trapped air, he felt a sudden soundless vibration that clutched at his throat. Then the low humming began, growing almost imperceptibly out of the void; and above and under and through it he heard Madame Joseph's voice in the unhurried pattern of the Great Invocation:

Pater noster adversus, rex et imperator, deus et diabolus, venite, venite, venite, ex sepulcrum universum . . .

Mel Williams stared incredulously at the revolving tapes behind the altar. Tapes that should not have held the voice of Madame Jo.

. . . upto in terra . . . upto in inferus . . .

The choking, animal stench began to fill the Chapel.

Eia! Eia! Eia! . . . deus et diabolus . . .

In Madame Joseph's quietly intense voice, the ancient phrases, in their ritual sorcerer's Latin came from where?

Horton-Crawley stood transfixed, staring at the altar. The bright rainbow colours were already dimmed. The intensity of the humming sound increased to a sharp revolving diamond-point that drilled mercilessly at his mind. And now even the flames of the candles began to die. Each seemed to withdraw into the body of its own black cylinder of wax, diminishing until at last it was no more than a tiny spark, infinitely distant. In the moment before they were extinguished completely, he saw the girl on the altar reach up her arms, arching her body towards a black shape that was imperfectly moulded from the sudden darkness.

From somewhere even more remote in the darkness, someone screamed. A shrill, terrified scream that went on and on. The other girl? The stench became unbearable. It was as though his mouth and nostrils were pressed against the hide of some foul-smelling beast, rank with its own ordure.

Eia! Eia! Eia! cried the voice of Madame Joseph, and with each repeated syllable the pressure increased, the shrill dynamo humming grew in intensity.

. . . upto in terra . . . upto in inferus . . .

Horton-Crawley was down on his knees, fighting to survive. The blackness now was absolute. Everywhere was the stench, the feel, the sound of Evil. Desperately, he searched in his pockets for the small crucifix that Madame Jo had given him. Dragging it out at last, gasping and choking he fumbled with it in the dark. His hands clumsy with fear, he realised that it was reversed, the head pointing down to the sick earth under his knees. Frantically, he tried to turn it, but it was held fast. Something, someone, some disembodied force, had the tiny charm in an iron grip. It was held, seized by an invisible power that all his strength could not overcome. The small fragment of carved bone was immovable, though he exerted against it all the force of his powerful body, reinforced by the fear that possessed him. At last he relinquished his hold on it, and instantly it was pulled away into the darkness. His last protection gone, he turned and began to crawl away in what he thought was the direction of the curtained doorway. But in the darkness and the din his sense of direction was confused. And the dark was now full of movement, and whispering, and foul shapes that gave obscenely under his outstretched hands. Wherever he crawled, his hands encountered this soft and yielding flesh, though his fingers gave him no clue as to the form that it took. *Monstrous toads, they could have been, like moving bags of churchyard slime. Corpses, long-dead, now summoned from uneasy graves . . .*

"God," he prayed, "let me stay rational. Let me accept that all that I *think* I feel is only illusion. Let me be sure that if light were to come, I should not see what my groping hands are so positive is there."

But did corpses move, or churchyard toads stretch out small leathery hands to claw and grasp? As his own hands searched among the loathsome crew for the way of escape, he felt himself seized by a thousand lecherous paws. This way and that he was dragged; turned on his back as helpless as a stranded turtle. He felt his clothes being stripped from him, until at last he was as naked as the two girl acolytes. Foul effluents flooded over him. The stench of corruption rose like a miasma in the darkness. Above all, was a sensation of sudden cold. Not only had light been withdrawn. Warmth, too, had gone. The floor of the Chapel was itself cripplingly cold. So was the unknown unidentifiable flesh that surrounded him. So, too, were the small leathery hands. He remembered suddenly, amidst the chaos and the terror, that the legion of those who had claimed to have had sexual relations with the Devil had invariably said that his member was cold, his semen like ice.

What had been summoned in that last calm invocation in its curious sorcerers' Latin? Madame Joseph's voice no longer called. The shrill humming had increased in pitch until it was now poised on a high threshold beyond which it would be lost. But at that level it was unbearably painful. Under and round and through it, the whispering grew louder, a vast susurration of unintelligible sound.

Naked and terrified, he managed at last to stand upright. It took all his strength, and with him he dragged a foul horde that clung to him with their cold leathery hands, their bodies swinging obscenely against him. Silently, sick with revulsion, he fought to fling them off. But their substance was as elusive as quicksilver, and their cold hands clung to every orifice and protruberance; even, to his utter horror, to his lips and nose and hair. Like monstrous leeches they swarmed and clung and would not be removed. As he stood swaying, another horde came hissing out of the darkness, climbing over those that already hung from every fold of skin and patch of hair. The Chapel was alive with them, and standing there, covered in the foul creatures, with wave after wave swarming up from the noisome floor, it seemed that they must be without number, their vast battalions stretching back along the endless sewers of hell to the throne of the Prince himself –

Then through the din came a new Voice; strong, arrogant; saying: *Where is the unbeliever? Where is he who denies the power of darkness?* And the soft sibilant whispering rose to a frenzy all about him. He tried to cry out, but the loathsome shapes hung everywhere about his face; the small cold hands were in his mouth, gripping his tongue; so that all that came was an inarticulate moaning that was lost in the greater clamour.

Alan Sebastian Horton-Crawley, do you still deny the existence of the power of evil?

The voice echoed about the darkness inside the Chapel, and suddenly the susurration ceased. The hands released their hold, the loathsome quicksilver shapes withdrew. And in his own voice, suddenly freed, he answered loudly, with an unexpected return of courage: "I accept that the human mind can be the subject of hallucinatory effects that can appear real –"

The Voice interrupted him.

If the effects you have just experienced are hallucinations – if I too am merely a hallucinatory effect – then why bother to argue with me?

"Perhaps I am not arguing with you. Perhaps even that is only hallucination."

If you cling to that belief, then your argument is like a series of little boxes, one inside the other. Each is covered by the one before it. Each in turn covers the next.

The sweet reasonableness of the Devil . . .

But if you wish to achieve your heart's desire, you will have to learn to accept. Now answer the question that has already been put to you. Do you, Alan Sebastian Horton-Crawley, accept that the utmost power of evil shall be invoked in the solution of your problems, or are there any lengths to which you will not go in the pursuit of your ambition?

There was a single short sharp hiss of indrawn breath from the waiting multitude, then silence again in the Chapel. Horton-Crawley stood there, naked in the darkness, aware of the silent swarms of whatever it was that had bones of quicksilver and small cold leathery hands. After that one sharp unexpected inhalation, the silence, like the darkness, was absolute.

At last, slowly, reluctantly, he heard his own voice say: "I accept the invocation of the utmost power of evil –" And in an instant the waiting hordes flung themselves upon him, seized him, lifted him from the ice-cold floor and bore him away and away into the humming dark, until his consciousness was reduced to a small pin-point of awareness at the end of a black tunnel; until at last even that, like the candle flames on the altar, faded and died.

(2)

Mel lay on his back, his head a foot away from Sarah's. They had been quarrelling ever since he and Barry had returned from Axel Heath, after leaving the unconscious Horton-Crawley in his car by the ford.

Each of them had retained a different impression of the events of the night. Mel, behind the altar, working his tapes and his electronic flashes, had heard the voice of Madame Joseph, and was still demanding how the hell it could ever have been imposed on the background that he had himself prepared for the ceremonies in the chapel. He had seen the candles doused, had stood bewildered in the dark until they had been re-lit. Or, rather, until they had re-lit themselves.

But that was almost all he had experienced. The usual question had been put to Horton-Crawley, who had denied the power of evil. Then Madame Joseph's voice had unexpectedly recited the Great Conjuration. The flames had dimmed, and in the darkness there had been only the high-pitched humming sound that had deadened his awareness of everything else. He had not heard the exchanges between Horton-Crawley and the new Voice; nor had he been aware, as Horton-Crawley had, of the whispering hordes of slack-bodied creatures that had swarmed out of the blackness and the sudden cold. When the humming was at last silenced, he had heard Horton-Crawley's voice saying: "I accept the invocation of the utmost power of evil –", but the words had ended in a sudden cry. Released from his own immobility, he had heard Barry's voice, shouting for a light, and he had fumbled about amongst his equipment for a torch. But then the candle flames had grown again, flowering from nothing, climbing into the troubled air and pushing back the darkness. On the altar, Janey lay trembling and spent. Sal stood a yard away, shivering, her arms crossed over her naked breasts. Barry, in his role of the Goat, climbed down from his high platform. On the floor of the Chapel, Horton-Crawley lay fully clothed, his hands stretched out as though to fend off some invisible attacker. He was unconscious, breathing slowly and heavily. His mouth was open, fixed in the shape of that last terrified cry.

Mel had gone down on his knees, and had opened one of the unconscious man's eyes. Only the white was visible, an oval of blankness in the still silently shouting face that seemed frozen into a pattern of utter horror. And as he had looked up again, he had seen Barry and Sal, locked in each other's arms.

Mel had kept quiet during the journey to Axel Heath, in case the big man recovered his wits on the way. But when they had bundled him, with some difficulty, into his own car, and the van had been turned and headed back for the Chapel, the quarrel had started. It had blazed up afresh when they had collected the two girls, and it was still going on now that Mel and Sal were in bed at home.

Sal said: "For Christ's sake, how many more times? What would I want with a hairy bloody school-teacher?"

"It adds up," Mel said. He had said the same thing, or something like it, a dozen times already. But in this sort of quarrel, the same weary points are brought out over and over, like the tired blows exchanged between a pair of fighters almost at the end of their resources. "You took the kid –"

"Christ, Mel, someone had to!"

"You're not his wife –"

A small spark re-kindled something of the earlier anger.

"What's that to do with it, for God's sake! This is supposed to be a joint effort, isn't it? We're all in it together."

"If only I'd known, at the beginning –"

"If only you'd known!" She mocked him. "You didn't think any further than *leave it to Barry; he'll fix it.* Now he's fixed it, and you're scared –"

"Christ, who wouldn't be? What went on tonight?"

"How do I know? Maybe Horton-whatsit had had too much of the drink. Maybe Barry mixed it wrong –"

"It's not only that –"

"The spooks, is it? The bloody spooks. Is that it?" Her voice was only a degree away from hysteria.

"You were scared enough. You said so. Otherwise, why'd you have to tangle up with Barry?"

"Sure I was scared. It was spooky all right, the lights doing that. And him out cold on the floor –"

"You didn't have to tangle with Barry –"

"Oh, for Jeez' sake, I told you, he was nearest. I didn't stop to think –"

Mel said: "I don't know what's going on. How'd they rig the tapes? That's what I don't know."

"How'd *who* rig the tapes? And why would anyone want to?"

"It could only be Barry, and the old woman –"

"But *why*? Why would they want to do that?"

"I don't know," Mel said stubbornly. "But, by God, I'm going to find out."

Janey said for maybe the hundredth time: "It *must* have been you! For Christ's sake, Bar, it *must* have been you!"

She had been lying on the altar. Horton-Crawley had repeated the words of the oath over her naked body, as they had intended, but his hands had wandered and she had been unable to stop the inevitable arousal of passion. She had felt the strength, the virility of the man, even in the touch of his hands. She had tried to lie still, but the big man's hands had caressed her with insolent deliberation. She had felt very little for either of the others; for Cargrove or for Pierse Delany. Except, perhaps, a slight shudder of distaste at the physical contact. But this man was different. Force flowed from him. And the forces in her own body leaped at the deliberate probing of his strong square hands.

But suddenly she had seen a look of horror and revulsion transform his face. He had snatched his hands away from her as though she was unclean, holding them out in front of him, the fingers hanging down. There might have been something unspeakable dripping from the ends of them, and as he hurled himself backwards, away from the altar, a cry escaped him. A cry of shock and horror. Through the fine silk mask that made her seem almost faceless, she saw him standing there staring at his hands, staring at her. Until suddenly whatever it was that he had seen, or thought he had seen, must have disappeared. His face slowly cleared, and he let his hands fall limply to his sides. Barry had started to repeat the standard question, but Horton-Crawley had interrupted him with his denial of the power of evil.

And then it had seemed that the world had stood still. For an endless moment, there was absolute silence in the Chapel. It was as though the bravely-spoken words had been received, and were being assessed. Still burning with the fire that his hands had kindled, she had moved once, convulsively, then she had lain still. And then the soundless vibration had set its iron bands about her throat. And following that the low dynamo-hum that had risen in intensity to the pitch of a high-speed diamond drill. And above and under and through it she had heard the totally unexpected voice of her own mother, repeating the words of the Great Invocation from the *Grimorium Pristinum* of the hunchback Octavius Gibber . . .

The flames of the candles had begun to die. The strange shrill sound had drilled at her mind. The darkness had crept from the far corners of the Chapel towards the altar. And in the last second, before the light failed completely, she saw indistinctly the dark male hairy outline of Barry, as the Beast, crouched above her. Helpless in the grip of her passion, her mind dulled by the shrill diamond drill from the power-house of evil, she had reached up for him, and had felt the sudden weight of his body on hers. As the darkness became absolute, the heat of her desire was pierced by an arrow of pure ice. It was ecstasy and agony. In all her often unsatisfactory relations with Barry she had known nothing even remotely like this swift hard stabbing pain.

Whimpering like a child, she had curled her fingers into the matted hair that they had sewed and glued onto the fine body-stocking that he wore for the ceremonies. The stocking covered him completely, except for an opening in front through which his organs hung free, half-concealed by a tangle of hair. On his head, he wore either the fine silk that made him appear almost face-less, or the leering goat's-mask from Parrott Lane. But now his lips were free, crushing hers. The rank animal-stench was suffocating. In the warmth of her body the arrow of ice melted into a river of snow. And, then, without a word, he slipped from her grasp, and she was left alone and spent in the humming darkness.

"It *wasn't* me! How many more times do I have to say it? I never moved. I didn't take the mask off. I was up on the shelf, I tell you. All the time. Until the lights came on –"

"But I *felt* you! The hair –"

She was trembling. In her loins was still a core of icy cold.

"You imagined it."

But he was excited. She knew that. His half-blind eyes were feverishly bright. His lips shone wetly in the light from the bedside lamp. Suddenly she lost control. Throwing herself at him across the bed she began to beat at him with her fists clenched.

"For God's sake, what are you doing?" she screamed at him. "Are you trying to make me think I'm as crazy as you are? Is that it? Is it? Is it?" In her frenzy, most of her blows went wide, but enough of them landed on his face and shoulders to rouse him into fighting back. He seized her wrists; held her, still struggling; tried to force her back to her own pillow.

"For Christ's sake, listen, can't you! All that happened was what I've tried to do from the start. For the first time we created a true atmosphere. *A climate of evil*. That's what the books call it –"

"The books!" she shouted back at him, with renewed fury. "I'm sick of the bloody books! I'm sick of being told we have to do what the books say! Was it in the books that you had to screw me on the altar?"

"I didn't, for God's sake!"

"You did! You did! Christ, do you think I don't know –"

Suddenly he released one of her wrists, and struck her hard across the face with his free hand. Contemptuously, he said: "You're hysterical, that's what. The books, if you'd trouble to read them, are full of claims by hysterical females that they've been screwed by the devil –"

The hand he had released came up like a scythe, her long nails tearing into the flesh of his face. As he flung himself back, the blood began to flow.

"Don't say it! Don't say it!" she screamed. "It wasn't that! It wasn't. It was you! It must have been you!"

With a sudden swift movement, no longer pinned down by his weight, she twisted over to lie on her stomach. Sobbing wildly into the pillow she repeated over and over, while he held a towel to the blood from his damaged face: "No! No! No! It wasn't that! It wasn't! It was you! It was you! It was you!"

CHAPTER TWO

(1)

Someone, and soon, is going to start asking questions . . .

That is what Harry Taylor said to Barry Simpson, out on the sand-dunes by the estuary.

*

"Is your name Peter Fletcher," counsel for the prosecution said, "of Bridgwater Mansions, Kensington Square, London?"

"It is."

"And are you a free-lance journalist and photographer?"

"I am."

"Was your father, Charles Fletcher, also a professional photographer?"

"Yes."

"And was he reported missing, presumed drowned, in a sea-disaster involving a vessel known as *Seamew*, some 20 years ago?"

"He was."

"A disaster which occurred off the town of Westport?"

"Yes."

"But his body was never recovered?"

"No. Legal presumption of death was obtained."

Counsel paused to let the jury digest the information so far established. Then he said quietly: "Mr. Fletcher, will you please tell the court why you visited Westport for the first time in August and September of last year."

*

As Peter Fletcher had gone up in the lift to the tenth floor of the Clay Building, off Chancery Lane, in London, he had wondered for the hundredth time what had prompted them to send for him in such an almighty hurry. He'd been photographing marine life off the East African coast, and they had sent a chopper to pluck him quite literally out of the water. Sixteen hours later he was in the lift in the Clay Building, still wondering what the hell it was all about.

Waiting for him was Ed's secretary, Midge; a small, intense girl with a C.C.I. badge hanging from a gold chain round her thin white neck. Unsmilingly she said: "Hurry, please. He's due in conference in ten minutes." She set off along a corridor that could so easily have been part of a modern hospital. Here and there they passed other equally intense-seeming girls, and dedicated-looking young men, all wearing similar badges, though not all on gold chains. *Clay's Crime Investigator* is published monthly, from Clay House, along with a score of other journals, and this was the H.Q. of C.C.I. (London). The New York H.Q. is larger and noisier. Paris, Munich, and Rome, are smaller. C.C.I. (Sydney) is still housed in a temporary shack-like building near the harbour. In Tokyo, you are even now politely frisked before they will allow you through the decorative portcullis that guards the C.C.I. wing of the Clay Building on Ginza Park. But here, quietly sandwiched between London's Chancery Lane and Lincoln's Inn, it could have been a high-class clinic for the treatment of top-class nervous breakdowns. Ed himself would have made the perfect Director of such an establishment. Quiet, watchful, sparing in the use of words, he was sitting at an almost empty desk when Midge opened the door and Fletcher found himself for the second time in his life in the sudden hush of the sound-proofed Editor's Room.

"Peter, this is Elizabeth Frele. I want you to work together."

No greeting no enquiry as to the state of his health, no

apology for fetching him back nearly five thousand miles. He looked for Elizabeth, found a long, lean, untidy-looking creature lounging in a black armchair. Under a tangled mass of sand-coloured hair, she looked sunburnt and cross.

"Where did he fetch *you* from?" he asked her.

She shot a glance of pure hatred at Ed.

"Morocco."

"You didn't *have* to come. Or did you?"

"Did *you*?"

"If I wanted the money."

"What makes you think I don't need money?" she snapped at him.

Ed said: "Liz's mother died on *Seamew*. Like your father, Peter." It stopped their small sparring match in mid-blow. They both turned back to the quiet man at the big desk. "She was Marion Frele. She was a painter and illustrator, using her maiden name of Marion Reynolds. Well known at the time. Liz has much the same talent. She also dabbles in archaeology. She's currently on a dig at a new site south of Meknès."

"*Was*, not *is*," Liz said.

"You can go back. Today, if you wish."

"Without the money? You're joking –"

"I have six minutes," Ed said. "Then I'm in conference. I want to be able to tell the meeting that in principle it's all settled. The details can be worked out later."

Fletcher said: "She's probably two jumps ahead of me. Can't you fill me in on why you want to talk *Seamew* now?"

"That's a fair question. In the last few weeks there have been two deaths by violence in Westport. One, an explosion, could have been accidental. The other, the kidnapping and subsequent murder of a child, could not. It was from Westport, a little over twenty years ago, that *Seamew* sailed on her last trip, carrying your father, Pete, and Liz's mother. The mystery surrounding the loss was never resolved."

Pete Fletcher was still standing. He looked down at the angry, sunburned face of Liz Frele.

"But, hell – that's twenty years ago –"

Ed glanced at his watch again.

"We had a telephone call. On Monday. From a stranger who wouldn't give his name." Apologetically: "We get dozens, every day, of course. Mostly from nuts of one kind or another. But this one had done his homework. He knew a heck of a sight more than the average nut could ever know about *Seamew*. He even knew the official comments on the inquiry report – comments that are never made public. And he suggested a possible link between *Seamew*, and these two recent deaths by violence –"

Pete said again: "But twenty *years* . . ." And Ed spread out his hands.

"I know. Not an obvious pattern. Not even a regular one. But there are several intriguing features about the affair. For instance, we recorded the conversation, as we always do. Listen –" He pressed a button on his desk, and from behind a grille in the wall opposite the windows they heard:

"Hello – yes, this is Bill Hodges, C.C.I., London . . ."

There was a pause, then:

"I'm the Assistant Editor. Anything you have to say, say it to me . . ."

Another pause, then:

"Yes, I remember the *Seamew* affair."

Ed switched off the recording.

"Notice anything?"

"The other half – the caller – shouldn't that be on the tape?"

"It should be. There's nothing wrong with the machine, or the tape. But not a word of anything the caller said was recorded."

Liz said: "It could be an elaborate trick. Who's Bill Hodges?"

Ed smiled faintly.

"Who is the Archbishop of Canterbury? Bill doesn't joke about his work. Especially when it's going to cost as much as this affair will. And, anyway, his secretary, who's as reliable as he is, heard it on the extension. She verifies word for word. They were on night stand-by and there wasn't much else doing. Another curious thing. The call came through precisely at midnight. Every call is clock-noted, automatically, for time commenced, time finished. This one was noted T.C. 2400 hours."

Liz looked up suddenly, and Pete noticed that her hands were tightly clenched, the knuckles showing white under the dark-brown skin.

"And – time finished?" she said.

"2400 hours."

Try as he would, Pete could not stop a small cold creeping of unease. Liz sat staring at Ed across the desk.

"But that's ridiculous."

Ed looked again at his watch. He half-rose from his chair, resting his weight on his big, capable hands on the desk in front of him.

Pete said over-confidently: "But, for Christ's sake! The clock stopped –"

Ed nodded.

"Sure. Sure. And so did every clock in London. They checked, and double-checked. And I don't doubt a word of either of their stories. They had a three-sided phone session that according to the length of tape used must have run to all of four minutes. But there's nothing of the caller on the tape, and it's clock-timed at no time at all."

As he thrust himself upright, he said: "This could be interesting. See Bill when he comes out of the meeting. He'll fill it in for you. There's a salvage team already on the way to Westport. They'll try to locate *Seamew*. And we've got three men already in the town, as of last night. But we want the human angle on the boat. *Son and daughter of victims in bid to solve riddle of the past.*" Half-way to the door, he said: "You know what we're offering. That's in any case. If it breaks good, there'll be a fifty per cent bonus. Are you both on?"

Pete turned his head, saw for the first time that the long, lean, awkward creature in the chair was a frightened girl.

"No," he said.

"Good man," Ed flung back at him as he opened the door. "See Bill and fix the details. You can travel down immediately after lunch."

Too late, to the closing door, Pete shouted: "I said no, blast you! No!" But then he heard the voice of Liz Frele behind him.

"Don't be a fool! I told you. I need the money –"

(2)

HORTON-CRAWLEY . . .

Slowly, painfully, consciousness had returned.

At first it was no more than an awareness of light. Bright, painful light that probed pitilessly into the great caverns of darkness in which he had floated for what had seemed like endless aeons of almost-forgotten time. He moved his head, to escape from the bright probe, and pain shot through his tortured muscles. As he moved, the source of the light shifted a fraction, and he was aware of a face, immeasurably old, lined and pock-marked, the mouth twisted into an evil leer.

It was some time before he realised that he was in the driving-seat of his own car, fully clothed, with a frightened, half-witted countryman peering at him by the light of a torch thrust in at the open window.

It was three-thirty a.m., and still dark, when he started the car, having pushed a five-pound note into the hand of the startled countryman. What the fellow was doing out there on the open moor, at that time of night, he never knew. Neither did he know why he had felt impelled to give him the note. He had done nothing, except to shine the torch in his face, and to terrify his first waking moments. Perhaps it was the relief of discovering that, ugly and half-witted though he appeared to be, he was at least of this world.

He drove on mercifully empty roads as far as the main highway, and was fifty miles from the Moor when dawn broke. At home, he let himself into his empty flat, made coffee, left a note for his daily housekeeper, and fell into bed. It was late afternoon when he awoke, and the woman had been and gone, leaving food in the oven. He showered, and scrubbed the pentagram from his breast. Then he telephoned the office, and ate whatever it was in the casserole in the stove. He moved as though he was living in an artificial world, going through a pattern of meaningless behaviour that had been designed for him by someone else. In the early evening, he went out, walked through streets of closed shops, drank a couple of whiskies in a bar. He entered a cinema, but came out after less than an hour. By ten-thirty he was back at the flat. Another drink, an hour's television, and as midnight approached he was lying in bed, with the lights on, waiting.

How had he known that the phone would ring, precisely at midnight? He didn't know. But as the hour approached his sense of expectancy increased. The clock by his bedside touched the twelve, and the shrill sound of the telephone cut through the waiting silence.

"Yes?" he said. And: "Horton-Crawley –"

There was a long pause, then a voice that sounded distant, impersonal, remote – he resisted the word *unhuman* – said: "Alan Sebastian Horton-Crawley, you have seen that the kingdom of darkness exists. You have accepted that the utmost power of evil shall be invoked in the solution of your problems –"

"No!" he said. "No, I withdraw –"

"It is too late," the remote voice answered. "Power has been released. It cannot be recalled."

"What are you going to do?"

"That you will know in due course. But what you desire will be accomplished."

"And if I no longer desire it?"

"You still desire it."

Horton-Crawley looked carefully round the bedroom. Something had caught his attention, but at first he had no idea what it could be. A movement? There was nothing. The wall-lights shone brightly, and a reading-lamp over his bed threw a pool of even brighter light over the small table that held the telephone, a note-pad and pencil, a book, the clock . . .

The clock!

He realised with a sudden jolt of fear that the hands still pointed to the hour. The small second-hand was motionless. Precisely at midnight, as the telephone had rung, the clock had stopped.

In his ear, the voice said: "You still desire it." Had he heard the words before? Or was this the first time they had been spoken?

"No," he shouted into the telephone. "No! I no longer desire it –"

"It is too late," said the voice.

"I shan't pay –"

"You will pay. Or we will exact payment from you."

"The police –" he said wildly, and the voice cut through his words like a knife through flesh.

"What can the police do? *Watch!*"

The two wall-lights slowly dimmed. The light from them faded until there was only a dull red glow. At the same time, the light from the lamp over his bed changed to blood-red, and began to flicker. The room was suddenly filled with moving shadows. The low humming began, and as he crouched back against the head of the bed, he saw the far wall of the room begin to dissolve into a whirling mist.

"No!" he screamed. "*No – !*"

And the calm remote voice said: "Do you accept our terms?"

"*Yes!* Yes, I accept –"

The humming ceased. The room steadied. Slowly, like the candles on the altar, the wall-lights brightened. And as the flickering light over his head changed back to a clear white, the telephone dropped from his trembling hand. He fumbled for it, replaced it, and almost at once it rang again. As he stared at it, he became aware that the clock had restarted. It still showed midnight, but the second-hand was moving. The telephone shrilled again, and again, until at last he stretched out his hand, picked it up, and held it to his ear.

"Horton-Crawley," he said, and ran his dry tongue over his lips. From far away came the remote, impersonal, unhuman voice: "Alan Sebastian Horton-Crawley, you have seen that the kingdom of darkness exists. You have accepted that the utmost power of evil shall be invoked –"

"Leave me alone! Leave me alone, for God's sake! I've already told you I accept –"

"That was last night –"

"No, tonight! Not thirty seconds ago –"

The voice cut at him with its razor-sharpness.

"What do you mean, tonight?"

Horton-Crawley stared at the wall-lights, at the bright bulbs that now burned steadily.

"Just that. When you rang before –"

When the clock had stopped, and time had stood still, who had rung before? For a long time, the line was silent. Then he heard: "That which you desire will be accomplished. Be prepared to pay the price. That is all."

He lay and stared at the telephone for a long time. But it didn't ring again. And after a while he climbed out of bed, swilled away the drying sweat from his face in the bathroom. Then he fetched a bottle and a glass from the living-room. At one-fifteen he fell asleep, drugged by the whisky he had drunk, leaving all the lights burning.

(3)

BARRY SIMPSON stood on the Promenade, watching the dark heaving sea. He had telephoned from a public call-box near the Skating Rink, dialling just at midnight. But what the hell had the big man meant with all that talk of *tonight*? And: *not thirty seconds ago*? Who else had telephoned? And who had left the local newspaper so conveniently in the call-box, where he couldn't fail to see it, even with his half-blind eyes? Mel? But why should Mel? Mel anyway was scared out of his small provincial mind. All Mel wanted was out. Out and back. Back to the time before they had started the game.

The paper was the mid-week edition of the *Westport Gazette*, dated Wednesday, September 14th, the day that had begun at midnight, only a few minutes earlier. As he had replaced the instrument, he had seen a headline on the front page: *Seamew Mystery to be Re-examined*. Underneath was a garbled paragraph that took five hundred words to say only that it was rumoured that a London crime magazine was sponsoring a salvage attempt.

But why now? Why *now*, for God's sake? Twenty years after . . . It was exactly as he had imagined it, when he had used the possibility of such a re-opening as a threat to intimidate the old fool who was now his father-in-law. It only needed young Fletcher, and the fantasy would be complete . . .

In the little lighted call-box, his eye had suddenly caught a note at the foot of the column. *See back page*. With a sick feeling of absolute certainty he had turned the paper over, had found the stop-press reference at the foot of column three: *Son and daughter of Seamew victims to aid in search*.

Now his eyes were fixed on the black heaving breast of the sea, but in his mind he saw a panorama of the game;

past, present and future. He saw himself, lying in the bushes above Fisk's cottage; waiting for him to go down to the *Red Lion* bar for his evening drink; slipping down the bank as soon as the car disappeared along the unmade lane; old socks over his shoes, his hands in rubber gloves. A window forced in the kitchen. Simplicity itself. A thin knife-blade was all that was needed. A minute to assess the lay-out of the cottage. Another to examine the stove. The main supply pipe came in from an outside storage cylinder through a hole cut in the window-frame. Inside, it branched to the stove, and to a water heater that was fastened to the kitchen wall, with pipes leading through to the bathroom beyond. The pilot light was *off*. The stove was obviously an old one. Mother Geeson let her cottage for what she could get, and spent the absolute minimum on upkeep and replacements. A length of flexible tubing carried the gas on the last few feet of its journey to the stove; a limp, lifeless artery that hung cobweb-incrusted between the window and the inlet at the back of the oven.

With the tips of his gloved fingers he pulled the limp tube almost to the end of the nipple into which it fed its gas, turned on a burner, lit it, tested the join for a leak. No leak. Good. He turned off the burner, looped a length of fine wire round the flexible link and threaded it back through the hole in the window-frame that held the inlet pipe from the cylinder. The hole had been roughly bored, years ago by the look of it, and there was room for a dozen wires to lie alongside the pipe. But he didn't need that number. All he needed was the thin double wire that was looped about the limp artery. And another, double and insulated, leading to a tiny length of high-resistance wire down behind the stove.

Eight minutes after entering the cottage, he was outside again. The loose catch of the window was in place on the inside, drawn back with a loop of the same thin wire that was hooked around the flexible tube. Wire that was then drawn clear, leaving no trace. He kept on the heavy socks until he was clear of the unkempt cottage garden, and well into the adjoining field. Then he removed them, and walked briskly back to the road, and so to his waiting car.

At three a.m. he was back in the garden. The night was moonless, but stars showed here and there between banks of light cloud. Fisk's car stood at the end of the track. The cottage was a small dark oblong in the lesser darkness of the night. Soundlessly, the thick socks again over his shoes, he moved along a brick path to the kitchen window. He ran his gloved hands over the smooth bulk of the cylinders, found the thin uninsulated wire, hesitated for a second, then pulled hard on both strands. In theory, the loop inside the cottage should have pulled the flexible tube clear of its nipple. He then pulled on one strand only, and the wire came away. Working carefully, methodically, he rolled it, and put it away in his pocket. From another pocket he took a small piece of wood, about four inches long. This he inserted between the spokes of the wheel-tap on the cylinder and exerted pressure to turn it. The wheel was firmly in the *off* position. Fisk must have turned it when he came back from the bar, and it was important that any finger-prints that might be there should not be rubbed away by the gloves . . .

In theory, now, gas was escaping into the kitchen. Fisk's bedroom was next to it on one side, the living-room on the other. The internal doors were old and ill-fitting. Even if the door of the bedroom was closed, there was a half-inch gap underneath through which the gas could creep, to build up again on the floor around the bed.

Then had come the hardest time of all. The long wait, until sufficient gas should have escaped into the small cottage. Thinking back, as he stood on the deserted Promenade, he remembered how he had sat on the high bank, waiting, straining his eyes through the night. The tiny glow from his wrist-watch had only emphasised the slowness of the passage of time. He had told himself that he would wait for an hour. But at five minutes to four he could stand it no longer. He slid down the bank, moved soundlessly along the brick path. In the hole in the window-frame, two wires were still in place, lying parallel to the gas-pipe. They ended in a coil wrapped round a cylinder of cardboard, which was tucked away out of sight behind the reserve cylinder. Taking the coil in his hand, he retreated along the path, paying out the wire as he walked. He stopped, thirty yards from the house, with all the wire unrolled from the cylinder. He took one of the two ends, each of which had a metal terminal attached, and connected it to a battery that was strapped to his shoulders. Then he lay down on his face in a hollow by the gate, and with infinite care connected the second wire to the opposite terminal.

There was an instant's pause, then the night was split apart. His arms over his head, his face pressed into the dusty soil, his first thought was that he was too close, that he had underestimated the power of the explosion. Debris rained about him. Something struck him a numbing blow on his left shoulder. But then, as suddenly as it had leapt into violent life the force of the explosion died. The night rushed back, spread its dark wings protectively over the shattered cottage. There was no fire. The force of the blast would have acted as its own extinguisher. Lifting his head, he saw the lower stars through a cloud of slowly settling dust. Then he was on his knees, winding in the wire until he felt a pair of jagged ends. Stuffing it in his pocket he stumbled awkwardly away, over into the field, and so back to his car. Janey was asleep when he let himself into their apartment. At breakfast she said: "Where did you go, Bar?" But he hadn't answered her, and she hadn't pressed it. He'd got through morning school somehow, and in the break one of the junior masters had told him that Ray Fisk was dead . . .

In the empty town behind him, a clock struck one. An hour since he had spoken to Horton-Crawley. But who or what had spoken the same words not thirty seconds before him?

Fisk was dead. Irrevocably dead. All they wanted now was the money.

Out at sea, a light moved against the black heaving water, a small speck of whiteness in the watery dark. A fishing boat? The drowned ghosts of Skipper Roberts and young Johnny Adeay, perhaps, on *Seamew*, taking their phantom passengers on their never-ending journey to the Sanctuary? Or Peter Fletcher and Liz Frele, out there already, dredging at midnight for the bones of the past?

He couldn't go home. Alone, on the empty Promenade, under the strings of coloured lights, he leaned against the salt-incrusted wall beyond which the sea, at the flood, stared back at him, fretting and heaving in its huge primeval strength. This was a drowning sea, drawing its restless energy from a million bodies, like those of Skipper and young Johnny, and all the rest, all of whom it had sucked dead before spewing back the husks on to the land from which they came . . .

Young Andrew Delany had been the next in the game. He remembered Pierse Delany's voice, high, querulous, itself as petulant as an aggrieved child's as he had stated his problem. There had been only one solution. Careful observation had established a pattern. And with Sarah's help . . . The disposal of the child had given him no trouble.

All that then remained was to wait for the money. But first the child's death had to be established. To have been kidnapped, merely to be missing, was not enough. When the first frenzy of search had died down, he had taken the body up to the Moor on a pouring wet night when tyre marks could not possibly have lasted for more than a few seconds. The body had been found on the following morning, by one of the mounted rangers.

The money . . .

All that still remained was to wait for the money. But it took time to settle an estate, even when a death was so clearly proved. Especially when the cause of death was so obviously murder. And it would take even more time to draw such a sum in cash, without comment. But if Pierse Delany tried any tricks . . .

Meanwhile, there was the far greater problem of Horton-Crawley.

With a small tremor of excitement he recalled the events of the previous night, when for the first time a true *climate of evil* had made itself felt. For Cargrove and Pierse Delany, they had put on their show, and had relied on the hallucinogens in the drink. But with Horton-Crawley, the evil had seemed a thing apart, a climate of their own making. None of the four of them had drunk from the cup, of that he was quite certain. He had prepared it himself, with the usual quantities of the hallucinogens R.S. 80, and R.S. 81, from the usual source. Sal had been in full view as she had carried the Cup to the big man, and she had stayed in view, holding it, while Horton-Crawley was persuaded to drink. He had seen him drain the cup. There would not have been even a spoonful left for her, assuming, which was unlikely, that she had wished to try it.

If the manifestations had indeed been hallucinatory, then why had they all experienced them, to some degree or other? Mass suggestion, and mass hallucination, are terms confidently used. But what do they normally mean? Mass deception, by a common conjurer? That was not the same thing at all.

Or *was* that it? Madame Joseph had intervened. Somehow, her voice had been injected into the pattern of the ceremony. *Eia! Eia! Eia!* she had called. *Deus et diabolus* . . . And the climate of evil had become a palpable thing. The candles had dimmed to nothing, then had been rekindled. They had all heard the shrill, painful, humming sound, and the words of the Invocation, though Mel had sworn that his tapes contained nothing at all of Madame Jo. And Janey had suffered the common delusion of most witches, that she had known intercourse with the devil.

This was no common conjurer's work, he told himself.

And yet he could not wholly accept that it had been a conjuration in the grand sense. At intervals during the day he had tried to see Madame Jo. But she was elusive. And Ted Modley had refused to talk. So he was no nearer discovering how the trick had been done. If indeed it was only a trick.

He shook himself, and turned his back on the sea. "Of course it was a bloody trick," he said aloud. "If it wasn't –" It was then that the thought struck him. Mel was responsible for the tapes. And Mel wanted out. But he also wanted the money. *Someone* had telephoned to Horton-Crawley. If Mel was working on his own. . . .

Suddenly, viciously, he kicked at an empty carton. It rattled across the deserted Promenade, and in the same instant the rows of coloured lights along the sea-front were switched off. Always, at about this time, they were switched off. But the sudden withdrawal of light was alarming. For the first time he felt the stirring of real fear. All around him was a sense of menace. The dark sea was a vast swollen belly, replete with the souls of the drowned. It was almost the end of summer, and the empty Promenade was like a dream sequence in a Bergman film, unreal, insubstantial, a cardboard place of death.

In the Royal Hotel, a single light burned, high up in a tower bedroom. All the other buildings on the Promenade were dark, shuttered against the night. Behind him the sea moved, making small furtive sounds as it sucked at the land. The light in the tower bedroom went out. Everywhere, now, on land, darkness ruled. The town was a dead town. The sense of menace increased. He glanced again over his shoulder. What was happening, out there on the black sea, where the single light now moved so slowly that he wondered at last if it was indeed stationary, moored over the wreck of *Seamew*?

Why should they have come back now? Why *now*, for God's sake?

Something moved in the darkness. He called out sharply:

"Who's there?" There was no reply, but the movement was repeated, at a different point. It was less a movement *in* the darkness, than a shifting of the dark itself. It was as though the dark was no longer a mere absence of light, but a creature of body and substance; composed of an infinite number of parts.

Again the movement, silent and instantly suppressed. And again. It was as though the darkness was closing in, stealthily, along with the drowning sea. This way and that he turned his head. The movement was always to one side, almost at the limit of his vision, never directly in front. And as the darkness closed in, so he was aware of the creeping cold.

For the first time, then, he lost his nerve. For the very first time in all his life. With a small cry, he put down his head and ran. He moved awkwardly, unused to the motion. His arms flailed a little, beating like ineffectual wings at the night air. His feet, in their heavy leather shoes, pounded a rhythm of fear from the concrete Promenade. Past the shuttered cafés and the empty ice-cream parlours. Past the vast dark bulk of the Skating Rink, and into the mouth of the Arcade where he had first lain in waiting for Ted Modley. And here, in the echoing tunnel with its single lamp, his fear caught up with him.

He was trapped. Beyond the lamp, shadows massed, blocking his path. They had no form, no substance, these fragments of the dark. Each seemed rather to be the projection of something else; of something that remained invisible, yet had the power to cast its shadow into the visible world.

He stopped under the single lamp, turned, screamed like a cornered animal. The way he had come was also blocked. Everywhere, the shadows moved, massed, waited. In the history of the undead it is recorded that, otherwise indistinguishable from the living, they cast no shadow, even in bright sunlight. What, then, were these? These who cast their monstrous shadows, but were themselves invisible?

Then the low humming sound that he had last heard in the Chapel began to trouble the air, and suddenly, above and below and through it he heard again the voice of Madame Joseph, unhurriedly repeating words that were already familiar:

Pater noster adversus, rex et imperator, deus et diabolus, venite, venite, venite . . . ex sepulcrum universum . . .

The humming grew louder, shriller. The single lamp in the centre of the glass roof of the Arcade turned red and began to dim. Louder, shriller, the dynamo-sound drilled at his ears. Under the dying lamp he turned this way and that, as the shadows advanced.

Eia! Eia! Eia! Rex et imperator . . .

Words that he had heard in the Chapel, when the climate of evil had first been established. But now there were added words. Words that he had not heard before, though Madame Joseph had used them on that other occasion, in the séance room at Parrott Lane.

. . . *homunculus infimus non filius sed gener* . . . not a son but a son-in-law . . .

. . . *in nomine Béelzébuth, Lucifer, Astaroth, Chameron* . . . The names of the Princes . . . Then the words of the Solemn Charge . . .

The lamp was almost out. Only a faint red glow marked its place in the roof of the tunnel. And as it finally died, he heard Madame Joseph say his own name, seven times: *Edward Charles Barry Simpson.*

Janey had fallen asleep. She awoke suddenly, lay wide awake in the darkness.

"Barry?"

There was no reply. She reached out a hand, felt for him in the other half of the bed.

"*Barry?*" more sharply.

She reached out her other hand, switched on the light. It was already half-way between one-thirty and two. His pillow was uncreased. The chair by his bed, where he always flung his clothes as he took them off, was empty.

Two o'clock, for God's sake, or as near as made no difference. He'd gone out half an hour before midnight, to telephone Horton-Crawley from one of the public call-boxes in the town. No risk that way of the call being traced back. So what the hell was he doing now? Roaming about the empty streets? All the bars would have closed long ago. This wasn't the sort of town where a man could buy a drink at any hour, especially at the end of summer.

Sarah? Was he with Sarah? Had she gone out, too, with some excuse or other, leaving Mel at home while she and Barry . . . When the lights had come on again in the Chapel, she had closed her eyes, waiting for the last trembling waves of passion to die. When she opened them again, Mel was bending over the unconscious figure of Horton-Crawley, and Barry, without his mask, had the naked Sarah in his arms.

"She was frightened, for God's sake!" he'd said, when the four-sided row had blazed up on the way home. And: "Sure, I was," Sal had said. "I was scared clean out of my wits. I just didn't know what I was doing."

But they had clung, and kissed, and Barry had run his hands down her spine and over her buttocks with an air of – of what? – of almost proprietorial familiarity. As though it wasn't the first time they had made the journey. Or even the second. As though the contours were well-known, often-explored. And when they had moved apart at last, it was obvious enough, through the matted hair of the Beast-skin, that he was as excited as hell. And all this not a minute or two after leaving her in the darkness on the altar. All this from Barry, who normally –

Oh, God! she thought wildly. *If he's right . . .*

But the alternative was unthinkable.

In the Arcade, a finger of light cut through the darkness. It was like the bright all-seeing Eye of God that had so terrified Jimmy Roberts in the school on the Madawaska, and again in the séance room at Parrott Lane.

Barry Simpson was lying on his back on the tiled floor. How he had got himself down there he couldn't remember. He had heard the voice of Madame Joseph repeating his name, then the shrill humming sound had increased beyond the limits of tolerance. Now it was still dark, but the sound had stopped. There was only the hard rod of light against which he twisted his head and lifted his hands to shield his eyes.

"Are you all right, sir?"

The voice was infinitely reassuring. Through the cracks between his fingers he saw a pair of legs, and the lower part of a uniform jacket. *The police! Thank God, the police!*

"What happened, sir?"

He managed to sit up, moved so that he was leaning against the façade of one of the shops.

"I was attacked –" He broke off. This was the Law. Welcome though it was, he must be careful.

"Attacked, sir? By whom?"

"I don't know. I was going home –"

"Home from where?"

"I'd been for a walk."

"At this time?"

"I like walking at night."

"You had no other reason for being out at this time?"

"No."

Panic returned, but for a different reason. Why should the police –?

"Such as making a telephone call, for instance?"

"A – telephone call?" Oh God! So they knew!

"You were seen, sir. In the box at the back of the Skating Rink."

His mind skittered about like a beetle in a trap, looking for the way of escape.

"I telephoned my wife. To let her know where I was."

"That was thoughtful of you, sir. We'll check with her, of course."

"Why? Why should you want to do that?"

"We have our reasons, sir."

"As a matter of fact, she must have been asleep. There was no reply."

"I'm not surprised, sir."

"Why, for Christ's sake? Why?" He was blustering, still trying to find the way out. But underneath it all he knew that the trap had closed.

"I didn't mean I wasn't surprised that there was no reply. I meant I wasn't surprised that you should suddenly *say* there was no reply. You wouldn't want us to check with her, would you, sir?"

"There'd be no point. As she didn't answer."

"As you didn't ring her."

"Are you saying I'm lying?"

"Yes, sir. We know who you spoke to. Mr. Horton-Crawley, wasn't it?"

Barry tried to stand up, but a heavy foot pushed him back against the shop-front.

"What did you say to him, sir?"

"If you're so bloody clever, don't you know that as well?"

"Yes, we know it. But I would have preferred to hear it from you."

"Let me get up. I want a lawyer –"

"He'll do you no good. We know it all. Let me prove it to you. You said to Horton-Crawley: *Alan Sebastian Horton-Crawley, you have seen that the kingdom of darkness exists. You have accepted –*"

"Stop!"

"Why should I stop? I simply thought you would like proof of what I said. Proof that we know it all. And I mean all. How you fixed the explosion at Ray Fisk's cottage, for instance. And what happened to Andrew Delany. Clever, both of them. But we know."

Barry struggled again to rise, but again he was thrust back.

"Let me remind you," the calm, official voice continued, "of the last thing you said to Horton-Crawley. You said: *That which you desire will be accomplished. Be prepared to pay the price. That is all*. Do you deny that you said that?"

"I'll neither confirm nor deny. Not until I've seen a lawyer."

"I've already told you. He'll do you no good. You might as well answer my questions. Tell me, how do you propose to keep your promise to Horton-Crawley?"

"That's my business."

"It is also ours. You were going to New York?"

"I refuse to answer."

"But of course you were. How else could you have assured Horton-Crawley that that which he desired would be accomplished. But you would have been too late. Sir James Prynne is already there. He has been there for three days. In another three he will be flying back to London to prepare for the Special Meeting. He's staying in New York for only six days altogether, not ten as originally planned. Did you know that?"

"No."

"The only way you can earn your fifty thousand is to get yourself over to New York as quickly as possible. You must fix Sir James so that he cannot possibly get back to London for the Meeting. You must fix him properly. Do you understand?"

Barry put a trembling hand to his face.

"What are you saying? Who are you?" And more shrilly: "Who the hell *are* you, for God's sake?"

The light moved, swung to the end of the tunnel beyond which lay the sea. Massed about the entrance were the threatening shadows. It swung again, to the opposite end. There, too, the shadows waited.

"You're not the police!"

The light swung up at last to reveal the face of the creature who stood over him. He felt, rather than saw, the shadows closing in. A cry escaped him; a thin, hopeless cry of absolute terror.

"No, sir," the creature said with mock subservience, "I am not, as you now observe, the police. I should have thought the discovery would have been a relief to you. The police can hardly be your friends, under the circumstances."

"Who are you?" Barry managed to say again.

"I am one of those named in the invocation spoken by the one you know as Madame Joseph. Precisely which one is immaterial. Whoever comes has full and immediate access to all Power."

"And what do you want with me?"

The light moved again. The shadows now were everywhere, crowding in on the small patch of tiled floor, the nearer ones almost at arm's length.

"Sport," said the creature. "What do we ever want with your world, except sport? You will go to New York at once –"

Barry clutched at a straw.

"I've booked a flight. For Friday –"

"That is too late."

"Tomorrow? I may not get a booking –"

He hardly knew what he was saying. Or what was happening to him. He was stalling, playing for time in which to manoeuvre.

"Not tomorrow. Now." The light shone again on the creature's head. Its features were half man, half bird. Above a cruel raptor's beak, its eyes glowed red, unwinking. "Get up."

Barry shrank back against the shuttered face of the shop.

"Get up!" the creature repeated. Its eyes were like twin danger lamps. "If you do not, we shall tear you apart."

Barry pushed himself upright, stood with the feel of the shutters solid behind him.

"That's better. If you obey, all will be well. If you do

not –" The uniformed shoulders moved a fraction. Then suddenly the dynamo-humming filled the narrow tunnel. The finger of light died, but the creature's eyes still burned like live coals in the darkness.

"Now!" it said suddenly. The two glowing eyes moved closer, and Barry shrank farther back, farther still, realizing too late that the solid shutters were no longer supporting him.

CHAPTER THREE

(1)

In Westport-on-Sea, England, the first cold hours of Wednesday, September 14th, were passing over the sleeping town. In New York, it was still the evening of September 13th.

The difference in time is only a book difference. A clock difference. A difference sometimes of daylight and darkness, too, of course. But in the wider sense of *now*, it is the same instant masquerading under two names.

When Barry Simpson felt the void behind him, where a moment before there had been the comforting solidity of the stout wooden shutters, he fell back not into what was left of a summer stock of shell-boxes and dried sea-horses, pixie-brooches, and comic postcards, but into a dark carpeted space with a television set flickering in one corner.

The two red eyes still glowed, and in the faint light from the screen he saw the tall, almost human figure with its cruel raptorial beak.

"Stand up!"

He picked himself up from the floor, stood warily. The uniformed figure moved to the windows, drew back one of the curtains.

"Look!"

Beyond a pent-house terrace, a city that could only be New York sparkled like a huge diamond set in the black velvet backcloth of the night.

"Come!"

Through the open doors, through a litter of plants and chairs, under a glass roof, to the perilous edge of the terrace. He felt compelled to follow, but every step was an effort. His feet refused the commands of his mind. Instead, they moved forward of their own volition, following the uniformed figure, but slowly, without ever losing contact with the floor. Each foot slid forward a few inches, then stopped. The soles of his shoes scraped across the textured surface as though they were held to it by a magnetic force.

And now he saw, by the reflected light of the city, that ranged along the edge of the terrace, their backs towards him, were a score of what he recognised from films and television as unmistakably New York cops. He looked around for the soberer British uniform, but it had disappeared. Instead, there was only this unbroken line of uncompromising backs. And beyond them, the vast improbable panorama.

He opened his mouth to scream, but no sound came. He tried to turn away, but his feet still refused to obey him. He was held fast, locked in the humming power-field that was everywhere about him. And then, as he stood there, one by one they turned to face him.

One by one, they showed their identical faces. Each had the same raptorial beak, the same red eyes that glowed in the semi-dark. They turned with precision, one after another, from right to left. When they were all facing him, one of them stepped forward, reached out for him. Again he tried to scream, but nothing came. The creature's hand was ice-cold, scaly against the skin of his wrist; like the fore-foot of a lizard; reptilian, and unutterably repulsive. Without a word, it led him to the edge of the pent-house terrace, his feet sliding forward outside his conscious control. At the edge of the terrace, he stood facing out over the million lights of the city. He had no idea where he was in relation to the great shining blocks that were spread out far below, and to the few fantastic towers that soared even higher than his own vantage-point.

The creature spoke at last: "Look down." He felt hands at his back, and was forced to lean forward over the safety wall. Beneath was a swooning drop to street-level. The street itself was a ribbon of light, with cars, the size of matchbox toys, crawling. Terrified, he closed his eyes, but the image of the drop remained.

"Jump!" the creature commanded sharply. And again he felt the hands at his back. "Jump! You will come to no harm."

"No! No!" he screamed. But the screaming was only inside himself. Still no sound came.

"We are your angels," the harsh, grating voice said. "Do you not remember the biblical phrase: *He shall give his angels charge concerning thee: and in their hands they shall bear thee up, lest at any time thou dash thy foot against a stone?* Do you remember that?"

"Yes," he said. And though the word was only a thought, it seemed to be understood.

"I repeat. We are your angels. Cast yourself down, and we will bear you up."

"No –"

"Have you so little faith?"

Barry opened his eyes, saw the vast and empty void, the distant street, far below, with its crawling vehicles. His legs gave under him, but at once he was seized and held by two of the creatures.

"Why have you so little faith?" It was the same harsh voice. "Have we not proved to you that we have the Power? You have my solemn word that if you climb the wall, and jump, we will sustain you, so that no harm will befall."

"No!" Again it was no more than a wordless thought. But again it seemed to be understood. And: "Why should I?" his mind framed in panic. "In God's name, why should I?"

"To demonstrate your faith in us."

Away to the south of Manhattan, beyond the Battery, a line of searchlights crossed and criss-crossed endlessly; fingers of light probing the underside of the sky. He saw them, realised with a renewed sense of shock that he now *knew* from where they came. Governor's Island. How he knew that, he had no idea. But suddenly the whole vast panorama of the city was fixed and plotted in his mind. He saw it with eyes that knew everything. He saw it as though through a fiery haze, or a screen of blood-red glass. Or was it through the burning eyes of the creatures who surrounded him?

He saw it, too, from an even higher vantage-point. Suddenly, no building in the entire city was as high as this new elevation from which he now looked down onto the elegant arches of the Chrysler spire, the massive cliffs of Rockefeller Center, the spear-point of the Empire State. Without being told, he knew that it was the Eye of Evil through which his vision was now being channelled. He still felt the wall of the pent-house, hard against his protesting hands, but no building of man could ever have been as high as this new pinnacle. Revolving slowly, high above the southern end of the Park, the blood-red Eye transmitted first an overall impression, a sparkling tinsel picture, framed by dark water. Across the rivers, more lights troubled the distance. But it was on the Island itself that the Eye was focussed. And now, either by a trick of the light, or by the angle of vision, or perhaps by the evil that was in the eye itself, he saw, looking south, that where the long straight river of moving light that was Fifth Avenue was crossed by 42nd Street, the two formed a *crux immissa* – a Latin cross – but *reversed*, the long base stem seeming to stretch upwards towards the southernmost tip of the Island. Surrounding the cross, were cliffs of light, turrets of light; still pools, and tumbling cascades of light. Other Avenues, other streets, ran white and red. But their brightness was blurred into an indeterminate haze. Clear as the outline of a central motif in the blaze and smoke of a firework set-piece, was this reversed cross, unmistakable, on the breast of Manhattan.

"You must jump," said the voice again. "You *must jump* –"

The Hudson River was a dark artery in the bright jewelled body of the city. Away to the left, the East River drew a second dark furrow across the glare. But now it was not only the bright towers and the dark rivers that were unexpectedly familiar. The smallest detail was a part of his awareness.

In twenty thousand eating places, in uncountable apartments and hotel rooms, people ate, drank, fought, made love, watched television. Strippers bared, and surgeons carved. Prayers were flung into the glare: invocations swooped like trained hawks through the channels of evil.

In the subway at 42nd Street and Lexington Avenue, a man died by the change booth. No special reason; his time had come. But the Eye saw it.

"Jump!" said the Voice urgently. "You will come to no harm. But you *must jump!*"

In Greenwich Village, in a small café on Macdougal Street, between 3rd and Bleecker, a young Italian girl smiled at her ex-lover as she ran a long, thin butcher's-knife through his rib-cage to pierce his heart. As he died, she flung herself across his body, whispering a hundred passionate endearments. When the homicide squad arrived, she went with them quietly, radiantly, like a bride to a wedding-feast.

In a dimly-lit bar at 53rd and Park, two men, both a little drunk already, argued whether the next should be rye or bourbon. Whichever it was, it was agreed that it would be their last. On this, both they and fate agreed. They were to die in the same car, an hour later, in a multiple pile-up at the entrance to the Lincoln Tunnel, on their way home to Succasunna, where they ran a small light engineering plant. They were good friends, in New York for the day to sign a new contract, and their wives were sisters. The Eye saw the bar, heard the argument, was aware of the crash. Past, present and future were one to it.

"Jump, and you will be cradled in the arms of Power."

The words were like small, sharp probes, seeking a way through the barrier of his reason.

In his suite at the Waldorf-Astoria, Sir James Prynne adjusted his tie in front of his wife's mirror. She was collecting a few essentials for a safari that tonight would take them through Copacabana country into El Morocco. The Eye watched them. Through the Eye, Barry Simpson also watched them; saw Prynne, handsome in a grey-haired, grey-moustached way, studying his elegant young wife's reflection as she moved about the room. I happen to know, Harry Taylor had said on the dunes by the estuary, that Horton-Crawley and Prynne's wife ...

Abruptly, then, the Eye was withdrawn. He was back on the pent-house terrace, with hands still forcing him forward against the wall.

"If you refuse to jump, we shall have to take the initiative," the harsh voice said. And suddenly, like a whiplash: "Okay, fellows, *throw him* –"

The hands gripped. A terrible, soundless scream formed deep inside him. He felt himself lifted, swung, projected. For an endless, agonising moment he seemed to hang suspended at the zenith of the throw. Far below, sickeningly far down in the swooning depths, the small river of light flowed at the base of its deep canyon. The scream exploded, tore its way out through his rigid throat. From the roof behind he heard a burst of demoniacal laughter. And then he was falling, falling, falling. The lighted windows were tearing past, and the river of light at the foot of the canyon was racing to meet him. His scream fell with him, on a dying cadence, but in the street below no-one heard it. Even if they had, there was nothing that anyone could have done. Nothing, that was humanly possible.

Janey rang through to Mel at six a.m., British time.

Mel said: "For Christ's sake!" And: "How should I know?"

"Is Sal there?"

"Sal? Sure she's here. Where else?" Then less sleepily: "Has he run out on us?"

"I don't know."

Over the wire she heard him say viciously, in an aside: "Your lover – if he *is* your lover – is missing." Then she heard the crash of the falling telephone, and the line went dead.

But an hour later, a pale and terrified Melvin stopped his car outside Janey's door. She was still in pyjamas, sitting at the kitchen table listening to the radio news, a cup of coffee in front of her.

"Mel," she said.

He flung down a copy of the local paper.

"Have you seen this?"

The article about *Seamew* was ringed in red. She glanced at the headline, pushed back the dark hair that fell over her eyes, looked up at him across the table.

"Read the back page," he said. She turned it over; saw: *Son and daughter of Seamew victims to aid in search.*

"At a guess," he said harshly, "he's gone. He's heard of this, and he's gone." He was trembling, standing in the middle of the small kitchen, shaking as though with a fever. Suddenly he raised his voice. "For Christ's sake, don't you realise? He's gone! He's walked out on us – left us to carry it –"

Janey reached for her coffee-cup, lifted it half-way to her mouth. Then she put it down again, untasted.

"This is exactly what you and he –" She stopped, made a vague bewildered gesture.

"It's exactly what *he* dreamed up to tell your fool of a father! Even to young Fletcher being in on it. So who set it going?"

"He wouldn't –"

"It's just the sort of crazy bloody thing he would do! I told you before. He's mad. We were mad ever to listen to him –"

"You don't *know* it's him –"

"Who else? Who else, for Christ's sake? It's not me? Is it you or Sam?"

"Not me. Why should I?"

"Why should any of us? And it wouldn't be your old man. Or the old witch. They wouldn't do a fool thing like that, not after all this time."

"One of Barry's contacts?"

"But who *are* they? Who *are* his bloody contacts? He's never told me where he gets his info, or his dope. Who *are* they, for God's sake?"

"I don't know."

"Christ, you're a fine wife! You don't know much, do you? You don't even know where he is now –"

Suddenly she picked up the coffee-cup, flung the contents full in his face. Screaming at him, she seemed to have lost all control.

"I can't help that, can I? Can I help it if he walks out on me –"

He said: "You bitch! If that'd been boiling –" He shook his head, and coffee dripped from his chin. He dashed it aside impatiently, took a step forward, his hand raised. "If that'd been really hot –"

She shrank back, suddenly quiet.

"I'm sorry, Mel. But you shouldn't say things like that. I don't know what I'm going to do. I just don't know what's happened –"

He lowered his threatening hand, pulled up a chair, sat with his shoulders forward.

"Christ, if only we'd never started."

"I didn't know – I never guessed it'd go the way it did –"

A thought struck him.

"The money – has he had the rest of the money? For the first two jobs?"

"If he has, I haven't seen it."

"He wouldn't go without it."

"If he'd seen the paper –"

"How could he? It's only out today."

"It's printed early. He went out late last night. To telephone. He might have seen it. Or heard from someone."

"And gone off in a panic, without even coming back for a change of clothes? At least he could have done that."

"It doesn't seem likely. Unless he *had* got the money."

"Wouldn't he have come back for you?"

She sketched again the vague bewildered gesture.

"I don't know. We had a quarrel –"

"Over what happened?"

"Yes."

"We still don't know what *did* happen."

"No," she said, and shivered. The core of ice was still deep inside her.

(2)

"Mr. Fletcher," counsel asked, "will you please tell the jury what happened when you and Miss –" he glanced down at his notes "– Miss Frele, arrived in Westport?"

*

They had travelled down on the afternoon train, and early on their first morning they had been joined at a prearranged meeting-place by one of the three C.C.I. men already in the town. The rendezvous was the end of the promenade, where they met casually enough and strolled out along the edge of the sea with the dunes on their left. There was to be no secrecy about the salvage attempt, or about Liz and Peter's presence in the town. In fact, these were to be publicised as widely as possible. But the three others were to keep out of sight.

"There's a woman who calls herself Madame Joseph," the contact said. "She was married to *Seamew's* skipper at the time. Skipper Roberts. Try her, for a lead."

It was Liz who went first to the small box on the Pier. A sign on the door said WAIT. She leaned against the railings over the quiet sea that had once drowned her mother, and after a few minutes a woman came out, blinked at the glare, then walked quickly away. Madame Joseph peered after her, reached out to change the WAIT sign, but saw Liz. She stopped, and her pale face froze. Liz stepped forward.

"Can you give me a reading?"

"No," said Madame Joseph. "No, I've finished for the day –"

"It's only twelve o'clock –"

"I'm not well."

Liz said: "My name is Frele. My mother was Marion Frele. Also known as Marion Reynolds."

Madame Joseph said again: "I'm ill. I can't see anyone."

"You'll see me, Mrs. Roberts –"

"I'm not Mrs. Roberts."

"You were once."

"What of it?"

"How did you know who I was?"

"You told me."

"No, before that. You refused to give me a reading. Why?"

Madame Joseph's eyes hooded.

"I have certain powers. That is why I am here. There was something about you –"

Liz took another step forward.

"Do you want to talk out here, in front of everyone, or inside?"

"Neither." There was a long pause, in which Madame Joseph appeared to be listening. Then she said: "Come to my house tonight. Parrott Lane, number forty-three. Come at eight o'clock."

Then she went back into her small cell, and locked the door.

*

"Did Miss Frele tell you she was going to Parrott Lane?"

"Yes," Pete said. "Yes, she told me."

Mr. Arlingfold glanced at the jury.

"And you agreed that she should go there? Unaccompanied?"

"Yes. It seemed the best way."

"You did not think of the possible peril in which she might find herself?"

"At that stage we did not know the extent of the peril."

*

At the time when Liz had made her unsuccessful attempt on the Pier, Madame Joseph had known nothing of Barry's disappearance, or of the newspaper report. She had bought a copy of the *Westport Gazette* at the Pier entrance, but had not opened it until later. The boy who sold it to her had not been born when *Seamew* sank. To him she was Madame Joseph, or Mrs. Modley, and the name Roberts would have meant nothing to him, even if he had bothered to read it. No-one from the *Gazette* had contacted her before publication. This was because C.C.I. had refused to release the story to the editor without a signed undertaking that any interviews with the family would be by C.C.I. reporters only (these, in fact, to be Elizabeth Frele and Peter Fletcher, of *Disaster Orphans Seek Truth about Parents' Deaths*).

Someone, somewhere in the town, would have drawn her attention to the paper, sooner or later, but the fact remains that she had not read of the search until *after* Liz had tried to see her. And yet, instinctively, she had refused to give her a reading.

At lunch time, she telephoned Janey, and heard that Barry was missing. Then she rang Sal, and insisted that Mel should come to Parrott Lane. He arrived, in a state of nerves, at one-thirty, but he had no news, and no advice to give. Madame Joseph withdrew into the séance room, reappeared about six, spoke briefly with Ted Modley, then withdrew again. At eight, Liz Frele arrived, and was met at the door by Ted who told her that Madame was still indisposed, and deeply regretted that she was still unable to see her.

(3)

Thirty feet above the crawling cars and the few hurrying pedestrians, Barry's fall had been checked. He felt as though a harness was pulling against the momentum of his body. In a split second his fall stopped, sickeningly. A wave of nausea engulfed him, and he kept his eyes tight shut. Suddenly the harness was released. With another sharp cry, he felt himself falling again, and almost at once he felt the impact as he struck the ground. But it was not the sidewalk of the street below the penthouse. It was some time before he could force his eyes open. When he did so at last, he found himself back in the carpeted room with the television flickering in the corner. One of the cops was standing over him.

"Now are you convinced?"

He couldn't answer. He lay gasping like a stranded fish. The cop kicked him contemptuously, and said: "Get up!"

As he struggled to his knees, he realised that the room was crowded. As well as the score of policemen, there were creatures of all sizes, dressed in ordinary human clothes. Each had the cruel beak, the glowing eyes. In the darkened room, lit only by the reflected light from the screen and the glow from the city lights that struck through the one uncurtained window, they stood in irregular lines, watching.

The cop kicked him again.

"Stand up!"

No-one else moved. He stood, swaying a little.

"Look at the screen."

He turned towards it, saw the same hotel room that he had seen earlier through the bloodshot Eye. Lady Prynne was ready at last. A final glance round the room, and they moved to the door. The harsh voice said: "The first rule of the hunt is that the hunter should be able to recognise his prey."

A faint whispering came from the crowded room behind him, instantly silenced. On the screen Lady Prynne's face was momentarily in close-up as they waited for the elevator. Dark, small, beautiful, she wore with her diamonds an air of youthful discontent. Prynne stood near her, stroking his grey moustache. They could have been father and daughter, on their way to the end-of-term party of an expensive finishing-school that Margot Prynne was now ready to leave. Groomed, poised, but with an air of inexperience, she stood by the elevator as though at the gate of the world. She was, in fact, twenty-three, and they had been married over four years.

Horton-Crawley and Prynne's wife. Harry Taylor had said; but he had not elaborated on it.

The elevator came, took them away, and the picture on the screen switched suddenly forward in time. As with the Eye, past, present and future were one. At a table in the *Copacabana,* they were with a party of four others. There was a glimpse of a French singer, pouring his mercenary heart into a microphone, then they were on the move again, in a vast limousine that swam south from East 60th Street to East 54th. In *El Morocco,* they drank champagne, and were presently joined by two men who looked like old-style gangster bosses.

"The president and vice-president of T.W.P's North American suitors," the harsh voice murmured in his ear. "The main reason why Horton-Crawley wants Prynne out. They're ruthless, immensely able in the book market, and they could eat up Mowdell and never even burp."

The screen flickered, and the Prynnes were alone again in their vast limousine, heading the few remaining blocks south and west, back to the Waldorf-Astoria. They sat in silence, as far apart as the car allowed. Park Avenue was almost deserted. The clock in the entrance lobby showed one a.m. The picture followed them into the elevator, and back to their room.

He heard Prynne say: "I hope you're satisfied." Angrily

he began to undress. "Are you still working for Horton-Crawley?"

"Don't be ridiculous, James!" She was removing her diamonds, locking them away.

"You couldn't have been any more bloody insulting to them if you were!"

She slid out of her dress with a small shrug.

"I didn't like them. I thought they were crude."

"They're just about the smartest operators for twenty thousand miles in any direction," he shouted at her. "And that includes up! For Christ's sake, Marge, do you want to throw it away?"

She removed her bra, stood there like a Sun and Air Academy schoolgirl ready for a race.

"You can mix with them if you have to, in the way of business. But don't ask me to be your geisha. Not ever again."

It was oppressively hot in the crowded room. Barry said: "Give me a drink, for God's sake –"

"Which God?" said the creature through his cruel beak, and automatically Barry answered: "There is only one God."

The whisper passed over the room again.

"True," said the creature. "But which face of the one true God?"

"The other face," Barry said, and this time the whisper was louder.

"Good," said the creature. "Good, good, good." Raising his voice, he said: "Bring a drink for the hunter, who now knows his prey!"

On the screen, Margot was naked under the shower. Prynne was cleaning his teeth. The argument was still going on. Suddenly there was a commotion in the room behind. Barry swung round. One of the beaked creatures was on the floor. Two others were kneeling at his side. One of them took the beak of the fallen one in his hands, lifted off a mask to reveal the features of a young man in a dead faint.

Barry's heart leaped painfully. So they were only masks, after all ... Was all the rest no more than hallucination? The sort of trickery they had themselves practised at the Chapel? With a sudden movement, he seized the beak of the uniformed creature at his elbow, twisted it, tried to pull it away. There was a moment of horrified silence. Then a gasp from the crowd around the maskless youth. The cop raised both his hands. Power flowed between them, a sudden surge like the kick of a high-voltage cable. Barry was flung out and away, quivering, paralysed.

"You fool!" the harsh voice grated at him. "Haven't you yet learned to distinguish between the Princes and the Nobles of Darkness, and their disciples?"

More of the crowd had removed their masks. Someone opened a window on to the terrace. The uniformed creature said curtly: "Get up, and look at the screen. Look at your prey, hunter."

The use of his limbs returned. He stood, trembling. On the screen was only Margot, beautiful, fragile as fine porcelain, a nymph in the rain.

"No," he said, his voice barely audible. "No, it's the other one. Prynne –"

"How?" the voice cut at him, infinitely contemptuous. "How will you get Prynne? He's rarely alone. In the daytime, never. For a year they have quarrelled continuously, often in public. There was the making of a scene at *El Morocco* tonight; that is why the Prynnes left early. There'll be other witnesses to the quarrels. The staff at the hotel – their chauffeur – their London housekeeper –" She stepped out of the shower, reached for a bath-towel, began slowly, luxuriously, to dry herself. "If you play your cards right, Prynne will be charged, and will be held here in New York. Even if the lawyers get him away in time for the meeting, he'll be discredited. The Mowdell shareholders won't listen to a man with a charge like that hanging over him. British shareholders don't like violence."

"But if Horton-Crawley –"

"Think nothing of it. On his side, it's only a passing affair. All he wants is Mowdell, and ultimately Parian-Laing itself. This is the way."

Barry was still trembling.

"But I still don't know how –"

"You will be helped, when the time comes."

Again, the whisper filled the room. The screen went blank. Barry felt himself falling again. All around was darkness. The whispering faded. Abruptly, the fall stopped, and then from somewhere far, far away he heard the insistent ringing of a telephone.

The telephone was ringing by the side of his bed. Surfacing from a deep sleep, he reached out for it automatically, heard the harsh, grating voice say: "Edward Charles Barry Simpson."

"Yes."

"Be outside the Waldorf-Astoria at ten a.m. Repeat that."

"Waldorf-Astoria. Ten a.m."

"Outside. At Park and 49th. That's all."

The phone went dead. As he replaced it, he realised that he was in bed, in a room that was wholly unfamiliar. He was in pyjamas, and his clothes were scattered about, on chairs and over an open suitcase. The curtains were drawn across, but a small finger of daylight probed in. Crawling out, he walked cautiously over to the window, peered through the crack, saw an urban landscape with a distant bridge between irregular blocks. Sunlight lay obliquely in wide swathes. His watch showed eighteen minutes after twelve o'clock, but then he remembered that if this was indeed New York it would be early morning still.

He pulled back the curtains, and, still cautiously, inspected the room. Nondescript furnishings, faded walls. A printed notice by the door was headed *Murphy's Emerald Hotel* with a three-figure number on East 59th Street. How he had pitched up in bed there, he had no idea at all. One moment he had been in the crowded penthouse apartment, then the telephone had rung and he had found himself pyjamad and newly roused from sleep.

He showered, dressed, and went out into an unfamiliar corridor. At the desk, at street level, a morose septuagenarian glanced up from a tabloid, grunted, went back to a study of someone's forecast of the week's ball games.

Barry hesitated, said: "How do I get to Park and 49th?"

The cropped white skull moved a fraction. Pale blue eyes stared up over half-moon lenses.

"Whatsamadda wid you, bud? You lost your memory or sump'n?"

"Why?"

"You asked me that yesterday. No, day before yesterday. Soon as you booked in. Whatsamadda, son? You don't like New York? You wish you was back in Westport, England? Is that it?"

Barry murmured something, escaped to the street followed by the old man's complaining voice. The day before yesterday he had been at home. Unless today ... He stopped at a news stand, saw the day's papers: Wednesday, September 14. How the hell could –? He felt in his pockets, found dollar bills and loose change, a return flight air ticket with the outward journey from London noted as September 12.

On Monday, September 12, term had started. He had sent a letter saying he was ill and would return to work as soon as he felt well again; and on Monday and Tuesday he had lain low during the day, in case anyone from the school ... He'd had a provisional booking to New York for Friday, the 16th. But someone had travelled, in his name, on the 12th. And not only *someone*. It was someone who looked like him. Exactly like him. The old fool at the hotel would not have said what he did, unless he had thought he recognised him.

A demon can come in any form. Man or woman, child or animal. The likeness of the living; or of the dead ... So said the books. Suddenly a feeling of exaltation possessed him. For the first time, the full significance of what was happening to him was made plain. What had happened in the Chapel, with Horton-Crawley, was only the beginning. It was true that he had doubted. He had refused to throw himself down from the penthouse. He had tried to twist off the mask from one of the Princes. And still they had plucked him from the abyss, had shown him the face of his quarry, had given him his final orders.

At Park and 49th, at 10 a.m.

Somehow, in all the mock ceremonial, he had broken through to them. *And they were on his side.* There was no cause for fear. Of that he was now quite certain. He had killed twice, and no-one would ever be able to prove a thing. If necessary, and if conditions were right, he would kill a third time. He had a momentary feeling of regret that it should be Margot Prynne, for through the voyeur's eye of the screen she had seemed young and vulnerable and disturbingly beautiful. But if that was what the Princes required . . .

He had no idea where he was. This was presumably East 59th Street. And he wanted 49th. But how did the streets run? The part of 59th that housed Murphy's Emerald Hotel was a place of small shops and restaurants. The sidewalks were crowded, but he felt reluctant to enquire his way from any of the hurrying strangers. Looking east, into the morning sun, he could see the beginning of what he discovered later was Queensboro Bridge. He was on the north side of the Street, and he began in his new state of confident exaltation to walk away from the sun, away from the river, heading west. Suddenly he felt hungry, realised that he had eaten nothing for – how long was it? – the change in time was confusing. Cautiously, he studied the faces of the buildings on his right hand, came to an Automat, entered warily, watching what others did to get coffee and a cheese sandwich. Then he walked again until he came to an intersection of a wider thoroughfare running roughly north and south. Third Avenue. Here he hesitated. A taxi? Taxi drivers could be traced, could give evidence. But if he rode so far, and then walked? But how far? Unlike the moment of revelation of the night before, when the city had seemed as familiar as Westport, it was now a wilderness to which he had no key. Ahead of him, the buildings were taller. Beyond, to the south-west, were the giants, glimpsed through the smaller but still massive complexes between.

A clock showed twenty-five minutes to ten o'clock. In desperation he stopped an elderly man who seemed in less of a hurry than everyone else.

"Can you tell me how to get to 49th Street?"

The man stopped, stood ruminating.

"Why, sure, son. You want to walk?"

"How far is it?"

"Oh, maybe ten, fifteen minutes. Depends how fast y'walk. But what part of 49th? East 49th, or West 49th?"

"I don't know."

"It makes a power of difference, son."

His eye on the clock, he said: "Park Avenue –"

"Park and 49th? Will that be the Waldorf-Astoria?"

"That's just a starting-point. I know my way from there."

"Thought maybe you was living there, son." The old man chuckled. "Thought maybe you was on your way home from last night."

"Can you tell me the route, please?"

"Sure. Sure. I'll walk along with you. Nothing better to do. Show you some of the sights. You from U.K.?"

"Yes, but I'm in a hurry. I'm late. If you could –"

"Think nothing of it, son. I'll walk you there in no time." He looked up at the sky, still ruminating. "Now, like with most problems in this city, you got a choice. You can go by way of Third, or Lexington, and head west along 49th; or you can –"

"For Christ's sake!" Barry shouted at the old fool. "Can't you just *tell* me? Is is that away, or thataway?"

"Hey, there's no call to get tough with me, son! I don't like guys who ask a favour and then bawl me out."

Twenty-three minutes to ten.

"What goes on?" It was a cop, a big blond cop, standing a yard away, rocking speculatively on his heels. "What's the trouble, pop?"

"No trouble. Except the young feller –" He started on a word by word account of it all. "Wants to get to the Waldorf –"

The cop's eyes travelled over Barry.

"You staying there?"

"No."

"Then what for you want to get there so fast?"

"I know my way from there –"

"Your way to where?"

"To where I'm going."

Twenty-two minutes.

He started to edge away.

"Not so fast. You didn't say where you're going *after* you find the Waldorf –"

"For Christ's sake! I'm just looking. Just seeing the town. But I got lost –"

"Asks me the way, and then bawls me out," the old fool complained. "He's –"

"All right, dad. Leave him to me." Again that speculative up and down glance. "You want to get there fast. Is that right?"

"Yes. I –"

"Why, son? Why so fast? If all you're going to do is see the town. What's the hurry? This town ain't going to run away and hide."

"I haven't much time. I'm only here for a few days. If I could get a taxi –"

Twenty minutes to go.

"No-one's stopping you," the big blond policeman said.

In the end, by the time he had found a taxi, and the driver had edged him in a slow crawl through crowded Lexington to Park at 49th, it was two minutes past the hour. He stood at the intersection, waiting for whatever should happen next, and after another couple of minutes a maroon Cadillac slowed, stopped. A uniformed chauffeur reached out an arm, indicated the rear door. He climbed in, and the big red car whispered away into the traffic.

It was twilight inside. The windows were smoke-blue. In the filtered light the eyes of the two creatures burned red above their cruel beaks.

"You were a little late. But it doesn't matter," said one.

"What am I supposed to do?"

"Nothing," said the other.

A small screen flickered in the gloom. As the chauffeur let the red car float with the stream along Park, then cut quietly across Madison to Fifth, he saw the now familiar interior of the Prynne's suite. Prynne was leaving. He picked up some loose papers, thrust them into a small leather folder. As he was about to open the door, he stopped. On the carpet, a yard away, was a heavy Chinese vase. He put down the folder, picked up the vase with both hands, replaced it on a side table. He stood and stared at it for a moment, then he retrieved the leather case, glanced at his watch, and opened the door. A moment later, the screen showed him outside the elevator gates; waiting impatiently; forcing his way in as they opened at last, and finally disappearing.

In the bedroom of the suite, Margot was still in bed, drinking coffee and reading the New York *Times*. She looked very fragile, and very beautiful. When the summons came, she slid gracefully out, reached for a gold silk *peignoir*, and padded on bare feet to the outer door. As she opened it, Barry saw himself, or the creature who had impersonated him on the plane and in the hotel, force his way in. Margot retreated; said: "Who the hell are you?" A second later, the Chinese vase, held by the rim in one of the creature's gloved hands, was lifted, and as she turned to run back into the bedroom was brought up and over and down in a single vicious curve to smash against her delicate skull.

Barry gasped, and one of the two creatures in the car said: "You see why you need do nothing? It is already done."

"You may also see," said the other creature, "the pattern of events." Margot lay on the carpet, the vase in pieces around her. "The only significant prints on the vase will be Prynne's. If you remember, he picked it up on his way out. You –" he made a small deprecatory gesture with one hand "– the you on the screen – wore gloves, and held it by the rim. But why was it on the floor in the first place, you may ask. Because we put it there, deliberately." A small self-satisfied chuckle came from behind the cruel beak. "A pattern of quarrels; Prynne's fingerprints; the time of death, should she die . . . Prynne will have a great deal to answer for. Actually, she is not yet dead, though very near to it. And this makes the whole affair so much more interesting. She may die; or she may recover, though not for some time. If she recovers she may well be able to describe her attacker; and if she does so, he may also be remembered by a garrulous old man and a cop who argued with a stranger on 59th at 3rd Avenue; an Englishman who was agitated and who wanted to get to the Waldorf in a hurry. A routine hotel check may then lead back to Murphy's Emerald. You see the beauty of it all?"

Ahead was the East River. Barry was crouched in his corner, his lips drawn back in an involuntary snarl of fear.

"Where are you taking me?"

"To the airport, of course. Where else? We have already booked you out of the hotel. Your case is in front with the driver. Your flight leaves at five minutes after noon. You came over, accomplished your mission, and flew back at once."

"No!" The word came out like a small and ineffectual explosion. "No, there's something wrong –"

The two raptorial beaks turned slowly towards him. The two pairs of eyes burned in the twilight inside the car.

"Wrong?" the harsh voices said together. There was a pause, then one of them said coldly: "There is nothing wrong with the pattern, Mr. Simpson. It is perfect."

"If Margot Prynne dies," the second creature said, "her husband will be charged, and sentenced. There can be no other possible outcome. Horton-Crawley will become Chairman of Mowdell, and, ultimately, of Parian-Laing –"

"But if she doesn't?"

"She will not be in a fit state to tell her story for some time. Meanwhile, Sir James will be held under arrest; or on bail, on condition he does not leave the country. Either way, Horton-Crawley will achieve his objective."

"And what happens to *me*, doesn't matter?"

The creatures exchanged a swift glance.

"On the contrary, what happens to you interests us greatly. Why else do you think we have intervened?"

Barry's lips were still drawn back in the defensive snarl, but he was blustering now with more confidence.

"I know what's wrong! The dates! My documents show that I arrived in New York on Monday. I'm booked in at the hotel here on Monday –"

"Agreed. What of it?"

"I was at home until midnight on Tuesday – nearly two days after I was supposed to have flown –"

"Agreed again. But you were lying low, as you were supposed to be at school for the new term. Who can testify that you were in Westport on Monday and Tuesday? Only your fellow-conspirators. And their word is worth what, do you think? Precious little in the face of travel records, immigration records, independent witnesses – the word of Margot Prynne, if she recovers." Another swift exchange of glances. The red eyes locked together momentarily like twin laser beams, then broke apart. "The sport is only just beginning, Mr. Simpson."

CHAPTER FOUR

(1)

AT London Airport, tired grey eyes looked up at him.

"A short trip, Mr. Simpson. What was the object of your visit?"

"The Book Expo."

"Are you interested in books?"

"I'm a schoolmaster. I'm planning a series of educational text-books. It's important to see what is already being done in that field."

"Of course," said the official politely.

He handed the passport back, but as Barry moved away he saw the man's plump white hand pick up a pen and make a note in the end column of an official-looking list.

"Barry!" And: "Where the *hell* have you been?"

"New York."

Janey's face froze.

"I said where the hell have you been?"

"And I told you," he snapped back at her, viciously. "You can believe it or not. Take your choice."

"Where did you get that case?"

He flung the ordinary-looking fibre-glass suitcase into a corner.

"It came from a friend. Give or take the second letter."

It was late, and Janey had been in bed, asleep. Now she climbed out, stood running her hands through her thick dark hair. She stooped and touched the case. On the side was a sticker that read: *I stayed at Murphy's Emerald Hotel, New York City.* She straightened, and opened her mouth, but before she could say anything he flung his passport on the bed, and a handful of dollar bills and loose change.

"If you get the dust of my shoes analysed, it'll be identical with the dust of Manhattan."

"But you couldn't," she said uncertainly. "It's physically impossible. Twenty four hours ago –" She stopped, saw how fever-bright his eyes were. "Barry, love, tell me the truth."

But all he said was: "Suppose you tell me what's been happening here? Have you seen anything of the *Seamew* mob?"

"No. But one of them has been trying to get to see Mam. She's had to lock herself in." Still uncertainly, she said: "Barry, love, tell me. What's going on? I rang Mel. He didn't know where you were, either –" Again, she stopped. "How did you know about *Seamew*?"

"Local paper. I saw it before I left. Christ, love, make me some coffee, will you."

"Now look here, Barry Simpson –"

But he kicked off his shoes, flung his jacket over a chair, and lay on the bed.

"Don't argue, love. I've had about three hours sleep since I saw you last." He put his hands behind his head, closed his eyes. But almost at once he opened them again. Uneasily they roamed about the familiar little room. She saw again how fever-bright he seemed. His eyes were everywhere, refusing to meet hers, scampering like small nervous mice over the walls and ceiling.

"Barry, where *did* you go? Why didn't you tell me you were going off? Whose case is that? And where did you get that American money?"

Still he refused to look at her.

"One day," he said, "I might tell you. If the spooks don't get me first."

(2)

Ed's voice sounded strange on the telephone. Perhaps it was because it was only eight o'clock, and he was usually still in bed at that time. He sounded weary, but there was an edge of excitement to it that was unmistakable.

"There's been another telephone call. Untimed, like the last one. And unrecorded."

Pete looked out through the glass-sided box in the hall of the Royal Hotel. Through the open doors, he could see the sea, lying quietly at the iron feet of the Pier.

Ed said sharply: "Are you there, Pete?"

"I'm here." The small cold creeping of unease ran over him again.

"Have you seen the woman yet? Madame Joseph –"

"No. She refused to see us."

"Get in there. I don't care how you do it, but get in there. Today."

"All right."

"And Pete. There's someone called Barry Simpson. He's married to one of the Madame's daughters. He's just back from a flying visit to New York. Or so the caller told us. Check on him, too."

Liz Frele came out of the lift, stood looking about her for a moment. She was wearing dark blue slacks with a short-sleeved white shirt. Her sand-coloured hair had been brushed, and now fell straight to her shoulders. Even at that distance he was aware of the clear blue eyes in the sunburnt face that was now relaxed after a night's sleep. She seemed less anxious, less cross than when he had first met her. Almost beautiful, he realised with a sudden jolt.

Ed said: "For Christ's sake, have we been cut off?"

"No, I heard you. Why did this character go to New York?"

"We don't know. But the caller said to check."

Liz went into the dining-room.

"O.K. Will do, Ed."

"Oh, and Pete!"

"Yes, Ed."

"Be careful."

As he joined Liz for breakfast, at a table by the window in the almost empty dining-room, he saw again how quietly, but how watchfully, the sea lay at the iron feet of the ugly Pier.

They rang the house in Parrott Lane at intervals during the day, but no-one answered. Three times they drove up to the door, pressed the bell, and banged on the wood. Then to the side doors. But there was no reply. And the little cell on the Pier stayed firmly locked.

Inside the house, though they couldn't have known it, Jimmy Roberts was going about his daily routine with an embalmer's touch. He washed dishes, swept the kitchen floor, made the beds, all with an exaggerated caution that threatened disaster. Every time the phone rang, or the knocking came at the doors, he jumped with fright. But he had been told that under no circumstances . . .

*

"Mr. Fletcher," Mr. Arlingfold said, "were you and Miss Frele on good terms at this point?"

"Of course."

"There is surely no *of course* about it, Mr. Fletcher. I understand from what went before that you in fact originally refused this assignment from C.C.I., and that you were – persuaded, shall we say? – by Miss Frele, who was motivated not so much by any feelings of filial duty or affection towards her late mother, as by the cash reward offered by C.C.I. Is that not so?"

"That was so. But once I had taken the decision –" He broke off, shrugged.

"Yes, Mr. Fletcher?"

"I became very fond of her."

"And yet you allowed her to take this undoubted risk."

"How many more times do I have to say it? I didn't know the extent of the risk! How could I?"

*

They had spent most of the day, when they were not trying to contact Madame Joseph, in and around the harbour. The salvage vessel *Catfish* was back after a preliminary survey, and it was arranged that they should go out with her on the following day. How much the investigation was likely to cost, no-one outside the Clay Building knew. But *Catfish* was as modern as they come, with an instrument room like a computer deck.

At seven-fifty that evening, they tried again. He took her back to Parrott Lane in the car that the Clay empire had hired for them – a roomy Mercedes estate model that was also being used to ferry light equipment for *Catfish*. It was dark, and the Lane was empty. As they had already discovered, it was a cul-de-sac, gloomy and uninviting, though here and there a light showed in one or other of the houses that lined it on the north side. To the south were the Jubilee Gardens, dark now and full of shadows, except for an occasional string of coloured lights along the main paths. Pete let the Mercedes drift gently along, stopped a few yards short of number 43. The front of the house was in darkness, but a light showed from the side.

"Someone's home."

Opposite the house, under one of the few street lamps, a white convertible was parked without lights.

"I'll go up to the top, and turn. We might want to move in a hurry."

"Let me out here," she said. "I'll do a preliminary reccy."

"All right. But no more than that. Wait for me, before you go inside."

"Nothing would induce me," she said, "to go in there alone. I didn't like what I saw of Madame J., or her house."

She closed the car door quietly, and he saw her move warily across the front of the house. He let the Mercedes drift on, turned at the top, came back down the opposite side and parked a dozen yards behind the other vehicle. Leaving the car unlocked, he climbed out, crossed to number 43.

"Liz?"

The light was still showing at the side. He took a few paces towards it, passing the side door to the séance room.

"Liz – ?"

The lighted window was the kitchen. Through a gap in the carelessly drawn curtains he saw three strangers gathered round a table. At the head was Madame Joseph, or so he guessed her to be. Her eyes were hooded under her black hair. She was rocking gently, and appeared to be listening to something or someone outside the circle. Though he was not to know it until later, the others were Ted Modley and Jimmy Roberts. Some kind of a meal seemed to be in progress, but only Jimmy was still eating. As he watched them, a car drew up outside the front of the house; there was the sound of voices, and a door slammed. A moment later, he heard the bell ringing, a long urgent summons reinforced by a thunderous knocking. The car was driven off up the Lane, came back a few moments later at speed, passed the house and drove away. The ringing and the pounding at the door were repeated.

Inside the lighted kitchen, the little tableau remained frozen. Ted Modley lit a cigarette with fingers that trembled so that he could scarcely hold the flame to it. Jimmy looked up at his mother, then went on eating. Madame Joseph sat listening, her head on one side. Then she glanced at the window, said something to Ted Modley, and with a swift, darting movement he slid over to the sink, flicked the curtain over the gap. And at the same time, Pete heard impatient footsteps moving towards the side entrance.

Behind him was a small shed. He moved back from the

window, leaned against the door, which gave into a square of utter blackness in which he was suddenly seized, and a hand placed over his mouth to prevent him crying out. A voice hissed in his ear, and from outside he heard someone pounding now on the back door of the house, shouting to be let in.

*

"Mr. Horton-Crawley," counsel asked, "where were you on the 14th and 15th of September last?"

"I was on a short tour of the Middle East, on behalf of my firm."

"Your firm at that time was Mowdell Publishing?"

"Yes."

"And when did you hear of the attack on Lady Prynne?"

"Late on the evening of the 14th. I was staying the night in Beirut. At the Phoenicia. My secretary telephoned from London."

"And what did you do?"

"I cancelled the rest of my tour, and returned to London on the morning of the 15th."

"Did you try to contact Mrs. Josephine Modley?"

"Yes. I tried to telephone before my plane left. I tried several times, but there was no reply. So I cabled her from Rome, where I had to change planes."

"Saying what, Mr. Horton-Crawley?"

"That I would be calling at her house on the Thursday evening – the evening of the 15th – and that she had to see me. That it was vitally important."

"Were you upset at the news from New York?"

There was a long pause in the courtroom, a moment of absolute silence. Then Horton-Crawley said very quietly: "I was more than upset. I was heartbroken. I was also very angry."

"Why angry?"

"Because I thought that this was in some way connected

with my approach to the group that Mrs. Modley represented."

"So," counsel said, "you flew to London, and then what?"

"I hired a private air-taxi, and flew on to Westport. A car met me at the air-strip, and took me to Parrott Lane."

*

"Fletcher," the voice hissed in his ear. "I'm Ericson. C.C.I."

Pete relaxed. Ericson was one of the three. He had met Camber already, on the beach, but the others were names only: Ericson and Schramm.

The hand was removed from his mouth.

"Is Liz with you?"

"No. I thought she was with you."

"She dropped off to do a reccy, while I turned the car –"

Horton-Crawley was shouting and beating on the door. There was a sudden crash of glass, and through the half-open door of the shed they saw the curtains thrust to one side, and the big man's head and shoulders half in the kitchen. The three sat like waxworks in a tableau of horror, staring back at him.

"Will you open the door, or do I have to break it down?"

Madame Joseph said something, and Ted Modley slid crabwise to the door, pulled back the bolts. Horton-Crawley flung it open, disappeared inside. The door was closed. The curtains were drawn back over the shattered window and the kitchen was again lost to view.

"Where the hell is she?"

"I'll call up Schramm."

Ericson moved in the darkness, there was a small *click*, and Pete heard: "Schramm here."

"Ericson. Have you seen anything of Miss Frele?"

"She went down the side passage, two or three minutes ago. Just before Fletcher returned with the car. I haven't seen her since. Who's the noisy character who just arrived?"

"No idea. He's burst his way in. Seems put out about something. Let me know if Liz shows. Fletcher's worried."

"Will do."

The conversation had been carried on in small bats' voices. To Pete, Ericson said: "Schramm's over in the Gardens, up a cherry tree." And: "Have *you* any idea who this character might be?"

"No."

The light was extinguished in the kitchen. The whole house was suddenly plunged into darkness, and Pete and Ericson edged cautiously out from the shed.

"What the hell kind of people are they in there? Can they see in the dark?" Ericson grumbled. But then a faint light showed from an attic room at the back.

"If they've got Liz –"

"I don't see how. No-one came out of the house. There was no scuffling. I was here."

"Then for God's sake where *is* she?"

Ericson flashed a torch round the small square of lawn. Beyond was a high wall. Empty.

"She couldn't have come down here."

"Schramm said she did."

Ericson said: "He's up a cherry tree, for Christ's sake! Maybe he only *thought* she came down the passage."

Pete said: "If they've left the door open, I'm going inside."

"Don't be a fool. They could be dangerous."

"Will you lend me your torch?"

"I ought not to. I ought to keep you out here by force. But if that's what you want, brother –"

The back door swung inwards. The torch revealed an empty kitchen, an empty passage beyond. The waiting-room door was open; the room beyond it was also empty. From behind the closed door of what he later discovered to be the séance room, he heard voices; a man's voice, raised in anger, and a woman's. He moved warily to the foot of the stairs, sent his torch questing up into the darkness, then followed. On the first floor, nothing. Empty bedrooms, empty bathroom. He paused at the foot of the steep flight leading up to the attic. From above came the murmur of a single voice, male, with a strong Canadian accent. Then a door was opened, and feet clattered on the bare stairs. Pete drew back into one of the bedrooms, heard whoever it was go racing down, whimpering like a big hurt puppy. The street door opened, closed. Then the house was silent again; watchful; not even the voices from the séance room disturbing the echoing silence. He ran up the stairs to the attic, found it empty. *Then who the hell had whoever it was been talking to?*

Suddenly fear gripped him. Blind, unreasoning fear. *What went on in this house, for God's sake? And what had they done with Liz?*

Downstairs again. Half-way along the passage, under the staircase itself, was a curtain. Despite his fear, he stopped. Behind the curtain was another door. Opened, this revealed a flight of stone steps leading down to a lighted cellar. Cautiously, his heart pounding, he descended. The cellar was dry, and extended under the whole of the front portion of the house. It was divided into three bays by wide brick pillars, painted white, and in the third and last bay, under the séance room, Ted Modley was watching Mel's monitor screen, headphones clipped over his sharp little head. Tapes revolved, and as Pete drew closer he saw Madame Jo and Horton-Crawley in the room above.

Horton-Crawley was walking up and down, gesticulating. Madame Joseph was sitting in her chair, rocking gently. At last she reached out, and opened a small drawer in the table on which the crystal ball stood. She flung a key on to the polished surface of the table, and Horton-Crawley picked it up, hesitated, then made for the double door that led directly out into the side passage. As he disappeared, Madame Jo began to rock more violently, her hands clasped in a curiously complex interlocking grip. And immediately the dynamo humming started, grew rapidly, penetrated at last even down to the cellar below. And as Pete stared at the screen, he was aware of Ted Modley struggling to take the earphones from his head. He looked as though he had no strength in his arms. On the screen, the wall of the séance room began to dissolve. Modley screamed, clawed at the earphones, fell to his knees. And then Pete heard Ericson's voice, and the pull of his hands, urging him away. In the last second before he was dragged back through the cellar and up the steps he thought he saw on the screen the shape of the Beast, huge, hairy, obscene, formed out of the swirling mists. Together they fought their way up through the choking animal stench that filled the house like a foul miasma. The dynamo hum increased, rose to the shrill painful drilling sound that threatened to rob them of their wits. Choking, deafened, they stumbled through the kitchen, and out into the night.

"Liz?" Ericson hissed at him.

"She's not in the house."

"Certain?"

"Certain."

Outside, the air was sweet, the shrill sound no longer audible. Ericson whispered urgently: "We know who the man is, and we think we know why he's here. Camber came through with it a minute ago. He's trying to start the white car. It isn't his. It belongs to Mel Williams, the other son-in-law."

"She gave him the key. I saw it –"

"He's in a devil of a hurry. At a guess, he's going to meet the rest of the bunch. But Schramm fixed it earlier on. Just in case. Come and look."

Pete held him back.

"Ericson – what's going on?"

"We're not sure. But if it's what I think it is, it's nasty. It's very, very nasty. Even nastier than we thought."

Outside, in the Lane, the starter of the white convertible was being punished. Ericson murmured: "O.K., Schramm," into his transmitter, and immediately Schramm strolled into the pool of light under the street-lamp.

"Trouble?"

Horton-Crawley said: "The stupid bloody cow won't start –"

"Know anything about cars?"

"Nothing."

The starter whined again, died.

"I do. Shall I look?"

"Please."

In the quiet Lane, their conversation was clearly audible. Ericson whispered: "As soon as he gets moving, run like hell to your own car. Got the key ready?"

"Yes." Pete took it out, held it in his hand.

"We mustn't lose him."

"What about Liz?"

"If she's not in the house, there's no point in hanging around. Schramm'll be here. And Camber is coming in to cover. You and I'll follow Horton-Crawley."

"Is that who he is?"

"That's him." Ericson said: "He's pretty powerful in his own line, even if he can't find a loose lead –"

Suddenly the car started, roared into life. Schramm stepped back.

"Thanks! Thanks a lot!"

"Think nothing of it," Schramm said. "She'll be all right now."

As the convertible moved off, Ericson and Pete raced for the Mercedes. They were in and moving before the convertible had reached the end of the Lane. They saw it turn right, away from the sea. Schramm watched them go, then melted back into the shelter of the Gardens, and reclimbed his tree.

(3)

When Horton-Crawley had finally forced the Modleys to admit him, Jimmy Roberts had been ordered upstairs, out of the way. He had raced up the two flights, glad to be no longer a part of a drama that he could not even begin to understand. Pausing at the top, he had heard the sound of angry voices from ground level. Then he had gone in to his small dormer room and had switched on the light.

The succubus was lying on his bed, waiting.

"Jimmy –"

The voice, as always, was the voice of Sarah. The beautiful body lay relaxed and infinitely desirable. He stood there, staring at her, as he had stared so often before, like a yokel at a fair.

"Sam –"

The succubus moved a fraction, made a gesture of irritation.

"You know that I'm not Sam. It's a stupid name for a girl, anyway. I come in her likeness, but I am not her. Do you accept that, Jimmy?"

He said nothing. He simply stood and stared, shifting his weight about.

"Do you?" the succubus said, more sharply.

"Yes." Reluctantly.

"Then do you remember a certain day, early in the summer –?"

"No!" he cried. "No – I don't want to remember –"

"It was a day of bright sunlight. Painfully bright. It was a hot day. We were in your mother's room, lying on your mother's bed. Now do you remember?"

"No."

"I think you do, Jimmy. I told you then what you would have to do one day, and what would happen if you refused. That day is today, Jimmy." The succubus stretched out an arm. "Come, Jimmy. Come and sit down. Tell me what it is that you have to do."

"No!" he said again, in rising panic. "No, I can't – I don't remember –"

"Then come closer, and I'll tell you again."

He took a step forward, allowed his hand to be seized. The demon drew him down, kissed him, and with its mouth close against his ear it whispered again the thing that he had to do. The terrible thing. The incomprehensible thing.

"This you will do," it said. "For if you do not, you will die. And through all eternity you will never lie with me again." Words that he had first heard on that day of early summer; words that, despite his denials, he had never forgotten.

"No," he said again, trembling. "I can't do it –"

The succubus took his hands, his big, strong, work-hardened hands, and laid them on its body, its beautiful golden body that was the body of his half-sister, Sarah.

"You must," it said.

"No –" He seized the beautiful creature, held it close to him. Clumsily, he began to go through the preliminaries of love. Anything to divert his mind from the road along which the creature was driving it.

The succubus responded a little, letting him explore its nakedness, giving him its lips, its open mouth, the tip of its small soft tongue. But in the instant before the intoxication of passion clouded the horror in his mind, it drew away.

"Later, Jimmy –"

He clawed after its withdrawal like a dying man clutching at life.

"No," he said drunkenly. "Now –"

But the succubus said sharply: "First you must do what I have told you." Again it repeated the words: "If you do not, you will most certainly die. And through all eternity you will never lie with me again." And such was the power the creature had over him that it was the thought of losing it, even more than the threat of death, that made his fear unbearable. Terrible though the thing was that he now had to do, he knew that he would do it. The demon knew it, too; had known it from the beginning.

Somehow, he climbed to his feet, stood swaying and whimpering like a big hurt puppy.

"Take this," the succubus said, and handed him the silver knife that had been dedicated by Madame Jo; the same knife that had severed the head of the white goat all those years before. The sacrificial knife, that had been fumigated with herbs, sprinkled with holy water, purified by ritual.

"Go now," the succubus said, "and walk on the beach. Listen to the sea. And listen for the clock to strike midnight. When you hear it, go up into the town. Go to the address I told you. But don't attempt to go there until after midnight. If you try to do so, you will be prevented. Repeat that, Jimmy." Somehow, only half-intelligibly, he repeated the words, and the succubus smiled up at him with the guileless charm of an innocent girl, teasing her first lover. "When the moment comes, I shall be there, too. Go now, Jimmy. And afterwards . . ." The smile was frank and open, full of promise. "Afterwards, everything will be all right."

He was released. He wrapped the knife in an old scarf, tucked it inside his jacket, and stumbled away down the stairs, past the room in which Pete Fletcher was hiding, and out into the night.

The white convertible was being driven fast through the older part of the town. Ericson said: "At a guess, he's making for the moorland road. There's a place called Axel Heath that is what the country people call a Way Place."

Pete gave the Mercedes its head, closed the gap by fifty yards, then hung at that distance until the street lamps fell away, and the road began to climb. There were a few other cars about, but once they passed the Roddon turn the road was empty. There was a young moon, and Ericson leaned across and switched off the Mercedes' headlamps. The car swerved, and Pete had to fight to bring it back. Angrily, he exclaimed: "For God's sake! Are you trying to wreck us?"

He stretched out a hand to switch on again, but Ericson said: "Do you want him to know you're following him? From now on there'll be no other cars on the road. As soon as your eyes are tuned, you'll have to switch off altogether. Not even sidelights."

"I can't possibly –"

"You'll find that you can. On the open moor there'll be enough light to follow the road. And he'll stop at the Way Place."

"What does it mean? The Way Place?"

"Just what it says. A place where there is a way through. To the other world."

The convertible was almost up to the edge of the plateau. Its lights pointed up towards the few stars that the moon had not yet dimmed, then swung down in a wide sweeping arc as the road levelled. Pete said: "And for Christ's sake, what does *that* mean?"

"Exactly what it says. They are not uncommon."

"A way – *through*?"

"Between my world and yours," Ericson said. "Switch off the side-lights. You're almost over the rise. He mustn't see you."

Pete reached out, switched off, saw the road clearly ahead of him, a long straight silver line. On either side, the open moor was like a night-sea, only half visible in the faint light, broken and troubled. His hands held the wheel with an involuntary locking grip like that of a roosting bird.

"*Your* world," he managed to say at last. "*Your* world?"

He glanced sideways, saw the dark outline of the C.C.I. man, silhouetted against the moonlight. Ericson turned his face a fraction towards him. And now his eyes were like live coals, burning redly over a cruel raptor's beak.

Pete jammed on the brakes of the Mercedes, brought her to a screaming halt. He had his hand on the door when the creature said reasonably: "If you follow Horton-Crawley, he will take you to Miss Frele. If you give up now, you will never find her."

With the door half-open, Pete forced himself to say: "Who the hell *are* you?"

"Ericson, of course. Or anyone else I choose to be."

"What have you done with her?"

"With Miss Frele? I told you. She is where Horton-Crawley is going in such a hurry."

"Through the Way?"

The creature made a small gesture with one hand.

"Oh, no. She is still on this side."

Pete said: "I don't believe in your Way. I don't believe in you. I don't believe in any of it. This is some stupid trick –"

Another gesture, this time authoritative.

"Look behind you." And as Pete hesitated: "If you think I am going to attack you while your head is turned, you are wrong. But if you want proof, I will get out while you turn around."

The creature opened the near-side door, slid out. Pete looked out through the half-open door on the off-side. The moor lay broken and troubled in the half-light of the moon. And then, suddenly, he saw a movement. Straining his eyes, he saw the outline of a figure, stumbling over the rough heather and the ancient boulders. In an instant he was out of the car, had crossed the narrow road, and was racing over the broken ground.

"Liz!"

She raised her head, held out her arms to him.

"Pete! Oh, Pete –"

She was weeping, trembling uncontrollably as he reached her, as he took her in his arms and held her close.

"Liz! Darling Liz – what did they do to you?"

"Oh, Pete, it was horrible! Horrible! I didn't know where I was – or what was happening –"

He stroked her hair, her long soft hair that in daylight

was the pale gold of desert sand, but was now bright silver in the young light of the moon. She quietened a little, lifted her face, and he kissed her for the first time, out there on the open moor.

"We must get away. Quickly. Back to the car. Ericson –"

He turned, held her hand, drew her back with him. There was no sign of the creature who had called himself Ericson. The Mercedes lay quietly. He took her round to the near side, opened the door, kissed her again, and locked the door behind her as she climbed in. Then he ran round to the driving-seat, cast a last glance round the moonlit plateau. Inside the car, he was about to switch on when he heard Ericson's voice.

"Well, Mr. Fletcher?"

He froze, with his hand still outstretched, turned his head slowly. In the front passenger seat, where a moment before he had locked the door behind Liz Frele, he saw the outline of Ericson – not the beaked and red-eyed creature from beyond the Way, but the Ericson who had been with him in Parrott Lane.

"I suggest you drive on. Or you may lose Horton-Crawley. He'll be changing transport at the cross-roads on Axel Heath, if that means anything to you."

Pete felt again the sudden creeping cold of fear.

"But –"

"Surely you haven't forgotten what I said a few minutes ago. I am Ericson, or anyone else I choose to be. Male or female, that is no problem. Was there ever a Liz Frele? After all, you never saw us together, did you? Incidentally, you kiss well, Mr. Fletcher. It is one of the advantages of being able to change so completely, that one can enjoy contact with whichever happens to be the opposite sex at the time –"

With a sudden desperate courage, Pete flung himself at Ericson, seized him by the throat.

"Where is she? What have you done with her? Damn you, I'll kill you –"

Ericson lifted his arms, gripped the shoulders of his attacker. Power flowed between his hands, flung Pete back into his seat, leaving him shaking and numb with shock.

"You fool!" Ericson's voice was full of contempt. "Do you still not realise?"

Pete saw that the face was no longer the face of Ericson. The raptor's beak and the glowing eyes had returned. It was as though the change back had been necessary, before the flow of power could be released.

"For God's sake," he said, "what are you trying to do?" For a while he could say nothing more. He could only lean weakly against the car door, staring at the creature who should have been Liz Frele. But at last the numbness and the shaking died. Cold anger returned. "All right, just tell me. What am I supposed to be doing?"

"Following Horton-Crawley," the creature answered with surprising mildness. "But you have probably missed him by now. And with it, your last chance of finding the girl."

"If ever there was a girl," he said bitterly. The memory of that first sweet kiss, and the way she had clung to him, out there on the open moor, was unbearably painful. But he started the Mercedes, drove on without lights, because there seemed to be no useful alternative. The lights of the convertible had disappeared. But far away over the plateau a new light now troubled the horizon.

"That will be the transport that is coming to pick him up," Ericson said. Glancing swiftly to the side, Pete saw that it was Ericson's likeness again in the other seat. "You're not too late. But they will come this way. It will be better if you are not seen. There's a bridle track on the right, a little way ahead. It cuts through to the old green road, the track your ancestors first used more than five thousand years ago. If you drive carefully, you can turn left at the green road, follow it to the cross-roads by the ford. There, you can turn left again on to this road, which will bring you behind the van."

"The – *van*?" Pete forced himself to say.

"That is the transport that has been sent for Horton-Crawley. It is small and unobtrusive. And it has the added advantage that passengers can be pushed into the back, and cannot see where they are going. Turn sharp right in another fifty yards."

The bridle track was rough, but passable, kept clear by generations of horsemen and by the moorland ponies who followed the beaten way. As Pete strained to follow the line of it, he strove desperately to think what he should do. By following the instructions of the creature who called himself Ericson, was he being led into a situation from which it might be impossible to withdraw? But if he withdrew too soon, would he ever see Liz alive again?

Liz ... The way she had flung herself sobbing into his arms, and the sweet surrender of that first kiss ... Had it *really* been her? Was Ericson lying after all –

"Sharp left!" Ericson said suddenly. "Now you're on the old road. The crossroads is another half a mile due north. But take it slowly. Let the van get away first."

The van's lights blazed across the plateau. Pete slowed when he was still well clear of its line of approach. He stopped, switched off the engine of the Mercedes. Then he took a pair of binoculars from the front, and focussed on the road ahead. As the lights of the van shone at last on the signpost that looked like a white gibbet, he saw the unmistakable bulk of Horton-Crawley move forward. In the stillness, he heard voices raised in argument.

"He wants to travel in front. To see where they are going," Ericson said. To Pete, the voices were only sounds in the distance.

"He has a gun," Ericson said.

A shot suddenly sounded, a clear whip-crack in the night, followed by a scream.

"He's put a bullet in the driver's left leg." Ericson said unemotionally. "Unless he directs him to the Chapel, he'll put another in his right. Either way, H–C will have to drive."

There was more shouting, but then the van moved off,

its headlights bayoneting a great golden wound into the body of the night.

"You'll have to move fast."

Pete hurled the Mercedes at the crossroads, swung it into a sharp-angled turn, followed the rapidly receding lights of the van.

"If you know so much," he forced out between his rigid jaws, "why the hell do we have to do it the hard way? Why don't you just take me to the bloody Chapel?"

"Why do people climb a mountain by its most difficult face, when there are a dozen simpler routes to the summit? For the sport, Mr. Fletcher."

Long before they reached the town, the van turned off to the right, into the half-recovered wilderness that had once been an airfield. Pete switched off the Mercedes' engine a hundred yards from a gaunt workshop that was suddenly floodlit from the van's headlights. He let the car coast forward a little, sliding gently into the concrete yard of the neighbouring plot. Through the chain-mesh fencing that divided them, he saw the big man climb out into the reflected light, a gun in his right hand. There was an argument, then Horton-Crawley switched the gun to his left, reached into the van with his right. Then he ran through the headlights' twin beams to the big metal doors. He unlocked one, slid it back, and, leaving it open, disappeared inside.

"Why are you waiting?" Ericson said. "This is the Chapel, and Liz Frele is inside."

(4)

When Jimmy Roberts had left the house in Parrott Lane, it was still ten minutes short of nine o'clock. Three hours still to midnight. He had already eaten most of his supper when Horton-Crawley had burst in and he had been told to go up to his room. But he had taken advantage of the general mêlée to seize a half-empty packet of biscuits and an apple and to cram them into his pockets.

Now he wandered aimlessly along the beach, watching the small creaming waves licking at the wet sand. Above him, on the Promenade, the strings of coloured lights still burned, though there were only a handful of visitors left in the town. Soon they would be switched off for the winter. But not yet. He sat for a while at the foot of the concrete steps that led up to the closed entrance to the Pier. For want of something better to do, he ate the apple and some of the biscuits. Then he took out the silver knife and unwrapped it. Instantly, he heard the voice of the succubus. "Put it away, Jimmy. No-one must see it." Guiltily, he re-wrapped the knife, and stuffed it inside his jacket. He leaned back against the lower steps, and like an animal that is suddenly tired of its play, he dropped into a dream-haunted sleep, lying twitching and moaning until he awoke with a jerk, stiff and cold, and with no idea at all where he was.

Above him, the quarter-bells in the church of St. Luke began to chime. Then the single deep bell. Nine, ten, eleven. . . . There was an hour still to go before midnight, and he began to whimper again with the cold, and with the thought of what he must do when the hour was up.

Pete Fletcher slid out of the Mercedes, hesitated, said to Ericson: "If I try to get inside, what do *you* do?"

"Nothing. It's up to you."

Pete reached in through the window, took out the ignition key and the torch, slipped the key into an inside pocket. Then he went back to the road, and in through the entrance to the Melvill Electric plot. As he passed the van, he heard a deep regular moaning from inside. Opening the door, he saw Mel in the passenger seat. He was barely conscious. Blood still flowed from his shattered leg, collected in a pool on the rubber mat on the floor. Pete hesitated only for a moment. He had no idea who the wounded man was, whether he was friend or enemy. But if he was to get inside after Horton-Crawley, before someone closed the doors . . .

Inside, the darkness was absolute. He sent the torch beam probing, saw a car-sized space with a small patch of oil on the floor, and a couple of tyres leaning against the wall. On the far side were long black curtains, concealing whatever lay beyond. He switched off the torch, listened. Far away, he heard the whistle of a train, a deep-throated melancholy sound. A plane flew over high, barely disturbing the trapped air in this vestibule of the unknown.

Suddenly he was aware of a movement in the darkness. Turning swiftly, he saw twin points of fire, glowing a yard away.

"Ericson?" It was no more than a whisper.

"No."

He switched on the torch, saw the creature's curved beak-mouth.

"The one you call Ericson is still outside. The one you know as Elizabeth Frele is in the Chapel, through the curtains."

"The one I know as –" He couldn't finish it. Was it true. then? But where does truth end, he thought, and illusion start? He had accepted Ericson, and Schramm, and Camber, and the skipper and crew of *Catfish*. Even Ed himself . . .

"Where does truth end, and illusion start?" the creature said, reading his thoughts. "You will certainly not find the answer by standing here."

Horton-Crawley had gone through into the Chapel. But he was armed.

The creature said: "A gun is of little use against the powers of darkness."

Pete glanced back at the open doorway. If he ran for it, took the van, drove back into town or to the nearest telephone . . .

"The vehicles outside have been immobilised," said the creature. "There is no public telephone within two miles.

And even if you reached it –" The rest was left unsaid.

Pete moved suddenly. He took a dozen paces forward, opened the curtains a crack and looked through. The first thing he saw was the body of Liz Frele, naked, flung across the Altar between the tall black candles. In front, and a little to the left, was a hairy creature with the head of a goat. A yard away, holding his gun pointing at the Beast's heart, was Horton-Crawley.

"Take it off!" he was shouting. "Take it off, or by God, I'll shoot it off! Let me see your face!"

He lifted the gun a fraction, and Barry took off the goat's head, stood holding it in front of him as a wholly ineffectual shield against a possible bullet.

"Are you Barry Simpson?"

A moment's hesitation, then: "Yes."

"Did you attack Margot Prynne?"

"No."

"Then who did, for Christ's sake?"

"Her husband –"

"That's a lie! Why should he?"

"They'd quarrelled –"

"How do you know that?"

"Everyone knew it. I made it my business to find out."

"While you were in New York?"

"How did you know I was in New York?"

"My secretary checked the passenger lists. You were the only one from Westport. You were there for three days. You left immediately after Margot was attacked. Was that your idea of carrying out my wishes? Attacking *her*?"

"No. I went to try to stop Prynne –"

"How, for God's sake? How the hell could you have stopped *him*?"

"I don't know. I only know I didn't touch his wife. It was him. He picked up the vase. His finger-prints –"

Horton-Crawley let out a roar of anger.

"You bloody hairy little bastard! How do you know that? Go on, tell me! How do you know that?"

On the Altar, Liz Frele lay motionless. She could have been a long-limbed brown rag-doll, flung down by a thoughtless child. What had they done to her? For God's *sake*, what had they done to her?

Suddenly, a new Voice spoke from above the Altar.

"You ask how he knew that, Mr. Horton-Crawley? Because we made it possible for him to know it. And by that I mean that we made it possible for him to know that Sir James picked up the vase from the floor, thereby ensuring that his finger-prints –"

Horton-Crawley swung the barrel of the gun up to cover the space over the Altar.

"How many more of you are there?" He peered up into the shadows, shielding his eyes with his left hand. "Come down, blast you, whoever you are!"

"You would be well advised not to insist on that," the Voice said mildly. But anger, and possession of the gun, seemed to give the big man a reckless courage. He shouted: "Come down! Or I'll shoot!"

"Don't be a fool," the Voice replied. "It would achieve nothing. I was going to show you exactly what happened in the hotel in New York."

"No!" Barry exclaimed.

"Why not, if you're in the clear?" Horton-Crawley turned his attention back to him. "Why shouldn't we know?"

Desperately, Barry said: "Because I was never inside the hotel, but they made it seem –"

The Voice interrupted.

"See, and judge for yourselves."

The humming sound began, softly at first, then louder. One wall of the Chapel began to dissolve, and it was as though they were looking through a clouded window at the Prynne's suite in the Waldorf-Astoria. Slowly the clouds dispersed, and the scene was exactly as Barry had seen it on the small screen in the back of the maroon Cadillac. Only now it was life-size. James Prynne stopped, stared at the vase on the floor, picked it up and placed it on the side-table. Then he went out, and the scene switched to Màrgot in bed.

Horton-Crawley stood transfixed. As she drank her coffee and glanced through the pages of the New York *Times*, he remained silent. But when the summons came, and she slid out of bed and padded barefoot to the outer door, a cry like a sob escaped him.

"Margot!"

In the open doorway stood the likeness of Barry Simpson. He pushed his way inside, picked up the vase in his gloved hand, swung it up and over as she turned to run back into the bedroom ...

As the scene faded, Horton-Crawley turned back to the Altar, but Barry had gone, slipping away into the shadows. "You bastard! You bloody bastard! Where are you?" He turned his head from side to side, searching for him. He seemed almost out of his mind with grief and anger. "Where are you? Where the hell are you?" Then: "You – up there!" he shouted up to the space over the Altar. "I'll give you ten seconds to come down, whoever you are –"

There was no reply, and furiously angry he shouted again: "Come down! Come down, damn you!"

Still there was no reply. And suddenly he fired twice, the shots echoing and re-echoing back from the metal walls like a burst of machine-gun fire. But when the din subsided at last, the Chapel was quiet. No Voice spoke. Nothing moved. Pete glanced swiftly over his shoulder. There was no sign of the glowing eyes. It was as though all contact with the other side had been lost.

"Simpson!" Horton-Crawley shouted. "Simpson!" His voice echoed about the Chapel, but then that, too, died. In the candlelight, he stood undecided for a moment, then he moved cautiously round behind the Altar, his gun at the alert. And as he disappeared, Pete moved silently in through the curtains, crossed swiftly to the Altar, and bent over the body of Liz Frele.

She was unconscious, breathing faintly but regularly. He

heard Horton-Crawley behind the Altar, shouting again for Barry. Something, a box it may have been, fell with a clatter. Seizing her wrists he dragged her upright, slung her over his shoulder in a fireman's lift. Then he ran for the curtains, crossed the outer space, and emerged into the open in time to see the van being driven off at speed.

So the creature had lied when it had said that the two vehicles were immobilised. Unless, since . . .

The whole estate was deserted. He ran out into the road, round the angle of the chain-mesh fence, in to the next-door entrance. The Mercedes was still there, but Ericson had gone. He managed to open the passenger door, lowered her onto the seat, covered her with a rug from the back. Then he climbed in and tried the ignition. The car started. He switched on the headlamps, and in their light as he swung for the turn, he saw through the chain fencing that Horton-Crawley had come out of the Chapel, and was standing uncertainly. He could still only guess at the big man's part in the whole affair, and trigger-happy as he was he seemed to be a doubtful ally. As he swung the Mercedes out into the concrete road that had once been a part of the approach to the wartime runway, he heard a bellowing shout, and a short burst of fire. Two bullets hit the roof of the estate-car, but the angle of fire must have been partly blocked by the metal fence. Then they were away down the straight, swinging in a semi-circle at the end, where the hangars had been. A sign said: *Westport Town Centre*, and he turned the car half-left to follow it. But it seemed almost at once that the road was leading in the wrong direction. As it climbed, he could see the lights of the town away to the right; the distant sweep of the promenade, with the dark sea beyond. But then the lights picked up another sign: *Westport Town Centre*, and though he hesitated for an instant, it seemed foolish to turn back and to try to find an alternative route. Another mile, and the banks fell away on either side, giving way to the open moorland. More signs reflected the lights of the Mercedes, pointing this way and that across the heather and the tumbled waste of boulders with here and there a silver birch, ghost-like and weeping, like the elegant wraith of a dead love. *To The Sea; Grand Pier; Bed and Breakfast;* they shrieked at him, as he sent the car hurtling along the empty moorland road. *No Parking; Level Crossing; To the Harbour.* He drove the car through a forest of signs, none of which made the slightest sense out there on the deserted plateau. And then, when he least expected it, the road finished. It ran straight ahead, and died. The tyres of the Mercedes screamed as he jammed on the brakes. Even so, he could not stop in time. For twenty yards the car rocketed over the rough ground, as he wrestled with the wheel. Then it stopped, flinging him forward with a spine-shattering jerk, to strike his head violently on the edge of the screen. His last conscious thought was of Liz in the passenger seat. But it was a fleeting thought, instantly blotted out in an explosion of pain, and, swiftly following, oblivion, as the car ricocheted from the seven-foot high *menhir* that had finally halted its progress over the moor. Almost gently, at the last, it turned over on to its side, and lay with its wheels spinning impotently in the darkness.

(5)

"Did you, in fact, Mr. Horton-Crawley, achieve your ambition? Did you become chairman of Mowdell Publishing?"

"Yes."

"And almost immediately afterwards, of Parian-Laing?"

"Yes."

"And do you still hold those positions?"

Horton-Crawley, in the box, was a ruined shadow of his former self. He stood with his shoulders forward, his clothes hanging in loose folds, his face pale and deeply lined.

"What do *you* think for God's sake? When the truth exploded in my face?"

"The – truth?" Mr. Arlingfold said quietly, and Horton-Crawley raised his voice a fraction.

"That I had employed a group of charlatans and impostors to kill my chairman's wife –"

"Did you, in fact, do just that?"

"Yes, in *fact* that is what I did. Though it was not my intention."

"You are admitting that you hired them?"

"What is the point of denying it? In view of the tapes and the films –"

"Quite. And you still maintain that they are – what were the words you used? – charlatans and impostors?"

The powerful hands gripped the edge of the witness-box.

"Of course they are! What else can they be?"

"Yet you were prepared to pay them fifty thousand pounds –"

"Not to kill Margot! I loved her. We had planned to marry as soon as –" He stopped.

"As soon as, between you, you had ruined her husband?"

He made a small, hopeless gesture with one hand.

"I know that is how it must seem. But Prynne would have ruined Mowdell. He would have sold out to the North American combine –" With an effort, he straightened his shoulders, looked at the judge. "I had two loves. Margot Prynne, and the organisations I had helped to create. I considered that any means –" Another pause. "The weeks that Margot Prynne lay unconscious, between life and death, before she finally –"

He broke off again, and the tears began to run unchecked. Mr. Arlingfold coughed, shuffled his papers, then he said: "The American courts were quite satisfied that Sir James killed his wife. That Barry Simpson could not have done so."

But Horton-Crawley only wept, standing there in the open court, weeping for his two lost loves.

*

While Horton-Crawley's attention had been distracted by the sight of Margot Prynne, Barry had slipped away round the Altar, and through a small side door; still wearing, he swung left where the sign said *Westport Town Cen-* driving-seat of the van, and had swung it out and away before he realised that it was Mel who was lying unconscious and bleeding in the seat alongside.

There was a small illuminated clock on the dash-board. It said forty-eight minutes to midnight as, without thinking, he swung left where the sign said *Westport Town Centre*, and like Pete in the Mercedes a few seconds later, found himself driving on the open moor. The track was an unfamiliar one, but he drove on, knowing that he should strike the upland road to Roddon. But the track wound on, endlessly, and the road to Roddon eluded him.

Mel stirred, moaned, and Barry shouted at him: "For Christ's sake, what happened?" And: "Where's the road?"

Mel said: "The bastard – he shot me –"

"The road!" Barry almost screamed at him. "Where's the bloody road?"

Endlessly, the track reeled out of the darkness, was flung behind them under the wheels of the van. Barry drove like a madman, as though by sheer speed he might escape from the nightmare. Yet still the road went on and on, endlessly. The Moor was less than four miles across. But the distance clock already showed eight miles from the point where they had left the Chapel. Ten miles. Twelve . . . The time clock crept slowly round; eleven-thirty; eleven forty-five. And still out of the darkness came spinning the unfamiliar, featureless track.

Mel was flung about in the passenger seat, drifting between consciousness and oblivion. The van's headlights carved a golden tunnel through the body of the night, revealing nothing that was new. Only the road came pouring out of the darkness like a never-ending river; sliding away beneath them like time itself. Eleven fifty. Eleven fifty-five.

Twenty miles on the clock, and two minutes still to go to midnight.

And then, as the two pointers of the time-clock joined at twelve, like hands in a prayer, it was as though the power-field was broken. The cross-roads suddenly appeared, straight ahead, and he swung the van to the right, and headed for the town. Less than fifteen minutes later, he stopped outside the house in Leas Avenue where Sal and Melvin lived. He glanced up and down the empty road, climbed out and ran, hairy and almost-naked as he was, up the path. Seizing the handle of the door, he pushed against it. It gave, and he slid inside. In the same instant, he heard the distant sound of police sirens.

Jimmy, on the beach, had heard midnight strike from the church of St. Luke. Cold and stiff, he ran up to the Promenade, and through the empty streets to Leas Avenue. Sal opened the door, said: "Jimmy!" And: "What the hell do *you* want, for Christ's sake?"

"Let me come in. I have to come in."

She retreated, frowned, said: "What's the matter?" A hand flew to her mouth. "Is it Barry? What's happened to Barry?"

He pushed his way inside, kicked the door shut behind him, sent his eyes searching for the succubus.

"Are you alone?"

"Sure I'm alone. Mel's out with Barry –"

"The – succubus?" he stammered.

"The *what*?"

He had been certain that the succubus would be there. It had promised to be there. Without it, he was lost.

She said: "What the hell are you talking about? What do you want?"

And then, suddenly, he was aware of a movement to one side. He turned his head sharply, saw what could only be the succubus. It was another Sal; but now he saw them for the first time together, it was not Sal. Every hair, every freckle, every shade of eyes and skin was identical. But now, side by side at last, there was a difference. A difference of quality, more than of physical attribute. There was also one other major difference. Sal was clothed. The succubus, as always, was naked.

Sal followed his eyes, appeared to see nothing. The succubus nodded to him, said: "Now!" And blindly he took out the sacrificial knife, unwrapped it.

"What's that?" Sal's voice sharpened with sudden fear.

"Gloves," said the succubus. "Don't forget the gloves." And he remembered that he had been told to take a pair in his pocket. He took them out, slipped them on. The right hand of the succubus reached for the telephone.

"Wipe the knife!"

He wiped it carefully on the scarf.

"Jimmy, for Christ's sake, what –?"

"Say it," the succubus urged him. "Say: I kill you Sarah Anne Williams in the names and to the honour of Béelzébuth, Lucifer, Astaroth . . ."

He took a quick step forward, seized her by the hair, mumbled the words as he thrust the knife through her awakening scream to slice through the honey-brown flesh of her throat.

When the police – alerted by a telephone call, apparently from a woman saying she was Sarah Williams and that she feared for her life – arrived and pushed their way in to the house, they found Barry on his knees beside her body, his glued-on hair wet with her blood. Outside, in the van, lay the dead woman's husband, unconscious again. There was no sign of the gun that had shot him, but the sacrificial knife was still in the living-room, without any identifiable fingerprints. Medical evidence suggested that the woman had been killed at about the time the call to the police had been made.

When Mel recovered consciousness, and was told that Sal was dead, he cried like a child. Then over and over he repeated: "He shot me. The bastard shot me. And then he killed her. He was her lover, but she didn't love him –"

"*He?*" they said gently.

"Barry, of course! Who else? Who else, for God's sake?"

(6)

"Is your name Ernest William Sefton?"

"Yes."

"And were you until recently employed as manager of the marketing division of Lee & Brough Chemicals of Exeter?"

"I was."

"You no longer hold that position?"

"No."

"Will you tell the jury what you are doing at the moment?"

"I am serving a prison sentence for theft, and for offences under the Dangerous Drugs Acts."

"You stole dangerous drugs from your employers, by means of false records, and in one case at least by pretending that a consignment of such drugs had been stolen?"

"Yes."

"Did these drugs include heroin, and the hallucinogens R.S.80 and R.S.81?"

"They did."

"These hallucinogens, are they an extremely potent development of lysergic acid diethylamide, generally known as L.S.D.?"

"Yes."

"With even more remarkable and immediate psychotomimetic effects?"

"Yes. Their main advantage is their speed. They are very rapid indeed in their action."

"Producing, when ingested in quite small quantities – I quote now from one of your former employers' catalogues

– 'hallucinations, depersonalization, and thinking disturbbances'?"

"Yes."

"Of great value, I believe, in neuropharmacology and psychopharmacology, particularly in experimental work, as a means of producing abnormal behaviour patterns very closely akin to those met with in mental disease?"

"So I believe."

"But dangerous in the wrong hands?"

"So I also believe."

"And what did you do with the drugs that you stole?"

"I gave them to Barry."

"Barry Simpson?"

"Yes."

"*Gave* them, or *sold* them?"

"Gave them."

"With no promise of future reward?"

"Oh, yes, there were promises. He was full of promises."

"Did you know for what purpose he required these drugs?"

"More or less," Sefton answered.

"Let us be more precise. Did you know, for example, that he needed the hallucinogens for his so-called Black Magic sessions?"

"Yes."

"Did you ever attend any of these – these ceremonies?"

"No. I'm not a fool."

"That is a matter of opinion, of course, Mr. Sefton. But what of the heroin? Did you know where that was going?"

"Yes."

"Will you tell the court where that was, according to your knowledge?"

Sefton's elegant shoulders moved in a tiny shrug. His mouth pursed in a moue of distaste.

"To his father."

There was a small buzz of surprised comment in the

public seats. When quiet was restored, counsel said: "His *father*?"

"His so-called father. His putative father. His mother was the town whore –"

Here the judge intervened, but the point was made. Harry Taylor, then a junior clerk in the Bank, and already engaged to be married, had believed himself to be the father of Barry. Recalled, he admitted that for eighteen years he had paid for Barry's maintenance and schooling. No, he had no *proof*, and neither had the child's mother. But it was quite possible, and to avoid any scandal he had paid. He had not known at the time that it could have been one of a dozen other men, including Skipper Roberts, though he had heard that gossip later. Yes, Barry had found out, but not until he was grown up, and had already left the university. He didn't know how he had found out, but perhaps his mother had told him. Barry had made contact with him, had tried to borrow money, and had discovered in due course that he was hooked on heroin, and desperate for supplies. From this small beginning had grown the whole complicated plot . . .

Sefton gave the rest of his evidence quietly, but maliciously. He and Barry Simpson had met at university, had developed a close homosexual relationship that had lasted for nearly six years. Oh, yes, he knew that Barry had since married, but that was just a part of the plan. Or so he had said. As soon as the big money came in, Janey was to be ditched, and he and Barry would go abroad . . .

Small, slight, self-possessed, he agreed that he had known from the beginning that Barry was not entirely homosexual. "There was a girl when we were at college. But it didn't last. He always came back to me. He pretended to have an affair with the other Modley girl, Sarah. But that was a part of the plan, too. He just used her. The same as he used everyone."

"Including you, Mr. Sefton."

"Oh, yes. I realise that now. Now that it's too late . . ."

CHAPTER FIVE

(1)

"How was it," Mr. Arlingfold asked, "that you were able to become chairman of the two organisations – that you were able to steer the destinies of your small empire into safer waters so to speak – while the police were actually interviewing you in connection with the affairs at Westport and in New York?"

Horton-Crawley said: "The police didn't interview me until more than three weeks after the shooting on Axel Heath. Even then, it was very discreet. They didn't altogether believe –" He broke off, ran a hand over his forehead. Then he said: "Apparently no-one told them at first."

*

It was three weeks exactly, to the day and almost to the hour, after the Mercedes had hit the menhir on Axel Heath, when Pete Fletcher suddenly said: "Liz! Where are you, Liz? Are you all right?"

He was lying on his back, and it was almost dark, not quite dark because there was a faint light a long way away, but he was pinned by the legs so that though he twisted his neck and shoulders, and moved his arms, he was trapped from the waist down.

"Liz!"

He was aware of a movement in the near-darkness. Lights shone down on him, hands moved over him.

"Three weeks," someone said. "Almost exactly –"

The following morning, Liz came to see him, sitting on a chair by his bedside in the small private ward.

"For God's sake," he said, "tell me what happened."

She looked very brown and very beautiful, a creature of the sun; her long sand-coloured hair, newly-brushed, hanging down over her white shirt.

"You opted out," she said. "Two crushed legs and total amnesia. Until midnight last night, when you opted in again."

"The car –"

"You wrote that off."

"And you?" Even now, memory was an effort. "You were lying on the Altar – you'd opted out, too. Or had been knocked out." Like a long loose-jointed brown doll, she had seemed, flung carelessly down. "How did you get there? I dropped you in Parrott Lane –"

She reached out a hand to touch his face.

"I've been told not to excite you."

"For God's *sake*!" he said again. "What did they do to you? Tell me that, at least."

"I don't know." She withdrew her hand, sat with a small frown creasing her forehead. "I found it difficult to remember, too. The beginning was clear, but then it became confused. I think they gave me a jab –"

"Who did?"

The frowned deepened. "I don't know. I remember after you dropped me I went down the passage between the houses. The side-door was open. Not the one where the light was; the first door. Inside, it was dark. Someone called out to me, said would I give you something. I reached out for it, and he dragged me inside and put a hand over my mouth." She paused, shivered a little. "I was in what I supposed was the front room at Parrott Lane. Whoever it was held me so tightly I thought he'd cracked my ribs. That's when they might have stuck the needle in – I don't know. When he let me go, the room seemed bigger. There was an Altar, and candles, and a Goat with the body of a man. Someone called out for Barry Simpson, said: 'I've brought the girl. What will you do with her?' And the Goat – I suppose it was Simpson – said it was a man he was expecting, not me. Someone else said: 'He will come. And so will the other man, Pete Fletcher, in due course, looking for the girl. You must decide what you are going to do.' And the Goat said: 'How can I decide? You created the situation. You must provide the solution –' I'm not sure of the exact words, but that was more or less it. The answer to that was: 'No, Simpson. This is the point where we cease to break your fall.' "

For a moment they both stayed silent. Then Pete said: "The man he was expecting? Was it Horton–Crawley?"

She sat up straight at that.

"That's it! I've been trying to remember the name. Horton-Crawley! The police kept at me to try to remember, but I was pretty hazy –"

"The police," he said. "Where do they come in?"

She shivered again, and pulled up the collar of her shirt as though she was cold.

"Barry Simpson. Apparently he shot his brother-in-law, and killed his wife's sister with a butcher's knife. Both on that same night. He's been arrested, but he denies both the stabbing and the shooting."

"Horton-Crawley had a gun. He shot someone in a green van –"

"You'd better tell that to the police," she said.

*

The police had found a conspiracy of silence everywhere. Barry, in his tangled goat's hair, had been taken away and charged, but all he would say was that he had not killed Sal. He made no mention of Horton-Crawley, and neither did any of the others. *If anything goes wrong, if questions are asked, know nothing. Nothing at all. There's nothing to connect us with the customers; unless they talk first, which is unlikely. And if we can keep their names out of it, then maybe afterwards they can be made to pay . . .*

When the police had gone to Parrott Lane, for example, in the small hours, they had had to rouse Madame Joseph from her bed. Jimmy, too was asleep. Or at least he was in his room, and the police didn't ask to see him. Why should they? They were there simply to break the news to Madame Jo, and to Ted Modley, as the parents of the murdered girl. Parents who, when they heard it, said nothing.

Even Janey . . . shocked into a white-faced silence she became what many of the earlier jurists, and even the later psychologists, called *mute of anguish*.

When the police came at last to the hospital, Pete gave them only an edited version of the events of the night. For how can one tell a country police inspector in a neat grey suit that one has kept company with demons?

"Ericson and Schramm," he said at one point, and the inspector said: "They were with you?"

"Yes. Watching the house in Parrott Lane."

"But we have reason to believe that they were all three – with Camber as the third man – at a drinking party with the salvage vessel *Catfish*, down in the harbour. At least until midnight." A pause, then: "Did you know them before?"

"No."

"So you had only their word for their identity. You could have been deceived."

"Yes," Pete said.

"Would you recognise them again?"

"Yes."

"I'll arrange for them to come up here."

The inspector was already beginning to show signs of active disbelief. When Horton-Crawley was mentioned, he made a polite note of the name, but he seemed unimpressed. "Yes," he said, "we know that Simpson and Williams were playing with Black Magic. We've seen the so-called Chapel. A converted vehicle repair shop . . ." In his soft west-country voice was all the scorn of a man whose knowledge is tied up in small tight parcels, all neatly docketted and stacked away. "This man Horton-Crawley," he said, "is he local?"

It was Liz who passed the name to Ed; and a C.C.I. man who knew something of the Mowdell saga was sent round to see him. It was the big man himself who told the fullest story of all. His company safe, and his other love irrevocably lost to him, he seemed not to care any more, except for a burning desire to blast the man who, he was convinced, had taken Margot away from him.

*

Barry himself was in the witness-box for nearly four hours. *Why did he go to New York? To the Book Expo? But he didn't even know where it was being held.... All right, then, what else did he do over there? Where did he stay? Who else was in New York with him? How did he gain entrance to the Prynne's suite?*

A catch question this last one, for no-one believed for a moment that he had killed Margot Prynne. But why else did he rush off to New York for such a short time? Had the blow been intended, in fact, for Sir James, not Margot at all?

He was questioned at length about the Chapel, but refused to answer other than non-committally. At last they asked him: *Why did you kill Sarah Anne Williams?* And though he swore by all the seventy-two names of God that he did not, no-one believe him . . .

When Horton-Crawley had talked, the police had raided the cellar at Parrott Lane, and had found the photographs and the tapes, including those relating to Cargrove and Pierse Delany. Neither Ted nor Madame Jo had had the wits to get rid of them. And though no-one could prove who had killed Ray Fisk and Andrew Delany Jr., there was little doubt in anyone's mind once the evidence was heard. . . . Not that any of this appeared to relate *directly* to the death of Sarah Anne Williams. But *indirectly* – ah!

that was a different matter. In an effort to establish motive, the prosecution ranged wide. Sam, for example, and Sam alone, could have testified who stole the infant Delany . . .

Edward Charles Barry Simpson, the Clerk of the Court had read out, *you are charged with the murder of Sarah Anne Williams on 16th September last. Edward Charles Barry Simpson, are you guilty or not guilty?*

Suddenly, the lights had dimmed. The air had vibrated with the painful dynamo-humming. In the Judge's chair, sat the Goat, leering with its yellow teeth under its massive horns. Clerk and counsel, jury and police, reporters and public, all were revealed with the same cruel raptorial beaks. As the little court grew dark, a hundred and fifty pairs of eyes glowed fire-red.

Edward Charles Barry Simpson, the harsh voice said, *say that you are guilty!*

"No," he shouted, and clutched the wooden rail in front of him. "No! Of that, at least, I am not guilty –"

"It will make no difference," the beaked Clerk said, and the court burst into demoniacal laughter. From the leering Goat came an echo of the words: "It will make no difference . . ."

The humming stopped. The court was normal again. The Clerk was reading the charge to the jury. But from time to time, as the trial progressed, he was to see again the other face of justice, that is only a shiver of the curtain away from the one we accept as normal.

(2)

"Liz," he said, and reached out for her hand.

He had at last been transferred, away from Westport, to a private clinic in London. All at the expense of C.C.I. Liz was staying near, and came in twice a day. Of the three weeks after the night on the Moor, he remembered nothing; but his memory of everything that had gone before was now sharp and clear. On this day, four weeks after the crash, he said: "Darling Liz, when I'm out of these plaster pants, will you marry me?"

"Yes," she said. She leaned over the bed, bent lower to kiss him. "Yes, please, Pete."

And sharp and clear in his memory, he heard the voice of the creature in the car on Axel Heath: "I am Ericson, or anyone else I choose to be. Male or female, that is no problem." And: "Was there ever a Liz Frele? After all, you never saw us together, did you? Incidentally, you kiss well, Mr. Fletcher –"

Ericson and Schramm had been paraded before him. He had said: "I'm not sure. *Someone* was there, watching the house. But I'm not sure –" He was perfectly sure. But how could he argue? "They *said* they were you. It was dark, of course –"

Was there ever a Liz Frele? After all, the creature who had called himself Ericson had said, *you never saw us together, did you?*

"If ever there *was* a girl," he had said himself, bitterly, on Axel Heath.

But her lips were still infinitely sweet. Her hair fell in a cloud of palest gold about his face. At the trial, weeks later, when he was up and walking again, he said in answer to counsel's questioning: "I became very fond of her –" And this was the understatement of his life.

It was the sceptical, slow-thinking police inspector who tied up many of the other loose ends. Both Cargrove and Pierse Delany told him they had been approached, by telephone, by someone who knew of their financial difficulties. *Who could possibly have known?* the Inspector asked. Each produced a handful of names, and in each short-list, the name of their Bank Manager appeared. Enquiries among the friends of Harry Taylor revealed that he had once spoken of Black Magic at lunch in the Club. In an unofficial and wholly irregular search of his bachelor flat, a quantity of heroin was discovered, the batch and code marks leading back to Barry Simpson's homosexual contact, Ernest Sefton.

"I was a fool," Taylor said. "I should have kept my big mouth shut. But it's always been a failing of mine. And, anyway, I despised myself for having to pander to crooked bastards like Cargrove and Pierse Delany and Horton-Crawley, just to be sure of a regular fix. Talking in the Club in front of the others was like putting Delany alive on a spit and watching him roast. He was probably the meanest bastard of them all –"

"The absence of fingerprints on the murder weapon is of paramount importance," Mr. Arlingfold said in his closing address to the jury. "No gloves were found, remember. Can you accept, then, for one moment, that the defendant could have held the knife with something, some cloth perhaps, without that cloth being stained with the blood of the unfortunate girl? Could you even accept that in the shocked state in which he was found, only four minutes after the telephone call for help, he could have wiped clean only the *handle* of the knife, leaving the blade still red with the poor girl's blood, *and then disposed of the cloth?*"

At that point, the curtain shivered again. From the high chair, the Goat looked down at the darkening Court.

"The absence of fingerprints need not greatly concern you, members of the jury. In fact it need not concern you at all. The prisoner is not guilty of the crime for which he is standing trial. We all know that. But do not let that bother you in the slightest. The verdict must be the same, whether he is, in fact, guilty or not guilty. *You are not here to see justice done . . .*"

It was probably at this point that Barry lost touch entirely with the world as we know it. From then on, to him the Court was peopled only by demons, enacting a parody of the pattern of justice. Under the burning eyes of the Goat, lawyers in their wigs danced in the well of the court with women jurors who stripped off their clothing, piece by piece, and flung it to the howling mob in the public gallery. Over it all, was the painful, shrill, dynamo-humming sound through which came the final words to the jury.

Members of the jury, the Clerk shouted above the din, *are you agreed upon your verdict?*

He had to repeat it, again and yet again, until finally the foreman, a beaked and naked giant, was called up from the embraces of a female demon on the floor of the jury-box.

We are! the foreman shouted back, and for a moment there was silence in the court. Then the Clerk said: *Do you find the prisoner Edward Charles Barry Simpson guilty or not guilty?*

Of what? the foreman said, with a leer at the Goat.

It doesn't matter, the Clerk replied sharply. *You should know that. It doesn't matter in the slightest.*

Guilty, then, the naked giant said, and fell upon the writhing figure at his feet.

Instantly pandemonium returned. In the near-darkness, the creatures swarmed towards the dock, their eyes glowing. Cold leathery hands seized him, pulled him this way and that. Screaming, he tried to fight them, but it was no use. Even above the din he could hear the cracking of his own bones, and the ripping of his own skin and muscle and inner fibre as they tore him apart at last.

*

"Members of the jury," the Clerk said, "are you agreed upon your verdict?"

"We are," the foreman replied.

"Do you find the prisoner, Edward Charles Barry Simpson, guilty or not guilty of murder?"

The foreman: "Guilty."

Suddenly Barry began to scream. He held his hands before his face as though to ward off an attack. "No! No!

No!" he screamed, and began to struggle, flinging himself about in the narrow wooden space like a man possessed. Two warders seized him, but he fought on, screaming, kicking, biting. A fine froth appeared at his mouth. Two uniformed policemen went to the aid of the warders, and he was carried at last, still threshing like a hooked fish, down the steps to the cells below.

*

Extract from the report of Dr. Heinrich Schlitz, police psychiatrist, and Dr. Ernest Hart-Jones, psychiatric consultant to H.M. Prisons:

"... Simpson has described to us, under hypnosis, the apparent delusion which underlay his violent reaction in court at the time when the jury's verdict was made known. He was then, and still is, under the impression that he is menaced by demons ... In our opinion he is no longer fit to plead ..."

Epilogue

FORTY FEET below, the sea still frets against the iron legs of the pier; sending, when the weather is fine, ripples of reflected sunlight up through the narrow spaces between the boards. In summer, Madame Joseph still sits in her small dark cell in which the bright cherubim quiver against the ceiling like moths trapped in a darkened room. She has never, since the night of Sal's violent death, repeated the words of the Great Conjuration.

In the house in Parrott Lane, Ted Modley sleeps alone now, in what used to be the girls' room. He is afraid of Madame Jo, and he cannot forget what happened in that summer. Jimmy still sleeps in the attic room, but the succubus no longer shares his bed. It was surely of the utmost irony that in obeying the instructions of the beautiful image that he loved, to ensure that he should not lose it, he somehow destroyed it for ever. He still carries deck-chairs in the season, and when he is not at this strictly limited job, he moves about the empty house doing his routine work with what has already been described as an embalmer's touch. At night, he tosses in his attic bed, seeking relief in the only way he knows, as he used to do in the school in the Madawaska all those years before.

Janey is about to be released from her marriage to Barry, who is in an institution for the criminally insane. One day, soon, she may well marry a limping Mel. Both were charged with conspiracy to obtain money under false pretensions, in that they had held out promises of help from supernatural powers in return for cash. Both were fined. But to the surprise of most of the town, no further charges on the more serious aspects of the affair were brought against them. Perhaps it was felt that to prove the extent of their participation, in the absence of Barry, would have been too difficult . . .

*

Catfish searched the sides of the deep channel for a month, but *Seamew* was never found. The *Investigator* published its own version of the affair, and Ed seemed satisfied enough. At least, he paid the promised bonus to Pete Fletcher and Liz Frele, who were married a week after the trial ended. For a working honeymoon, they went back to the East African coast where Pete had been photographing marine life when the C.C.I. chopper had plucked him, quite literally, out of the water. Together they dived in the clear warm depths of the Indian Ocean, wandering like companionable spirits through the avenues of coral and the herds of bright fish, Liz's long sand-coloured hair trailing behind her like a mermaid's bridal veil. Returning to base, they ate their evening meals in the same companionable intimacy under the palms, the Southern Cross hanging like a bright jewel on the breast of the night. Then to bed in a palm-thatched hut within sound of the waves pounding on the outer reef, to waken to another day of sea and sand and the cool blue-green world under the water.

It lasted like that for just ten days, and for almost ten nights. But at midnight on the tenth night, the Swede who ran the island camp sent Hamisi, the head steward, to fetch Pete to the radio-telephone to speak to Ed. Grumbling, half-asleep still, he tied a towel round his waist and followed the grinning Hamisi through the groves of palms and wild hibiscus and casuarinas.

"Pete – is Liz with you?"

"Yes."

There was a long silence, to which the distance added its small background of mad cacophony.

"Pete, I don't know how to say this –"

Five minutes later, he walked back alone through the moonlit palms. As he neared the beach, he saw Liz slip out of the hut, and run swiftly along the edge of the creaming surf. She was naked, her hair streaming out behind her as it did in the water when they were diving through the canyons of coral. He began to run, shouting "Liz! Liz!" above the pounding of the incoming tide. But she ran on, seemingly oblivious.

All along the white beach, in the brilliant moonlight, a great concourse of ghost-crabs moved swiftly out towards the receding edge of each retracting wave, ran half-submerged away from the next advancing line of breaking surf. Each was harnessed to its own shadow, moving with it in close tandem. At his shouts, and the vibration of his running footsteps along the moonlit beach, they vanished, swift as silver arrows, each into its own small burrow in the coral sand, to reappear only as the danger passed.

"Liz!" he shouted, "Liz! Liz!"

A small wind stirred the tops of the casuarinas. The air was warm against his skin, caressing as a loving hand. Everywhere the ghost-crabs ran before him, disappeared, emerged behind him to resume their ritual moon-dance with the sea. He was gaining on her. Thirty yards. Twenty. Suddenly she swerved, ran into the creaming surf, dived through a breaking wave and he saw the regular motion of her arms as she came up swimming strongly out towards the inner reef. He plunged in after her, felt the sudden exhilaration as his body sliced through the cool clear water. From time to time he was forced to lift his head to check her progress, losing each time a fraction of the distance he had gained. A hundred and fifty yards from the shore, she turned, swam parallel for a while with the beach and the thunderous reef, then began to follow a curving line of return. Twenty yards out from the crab-haunted shore, an outrigger canoe rode the tide on a palm-rope tether, anchored to a lump of coral on the sea-bed. She stopped, reached up to grasp the side of it, hung half-suspended, half-floating in the moonlit water.

He swam slowly towards the canoe, grasped the palm-rope, hung close to her. Their bodies swayed gently in the limpid sea, like the floating fronds of ocean plants that are stroked this way and that by the movement of the tide, and sometimes are brought together in a brief moment of contact that is as light as the wing-brush of courting moths.

Breathless after the long chase, he said: "Liz –" and: "Darling Liz – why did you run away?"

Her long wet hair hung down over her shoulders, and over her moonlit breasts. Without answering, she let herself drift closer to him, so that they touched, parted, touched again. Their lips met, clung for an instant. Then he forced himself to say: "That was Ed. He tried to tell me that you're not here. That you've never been here. Or even in Westport. That you're still on the dig at Meknès."

"And you believed him?"

"No."

"Why not?"

He kissed her again, a sea-wet salty kiss.

"It would drive me mad if I allowed myself –"

"What else did he say?" she interrupted him.

"That you'd sent a cable, turning down his offer. But the cable was never delivered. Instead, you turned up at the office."

"How could I, if I never left Meknès?"

"Someone is at Meknès now. Someone who calls herself Liz Frele. A C.C.I. man from Rome flew over there to check."

"Why?"

Miserably, his eyes now tight-closed so that he could not see the hurt that he knew must be in her face, he said: "Ed had another phone call. Untimed, like the earlier ones. So he contacted Rome. They deal with North Africa from there. Their man flew in to Rabat, then covered the last hundred miles by desert-cat. Apparently it's a hell of a place to get at. But perhaps you know that."

"If you don't believe him, what difference does it make?"

"I want to *know*," he said stubbornly. "This isn't the first time –"

He cut it short, but it was too late. For a single instant she froze against him; then suddenly he felt her go. His hand released its hold on the rope, and he felt the water close over his head. When he surfaced, she was already half-way to the shore. Long before his feet touched bottom in the shallows, she was running lightly up the beach, barely disturbing the lines of foraging crabs. He followed, still calling her, his mind still fighting against the doubts that Ed's words had re-introduced into the idyll of their new life.

Outside the hut, he stopped. The night was alive with the churring of a million strident insects. From the outer reef, the ceaseless roar of the breakers underlined the shrill cries of the bush-babies and the distant throbbing of native drums. The entrance to the hut was a dark rectangle in a moonlit paradise. Inside was – *what*?

He couldn't force himself to cross the last few yards of silver sand. He remembered the thoughts that had entered his mind, and the words that had been spoken in the anteroom to the Chapel. *Where does truth end, and illusion start?* And: *The one you know as Elizabeth Frele* . . .

Liz –

Liz in the big chair in Ed's office, on that first day. Long and lean; sunburnt and cross under a tangled mass of sand-coloured hair. Hair that turned to finest silver in the moonlight.

Liz, whose mother had died on *Seamew*, drowning her talents in the same small patch of halcyon sea as his own father. But Liz's mother had been washed ashore at last; dead; along with all the rest, *except his father*.

Except his father –

What had the powers of darkness done with his father? Why should Liz's mother, but not his father –

The distant drumming subtly changed. A chorus of tree-frogs sounded close at hand, like small bells struck sharply with a silver hammer. On the beach, the ghost-crabs still trod their dance of death with the incoming tide.

Something moved in the darkness inside the palm-roofed hut. If he went in now, what would he find? A pair of eyes, gleaming in the dark like twin danger-lamps, over a cruel raptor's beak? The voice of the creature who was sometimes Ericson? If it was true what Ed had told him – if he were to pack up now, go to Meknès, and find the real Liz –

But how could he be sure, even then? And would the Liz at Meknès accept him? With whom was he in love, anyway – a stranger in Morocco whom he had never met; or this beautiful projection of that stranger, who was his wife?

Where does illusion end, and truth begin . . .

The drumming changed again, a fractional shift of emphasis that lent a new measure of urgency to the endlessly repeated patterns of sound that were woven under the stars to keep the spirits at bay during the long tropical night.

Suddenly, he made up his mind. He moved forward, stooped a fraction, walked in through the dark doorway.

"Liz?"

Inside the hut it was so dark that at first, coming in out of the bright moonlight he could see little but the lighter square of the bed, empty, and the long narrow window.

"Liz!" he said again. And: "Here!" came the answer, in Ericson's voice; from behind, between him and the open door. He swung round, caught a fleeting impression of two red eyes, a beak outlined against the open doorway. Then Liz was in his arms, repeating his name, over and over. The eyes, the beak, the voice of Ericson had gone, if ever they had been there at all.

In the warm tropical night, their bodies were already drying off, but her hair, her beautiful sand-gold hair that flowed silver under the moon, was still wet as he stroked it back from the sweet symmetry of her face.

"Liz," he said, and kissed her once, tasting the drying salt on her lips.

"Darling Liz," he said, and kissed her a second time, while the vibrations of the distant drums, trapped under the palm-thatch roof, changed their pattern yet again, almost imperceptibly.

"You bloody little devil," he said.

RITUAL MAGIC

by Francis King

An eye-opening account of the practices of magic and alchemy.

From medieval times to modern day, the practices of magic and alchemy have been in the hands of some of the greatest occultists of our times.

The secret rites and conflicts have remained the sole knowledge of each cult, never to be seen by the outside world.

Now Francis King relates those secrets and conflicts, including the struggles of Aleister Crowley and W. E. Yeats within the infamous Order of The Golden Dawn; the goat-sacrificing mediums of Keighley, the left-handed Bengali Tantricists and the sexual magic of an American Mulatto.

THE NEW ENGLISH LIBRARY